The Carda

ALSO BY JON STOCK

Riot Act

The Cardamom Club

Jon Stock

BLACKAMBER BOOKS

Published by BlackAmber Books Limited
3 Queen Square, London WC1N 3AU
www.blackamber.com

First published 2003

1 3 5 7 9 10 8 6 4 2

A CIP record for this book is available from the British Library

Typeset in 12.5/13.5 pt Garamond Three
by RefineCatch Limited, Bungay, Suffolk

Printed by WS Bookwell, Finland

ISBN 1–901969–18–5

FOR HILARY, FELIX, MAYA AND JAGO

"Which side do the Asians cheer for? It's an interesting test. Are you still harking back to where you came from or where you are?"

Norman Tebbit, 1990

"One is patriotic only because one is too small and weak to be cosmopolitan"

Anthony Trollope

Acknowledgments

Thanks to C. Sujit Chandra Kumar for his considerable knowledge of Kerala and cooking; Patrick French, whose book, *Liberty or Death*, revealed for the first time the true extent of Indian Political Intelligence's role in British India; Stephen Robinson for sending me to Delhi; Alec Russell for seeing beyond the headlines; Frank Hancock for listening in the early days; Mr Jonathon Bond for his encouragement and introductions; the Dominic family for their hospitality; Taiki Malhotra for the Hindi lessons; Andrea Stock and Val and Mick Goss for use of their computers; Stewart McLennan for his encyclopedic knowledge of computers; Judith Gray and Helen Simpson for their telling editorial insights; BlackAmber Books, a pioneering publisher; and, most of all, Hilary, for sharing India.

Part One

CHAPTER ONE

New Delhi, 1999

THE SPORTS BAR at the Radisson Hotel was not the sort of place where I normally spent an evening, but there weren't many choices in Delhi when you needed a break from India. The homesick headed for Djinns, an English pub attached to the Hyatt Hotel, where you could take calls in a red telephone box at the end of the bar. But I needed a break from Britain, too, some anonymity. And in this bland no man's land out here on National Highway 8, near the Indira Gandhi International airport, I could listen to a Filipino band singing the Beatles and imagine, just for a moment, that I was nowhere.

I wasn't, of course. All was *maya*, illusion. It was one of the first things I had learnt about India. Even in this quarantined, five-star environment, the subcontinent still managed to seep in. India was like that: airborne, irresistible. Eleanor Rigby soon gave way to a taped recording of Daler Mehndi. *Tukatukatuk.Tukatukatuk.* My taxi driver had played it all the way in from the airport when I first arrived, told me he was the Punjabis' answer to Michael Jackson. Somewhere outside a diesel generator started up. *Chugachugachug.* And then, in front of me, across sixteen television screens, Sachin Tendulkar flickered simultaneously into life. I was in India, no question.

Tendulkar was preparing to silence England's supporters, a few of whom were cheering meekly in one corner. It was the mobile phone set, engineers mainly, who in five years had changed for ever the face of communications across South Asia. Newspapers were calling them the "telecolonials". Young Delhiites, phones clipped to their belts like pistols, were laughing and talking up at the bar, flirting with each other in between overs. I had seen their cars on my way in, 7 Series bought by doting admirals and arms dealers for their precious children. The women had a brash kind of beauty in their tight, imported leggings; the men, wearing Nike T-shirts and Levi jeans, looked moneyed and cocksure. These were the notorious BMW kids of Delhi, famed for their wealth and wicked Western ways.

A second group of English fans was playing table football, burnt-out businessmen waiting for the midnight flight back to London. Sizing up the women at the bar, they began pulling suggestively on the spinning handles, tongues and ties loosened by too much alcohol. An anxious member of staff, one eye on the football, reached for a telephone. Before he could speak, the bar was erupting around him: Tendulkar, quick hands, heavy bat, had flicked an attempted bouncer for four. The TV cameras panned across a delirious section of the crowd, focusing on a banner: "We fail the Tebbit test and we are proud of it."

The barmen became distracted, huddled in a nervous group, arguing over who should approach the unruly *angrez*. I caught the eye of one of the businessmen, his bald pate scalded by Delhi's ceaseless summer sun. He stared through me as he finished his beer, wiping froth

4

from his mouth with the back of a hand before returning to the football. He was so full of lager it seemed to slop out of him, like an overflowing water butt. His eyes were small and distant, two beads floating in milky red pools.

Glancing at the man's paunch, his shirt shiny with spilt beer, I thought about Tebbit's cricket test. Then Tendulkar walked down the pitch to hit another boundary. All across India, in shops, buses and homes, I could picture them: men, women and children leaping up as one. It was too much for the businessman. Without warning, he grabbed the nearest person, one of the young men at the bar, twisted him round by his collar and headbutted him to the ground. The whole room fell quiet, as if we had all drawn in breath together. For a moment the businessman seemed to hesitate, looking down at the figure by his feet, then he was gone, running into the warm night.

I pushed my way through the gathering crowd, explaining that I was a doctor, and knelt down beside the man. His nose was broken but otherwise he was okay, just a little groggy.

"Is he breathing?" someone asked. "I can't see him breathing."

"He's going to be fine," I replied, discreetly checking for a pulse. The man was regaining consciousness. "Could someone bring a blanket, a jacket?"

The hotel doctor arrived a few minutes later and I gave him a brief summary of what had happened, aware that the rest of the Englishmen had already left the bar. I realised, from the unsteadiness of my words, that I was trembling. As we talked, one of the young Delhiites strolled over. His chest was unnaturally broad, pumped up, his head too small, way out of proportion with the rest of his body. Following a step behind him was a petite woman, barely five feet, with fragile arms and strong hair.

"Thanks," the man said. His shrunken eyes flitted nervously, assessing the scene, me. I took a card from my wallet and handed it to him, noticing the woman was wearing platform soles. Even with those, her head barely reached his chest.

"Let me know how he is," I said, my voice still unsteady. The man's blue T-shirt was so tight it looked like a layer of skin. "I'm sure he'll be fine."

"Raj Nair, British High Commission," he read, my card lost in his big hands. A smirk creased across his face, ruining its toned symmetry. He passed the card back to me. Then he turned and walked away, cradling his delicate companion.

Later that evening, as I was driven home, we followed a wedding band. They were squatting in the back of a Tempo truck, cradling their tubas and drums. The musicians' ill-fitting uniforms, white with crimson shoulder pads and gold tassles, seemed incongruous as they stared out into the night. They were like toy soldiers who had been put away in the wrong box. It was almost the end of the wedding season, a propitious time to get married if the stars were to be believed, and I had seen many bands in recent weeks, lying around outside gates in the afternoon heat, trudging in single file from one dusty venue to another.

I had seen the bridegrooms' horses, too, magnificent Marwaris from Rajasthan with their sickle-shaped ears and upright gait. Traditionally they had carried the bridegroom to meet his wife but these days he preferred to go by Japanese hatchback than horseback, riding for only a few short yards, first when he left the family driveway and later as he arrived at the chosen hotel. The bridegroom turned up looking relaxed and immaculate, unlike the horse beneath him who was breathless and steaming. At this time of year you saw them everywhere, galloping across town to make sure they arrived on time, ready to complete the charade.

After reaching Qutab Minar, we headed east towards Saket, one of South Delhi's more lively suburbs. Its chief attraction was the Anupam cinema, on the front of which was an Andy Warhol image of an Asian Marilyn Monroe. Already I found this stretch of road more terrifying than most. Shortly after Qutab Minar, the road widened, without warning, into an informal dual carriageway for five hundred yards and then closed up again. My toes curled over. At the point where the traffic was meant to return to single file we passed the carcass of a Blue Line bus that had driven straight into a tree on the central reservation. I felt like shouting, "You see, you see, everybody in this country is so bloody relaxed about driving, but look what happens. Look! People die!"

Instead I said nothing. Ravi, my driver, laid back, slowing down, shook his head in an ambiguous way. At least he had noticed the accident, made a mental note not to die in one himself. It was a fresh crash, he said, probably caused by brake failure. I wound down the window and looked at the twisted metal to the left of the driver, where the women usually sat. The bodies had gone, but I could still taste the scene, the warm, sticky carnage.

We drove on, squinting at the dusted shards of head-light spiralling past us. A private ambulance of some sort slipped eerily by, its siren so faint you wondered why the driver bothered. Sometimes the oncoming traffic seemed to be on our side of the road. Ravi never flinched. Occasionally he would flick his headlights but most of the time he just hooted, not aggressively, but as a way of acknowledging passing cars. Every car, in fact. If hooting was like a nod of the head, then Ravi knew everyone.

The last straw was when we slid inside a tree that was pushing up through the cracked tarmac of the out-side lane. I shut my eyes, understanding in a moment why my father had left India. My posting here suddenly felt like a lifetime. I could only begin to imagine the condition of the roads in his day. Nobody seemed to think that the tree's presence was odd. I looked back at it and then glanced at Ravi for signs of a reaction. Nothing. (He couldn't see the wood for the trees.)

I kept my face near the open window as we drove on. Swept-up leaves smouldered along the roadside in piles edged with faintly glowing embers. The earth was slowly releasing the heat of the day and the night air was still warm. It was only April but Delhi was already a firebowl, hot and powdery, hostile. I thought of the bodybuilder giving back my card, his look of com-prehension followed by rejection. There was no reason why he should have been more civil. One of my com-patriots had assaulted his friend.

We turned right into Sainik Farms, the residential colony where I had rented a temporary house while the British High Commission built more accommodation on the compound. Sainik Farms was probably Delhi's

8

richest suburb; I later discovered it was also illegal, although residents preferred terms like "informal" and talked of its imminent "regularisation" by the government. There was no official power or water supply. Instead we used diesel generators and drew water from our own wells. When the water dried up, we hired big, noisy boring machines and dug deeper. Locals called it the Republic of Sainik Farms. Its citizens were a mixture of corrupt politicians, struck-off doctors and underworld dons – an unholy alliance so influential in India that it was rumoured Pakistan had used Sainik Farms as the target coordinates for its nuclear arsenal. Their money was mostly new, much of it spent on hapless architects who were consulted, ignored and then ordered at gunpoint to carry out their clients' own kitsch, napkin sketches of Palladian excess.

My home, like the others, was described as a "farmhouse", although it was nothing of the sort. There was no farmyard or tractor or fields of sun-kissed corn. Farmhouse was a term used liberally for "elite effect"; it suggested land ownership, which in an expensive city such as Delhi meant wealth. It was also a harkback to the 1960s when Sainik Farms (literally "soldier farms") was set aside for army officers who were allowed to use it for agricultural purposes such as keeping chickens or cows. Nobody seemed to have questioned why these animals needed to live in marble palaces with twenty bedrooms, bathrooms attached.

My farmhouse belonged to a retired general and was constructed solely, of course, with livestock in mind. A sprawling one-acre estate, it boasted two water features (cascading ponds that lit up at night to the sound of Handel), a jogging track (a vivid blue gravel path, lined

9

with white stones, that meandered round the borders of the property to ensure outdoor exercise could continue throughout the soggy monsoon) and a crazy golf course built into the foothills of a Himalayan rockery. The house itself appeared to have been an afterthought. Tucked away in one corner, it was an uncharacteristically small, slit-windowed fortress designed to look like a log cabin, complete with a concrete veneer of knotty bark.

I had been in Delhi for a month and I was still not used to the idea of living in this house, or employing the staff that came with it. Every time the uniformed *chowkidar* opened the gates to let me in, I was surprised, turning round to see who was coming. Tonight, despite repeated instructions to the contrary, he saluted as we drove past, and saluted again when he opened my car door, stamping to attention for good measure. My landlord called him the sentry.

"At ease," I whispered, as I walked up to the oak-effect front door. He never smiled.

I was tired and headed straight to bed. In England sleep would have followed soon after, but bedtime in Delhi marked the beginning of a battle that would rage for most of the night. Moving systematically round the bed, I tucked my mosquito net under the mattress, covered myself in Jungle Formula and hoped in vain that the enemy would be kind.

I had no plans to visit India until I was posted here, no desire to discover my Indian ancestry halfway up a hillside in the Kullu Valley. I was too rational for that kind of thing, too English. I was also too old, not by much, but old enough to feel uncomfortable listening to Talvin Singh down at the Blue Note in Hoxton.

Now, though, I was in India, not by choice, but here nevertheless. And in those rare moments of solitude, I did wonder if this place of my birth would resonate, if it would tug at my sleeves in the stillness of the night. And if it did, how would I feel? What would I do? Would I still pass the Cricket Test?

CHAPTER TWO

THERE WAS A new woman on reception when I arrived at the medical centre, but I didn't expect to be stopped.

"Can I help you?" she said, as I breezed past. Her tone was emphatic.

"It's okay, I'm working here," I said. "Started last month."

"Can I see your pass?" she asked.

"My pass?" I said, laughing lightly. "Of course." She was only obeying orders. The medical centre was on the British High Commission compound and subject to the same levels of diplomatic security.

"Thanks," she said, as I handed it over. She gave it back immediately, smiling. "Sorry."

"No need. Did you start today?"

"Yesterday."

"And are we busy?" I asked, turning round the clipboard on the desk in front of her.

"Lots of babies. And a Mr Grade."

She looked up at me as if I should know his name. I could feel my mouth drying. I hadn't met him yet – he'd been away on holiday – but he had obviously returned.

"What time?" I asked casually, glancing at my watch.

"First up. There's also . . . " She paused, then nodded at the waiting area behind me. I turned round and saw the bald businessman who had attacked the Indian last night. The top of his head was still sunburnt, but it was his left eye that had brought him here. It looked as if the bodybuilder had caught up with him.

"Does he have an appointment?" I asked.

"Not yet."

"Keep him waiting," I said quietly.

The morning clinic was a fairly routine affair, much like a travel clinic in Britain. Injections for hepatitis B and Japanese encephalitis, advice on dysentery, tips on how to avoid dying in Delhi (don't drive at night), reassuring a newly arrived expat mother that one mosquito bite on her baby girl didn't mean that she had cerebral malaria, and listening to another mother who would only bath her child in imported bottled mineral water that had also been boiled. Today, however, was entirely coloured by the imminent arrival of Jamie Grade. I heard him first, chatting up the receptionist in a quiet, semi-serious way, and then he was knocking on my door.

"Come in," I said, feigning indifference, wondering what this legendary man would be like. Officially he was head of the political unit; unofficially he was king of spooks.

"Ah, Raj, good man," Jamie said, beaming, his hand outstretched. "Just who I was hoping to see."

I was expecting a suit but he was wearing khaki, empire-building shorts, a plum-red short-sleeved shirt and deck shoes without socks. He sat down, pulling one leg up across his knee, which he held there with his hand, and launched immediately into telling me a joke.

"There's this one-eyed man," he began, ignoring my bewilderment. "You don't mind, do you? I've been dying to tell you this one all day."

"Please, go on," I said, trying to take him in.

"It's a doctor's joke, you see . . . Anyway, this one-eyed man accidentally swallows his glass eye two days before a proctological examination. He decides to go ahead with the appointment, undresses at the surgery, bends over and waits. The proctologist walks in, takes a look up the man's arse and the first thing he sees is the glass eye glaring at him. 'You know,' says the doc, 'you really must learn to trust me.'"

I laughed, more out of politeness than anything else. Despite his sense of humour, Jamie must have been fifty. He was in good health, sandy-haired and fresh-faced, and everything about him was young except his eyes, which were flat and slate-grey and suddenly upon me.

"How are you settling in?" he asked, still smiling at his joke. I had to look away from those eyes, ancient and tired, violently at odds with the rest of his boyish face.

"Fine," I said. "I had a bad case of dengue last week, but otherwise the community is thriving."

"No hilariously embarrassing sexual problems?" he asked.

"Nothing I can share, I'm afraid."

"No. Of course not."

He looked at me for a moment, untroubled by the silence. Neither of us was fooled by his manner.

"Listen, I'll cut straight to the chase," he began, suddenly sitting forward. "We're planning to get you on stream in a couple of weeks, after you've toured the regions."

"Anything specific?"

"Not yet. I'm still congratulating myself. The perfect cover, don't you think? A doctor."

"An Asian doctor."

14

"Yes," he said, pausing. "Actually, that was our new High Commissioner's idea. Sir Ian. You met him in London, I think."

"Once," I said.

"Very New Labour, the whole thing. I wasn't so keen, myself."

"No?" I asked, wondering what he was about to say next. I had met people in Edinburgh, usually drunken medics at dinner parties, who had told me without a hint of anger or malice in their voice that there were too many Asians working in the National Health Service. But it was invariably late and they immediately put an arm round my shoulders and started slurring apologies. Jamie was sober and it was barely lunchtime.

"Don't get me wrong," he continued, looking straight at me. "Nothing personal about it. Really. Equal opportunities and all that – very important, crucial. Just not for all jobs. We've had a few problems in the past, that's all."

"Problems?" I asked.

"Oh, you know, the usual sort of thing. Last year London sent over a nice bloke from Birmingham, Javed I think his name was. He was here on a ten-week attachment with the political unit. The first time we took him over to the Ministry of External Affairs, the Indians asked him where he was from. 'Birmingham,' he said, in his best Brummie accent. 'But me parents are from Lahore.' The MEA never spoke to him again. They thought he was spying for Pakistan."

"And you think I'll have similar problems?" I asked.

"Not exactly. Your parents were from the south, no?"

"Kerala. But I was born and brought up in Edinburgh."

15

"The dynamics will be different, that's all I'm saying. You tell me. In my experience Indians aren't always overwhelmed to see people who have passed up their own country to live somewhere else."

"And they're delighted to see the British back in India, are they?" I asked.

"We have our own complicated relationship," he said, looking at me as an equal, it seemed, for the first time in our conversation.

He leant back, put his feet up on my desk and spoke for a while about my job in Delhi. I had heard so much about him that it didn't feel as if we were meeting for the first time. He had no wife or family – married to the job, according to colleagues. Nobody on the compound was in any doubt what that job was: station head of MI6. His cover job at the political unit suited him well, as his skills in that department were formidable. Rumour had it that he had managed to predict the correct prime minister for the previous three elections (no mean feat in a land which had seen so many governments come and go in the last few years), winning the office sweepstake each time.

Without thinking, he pulled out a packet of cigarettes and then checked himself, laughing, tapping the cigarette on the outside of the packet. Ironically, he said, it was safer talking in the medical centre than it was in his office, which the Indians had recently rewired. At least ninety per cent of my working day, he explained, was to be spent helping run the clinic. The rest of my time belonged to him, to MI6. His idea was that the High Commission, in the spirit of cooperation and free market enterprise, would make available its Western medical services to any Indians who could afford them. By that he meant politicians, civil servants and, with a bit of luck, some senior members of the Armed Forces. My role would be to gauge whether any of these patients had anything interesting to say about matters of national security. Those I deemed suitable would be worked upon further by the spooks.

"I can't understand it, myself," he said, getting up and walking over to the window. "In a country with so many top doctors, these people still go abroad for their treatment. Look at Jyoti Basu, chief minister of West Bengal, Marxist to the core, champion of the *swadeshi* movement, and yet he still flies over to London every six months for a *videshi* check-up. And then there's your lot" – my lot? – "from Kerala. The Communist Party of India – Marxist. CPIM. One of their distinguished leaders, Achuthanandan, developed a bit of a problem with his thymus gland. So what does he do? What would you do in Kerala, a state which produces some of the best doctors in the world? He flies to London, of course, and checks in for £15,000 worth of private care at the Royal Brompton. Paid for by the party, naturally, who had a whip-round, which is why his car goes via Highgate on its way to the hospital."

"Highgate?"

"Yes. He's a Marxist, remember. A patron of private hospitals, but still a Marxist. When he gets to Highgate, he walks across the cemetery and salutes at Marx's grave, accompanied by a few senior colleagues and watched at a distance by some of ours."

Jamie was in his stride and I let him talk. I didn't immediately warm to him, but there was something infectious about his enthusiasm, the lightness of touch underpinned by a sharp intellect. He understood India better than anyone I had so far met, perhaps with the exception of Sir Ian.

I told him that in my own mind I would always see myself first and foremost as a doctor – my father had been a doctor in Edinburgh. The approach from MI6, made at a medical conference in London, was flattering, I said, and gave me a chance to put something back. Neither of us mentioned the subject again, but we both knew that my attachment had more than a little to do with ethnic quotas. Unlike the rest of the civil service, MI5 and MI6 employed very few people of Asian or Afro-Caribbean origin. I hadn't come up through the ranks, I was not even full-time, but I would do. I was a useful statistic for the government and an unwanted complication for Jamie.

He left after ten minutes, told me to keep in touch. I had the same feeling of excitement as I had felt when I was originally asked, a sense of embarking on something that mattered, that would count. I also wanted to prove Jamie wrong, allay his fears, show him that I was the best man for the job. On his way out, Jamie passed the receptionist, who put her head round the door.

"That man at reception," she said. "I'm worried he's going to collapse on me."

"Send him in," I said.

The bald businessman stumbled in a few seconds later. He was in a bad way, which upset me greatly, of course.

"Watch the cricket last night?" I asked, looking at the bruising above his eye.

"Caught some of it," he said. "You must be chuffed."

"Why?" I asked, reaching for an alcoholic wipe. With a bit of luck, this was going to hurt.

"Winning so comfortably."

"We didn't."

The man let out a cowardly yell as I cleansed the incision. I wondered if he had even heard of the cricket test.

"Watch it with that," he said, pulling his head away.

"I have to clean the cut. How did you get it, anyway?" I asked.

He leant forward, gingerly.

"Car door," he offered. It was usually car doors, or low-flying pigs.

I showed him the door, armed with some suncream, but just as he was leaving, he turned to me, smiling. "I've got it now. You're from Southall, aren't you?"

By the end of the morning, I had vaccinated three babies against polio, lectured a pregnant mother about hygiene, and offered tentative advice to someone with a hilariously embarrassing sexual problem. I was just closing up to go for lunch when I heard a noise from the far end of the corridor. It sounded like a human cry. We had half a dozen beds in private rooms, but as far as I knew nobody had been admitted over the weekend. I heard the noise again, a faint wailing. Walking down the corridor I came across the director of the medical centre coming out of one of the rooms, locking it behind her.

"I didn't know we had any admissions," I said.

"He's just arrived," the director replied. She was a stout woman in her forties, matronly, severe, more concerned with management systems than patients.

"Why didn't somebody tell me?" I asked.

"Mr Grade didn't mention him to you?" she said, suspiciously.

19

"No," I replied, thinking back over our conversation. "I would like to see him."

"But nobody's allowed to see him."

I was shocked by her words, but she meant what she was saying, her body language suddenly protective of the room behind her.

"I'm sorry, but I am the doctor around here," I said, looking over her shoulder at the door. "I think I'm entitled to see my patients."

"Mr Grade's orders, not mine." She stood her ground, unflinching.

"Give me the keys," I said, as authoritatively as possible, not rating my chances. "I insist."

"I can't. I'm sure it's fine for you to see him, but you must check first with Mr Grade. Sorry, orders."

I couldn't believe what she was saying, her more conciliatory tone somehow making it worse. It was more calculated than stubborn. A minute later I was back in my office and on the phone to Jamie, demanding an explanation.

"Of course you can see him, how absurd," he was saying. "I can't believe I didn't tell you about him this morning."

"You didn't," I said, struggling to sound calm. "Who is he?"

"His name's Dutchie. He's a hippy, a low-rent traveller. We're flying him out tonight."

"Why?"

"Because he's our responsibility and we don't want an embarrassing scene."

"Our responsibility? Why ours?"

"Because he's a British citizen."

Jamie added that Dutchie had been hanging about in

Kerala when he got involved in something he shouldn't. That was all, but I knew he was not telling me everything. I took the keys from the director, her unchanged manner denying me any satisfaction, and walked back down the corridor, my brittle heels echoing my frustration. I unlocked the door and went in, accompanied by the director. There was one bed in the middle of the room, neatly made and empty. I looked around and spotted Dutchie curled up on the floor, beneath the basin. He had his forearms up against his face, shielding it from an imaginary threat, and his whole body was trembling. The director moved quickly forward to pick him up but I gestured for her to keep back and squatted down next to him. He was clearly in shock. It was not the sort of case I expected to see in the clinic – far too interesting – and I had nearly missed it.

Dutchie's head was clean shaven. His ears were full of rings and there was also a glistening stud in his nose. He was wearing a dirty white T-shirt and a faded maroon *lunghi*.

"Can I get you anything?" I asked. He flicked his eyes sideways at me for a moment and then turned his head away. I looked up at the director, who was standing by the door.

"Has he been given anything?" I asked.

"A sedative in Cochin at nine this morning. The nurse is giving him another one tonight, before the flight."

"What exactly happened to him?"

"Nobody knows. All we've been told is that he was found wandering around Ernakulam Junction in a semi-delirious state."

I looked at him again and noticed that his lips were mouthing something. I bent down, closer, wincing at the smell of his rotting clothes.

"What are you trying to say?" I asked, my ear close to his mouth.

He was barely audible, but I could just make out one word, "Kali", which he seemed to be saying over and over again.

I spent the whole evening at home, searching the internet for information about Kali and her fearful reputation. To judge from the large number of web pages in her honour, she was alive and well in modern India. One of the fiercest deities, she was the dark goddess of death, worshipped mainly in the north with sexual rituals and sacrifice, sometimes human. Her image was terrifying: she wore a garland of skulls and her lolling tongue dripped with blood. She wasn't all bad, though. Many believed that she represented the creative as well as destructive aspects of nature, empowering the downtrodden and abused women of India. Her manifestations were numerous: the destroyer of time, a sensual, swan-like woman, a prolific drug-taker (camphor, musk and wine), the embodiment of female desire, and a worshipper of young women with foreplay.

I thought of Dutchie again. All things considered, Kali seemed an entirely appropriate goddess for a drugged-up traveller. Perhaps he had just had a bad trip. But there was something else about him, his struggle to communicate, that made me think otherwise.

CHAPTER THREE

THE FOLLOWING EVENING, after a routine day at the medical centre, I was invited over to dinner with the only people I knew in Delhi who didn't work at the High Commission. Susie and Frank were easy company and they had been very good to me in my first few weeks. They had come into the clinic on my second day with their eldest son, Kashmir, who was suffering from a bad case of gastroenteritis. I followed up his treatment with a home visit, stayed for a meal, and we had been good friends ever since.

Unlike the rest of us, Frank and Susie celebrated being in India. I didn't understand why they did, but it made a welcome change from the paranoia of my colleagues, most of whom were desperate to jump on the first plane out of Delhi. Living in a state of siege behind the barbed-wire walls of the High Commission, they ate fish and chips at the compound restaurant on Fridays, and insisted on drinking cow's milk that was flown in twice a week from Tesco's. (One woman told me, in all seriousness, that a pint of the local product, buffalo's milk, contained enough DDT to kill an adult elephant.) They were trying, much like the bar at Radissons, or Djinns, to deny the existence of India. I didn't like the country much but I was living here and to deny it seemed futile. Meeting Frank and Susie was a bit like encountering a brilliant scientist who also believed in God. There had to be something about India that I was missing if two sane, rational and warm people had lived here for fifteen years and showed no signs of wanting to move on.

"Either you get India or you don't," Frank had once told me. If I was ever going to get it while I was here, it would be by spending time with people like him. He was an artist, currently obsessed with painting richly coloured abstracts of rural Rajasthan, and always seemed to be on the point of converting to Sufism. They lived in a *haveli* in Nizamuddin, a leafy, bohemian suburb named after a thirteenth-century Sufi mystic and favoured by journalists, artists and anyone else who wanted to experience the old city of Delhi without having to trek up to Chandni Chowk. Their trick, it seemed, was to incorporate the occasional Western comfort into their otherwise wholly Indian way of life. Guests could drink Kingfisher beer or Chivas Regal whisky all night long at Frank's place, but he also offered fine wines from France, procured, he would explain proudly, from a gold-toothed Mr Tricky who had good contacts in the African embassies. Mr Tricky's "Bordix", "Stemillion", "Bew Rividge" and "Pully Fussy" were particularly recommended, but for special occasions he would always insist on "Pippa Headsick".

There was a daily throng of people passing through their house – writers, photographers, intellectuals, almost all of them Indian – and that night was no exception. Frank led me through to an open courtyard at the back of the *haveli*, his arm round my shoulders. Nobody had shown me this sort of kindness in Delhi. In the winter I suspected he wore reassuring patterned jumpers, holed at the elbows. That evening, though, he was wearing white *kurta pyjama*.

Sitting on the edge of a pool in the middle of the courtyard was a writer I had met once before called Tapash. He was short, gnomic, with a grey-flecked goatee beard that didn't make him look any taller. Next to him was an ageing, unfamiliar man in a red turban and cream *churidar kurta*. He was talking to two women, one of whom was Susie. The other, an Indian woman, I had not met before. She glanced up at me, turning away as soon as our eyes met.

"Raj, how lovely to see you," Susie said, rising to kiss me on both cheeks. She tossed back her silk *dupatta* over one shoulder and turned to the others. "Tapash-ji you know, of course," she said, waving in his direction. Tapash stood up and greeted me with hands pressed together in front of him. "And this is Ranjit Singh, who used to be ambassador to London."

"Many years ago," Ranjit said, rising to shake my hand. I hadn't realised how tall he was until he was standing above me. He was well-built, too, naturally broad across the shoulders, no evidence of any gym visits.

"And this is Priyanka Pillai," Susie said. Priyanka held out a soft hand for me to shake, which surprised me. I had been preparing to greet her with a respectful nod of the head. I took her hand, feeling its warmth, and noticed that she was not wearing shoes. Her feet were slender, small gaps between her painted toes, the ankles gilded with silver chains. She was wearing a purple sari, which allowed a glimpse of taut stomach above the hip.

"Priyanka works for *Seven Days* magazine," Susie said, firmly, helpfully.

"Do you know it?" Priyanka asked.

"I've seen it on the shelf, at Khan Market," I said, struggling to appear normal, my scalp suddenly glowing.

"Raj, you need a drink," Frank said. "What can I get you? Bordix? Fresh from the Africas."

"Maybe later. I'll take some lime soda."

"One *nimbu pani*," he said, heading off towards the kitchen.

Frank and Susie employed a huge number of domestic staff, but they always seemed to be huddled in the corner of the main room, watching Hindi movies on a small but loud television set. I hadn't been to an expat house where the hosts fetched their own drinks. At the High Commissioner's official residence, generous gin and tonics were brought to you on silver East India Company platters by bearers in white starched uniforms and *pugris*.

I wanted to talk to Priyanka, but she had turned to Tapash. Instead I chatted with Ranjit about Britain, the only common subject that came to mind, but he wanted to know what I did at the High Commission.

"I'm a doctor," I said, glancing across at Priyanka. "One of two. My colleague is away on a tour of Bangladesh and Pakistan."

"Anything else?" he asked in perfect, almost overprecise English. His eyes were a little too moist, giving the impression they were permanently twinkling.

"I'm sorry?" I asked, wrong-footed.

"Do you do anything other than doctoring?" he said again, gently brushing down one side of his moustache. His eyes sparkled. I was flummoxed and he knew it. "I'm sorry, I shouldn't have asked," he said, leaning forward to touch my arm. "It's just that in my experience nobody at an embassy ever serves only one purpose."

"As far as I know I'm just the doctor," I said, laughing, regaining some composure, hoping that he would change the subject. "Occasionally I have to read last rites, but not very often."

"Don't worry about him," Tapash said, breaking away from Priyanka. "He thinks everybody at the British High Commission is a spy."

"Absolute nonsense," Ranjit said. "Although I do remember a first consul once tried to recruit me when I told him I preferred Margaret Thatcher to Mrs Gandhi."

I stood back a bit to let Tapash and Priyanka join our circle. They seemed close and I found myself wondering, briefly, if anything existed between them. Frank came over with my drink.

"What's there to spy about anyway, these days?" Frank asked. I could smell wine on his breath.

"Trade, nuclear technology," Tapash offered.

"But you've got the bomb," Frank said, pouring himself another glass of wine. I wondered how this conversation had ever begun.

"Oh yes, we know how to blow things up," Tapash continued, "but we can't crack a reactor, not on our own. We've been trying to build an indigenous nuclear submarine for years."

"That's all very well," Frank said, "but it still doesn't explain why *we* would want to spy on *you*."

"Frank, you're sounding positively colonial," Tapash interjected. "We've got plenty of secrets." He paused, looking at Priyanka. "Like my mother's recipe for *papdi chaat*."

27

We all laughed and I took the opportunity to glance at Priyanka again. She was tall, about my height, with an upright posture that suggested poise rather than arrogance. Her black hair was rich and effervescent, tumbling down below her shoulders. By anyone's standards she was beautiful, but it was her manner, her equanimity, that was touching something inside. It was a quiet confidence, a focused calmness, a trait that I hadn't seen too much of in Delhi.

"Were you here or in London when we tested the bombs?" Ranjit asked, making me nervous again.

"No, I was in Edinburgh," I replied.

"Raj has only just arrived in Delhi," Frank added.

"And did you join in the chorus of Western disapproval?" Ranjit continued.

"It took me by surprise," I said, beginning to suspect how much this man knew. "I think I squealed, more in shock than pain."

"A very medical answer," he said.

"I'm a doctor," I replied, shrugging my shoulders. I glanced at Frank for help.

"It was an interesting time," Frank said. I don't know whether he was bailing me out or just getting into his stride. "The fallout did funny things to your head. All my life I'd opposed nuclear weapons but I suddenly found myself defending India's right to test them. It was the hypocrisy that got me: it's all right for us, the first world, to have nuclear bombs, but it's not okay for a third-world country. They didn't want India to join the club."

"France were much more consistent," Ranjit said, turning towards me again. "They were very brave, no squeals."

"Were you scared at the time, worried that tensions might escalate?" I asked.

"Not really," Frank said, looking at Ranjit, who nodded assent. "I popped over to Khan Market, asked a few of the shopkeepers if they were stocking up, but they weren't. The bazaar always knows."

Ranjit had the unnerving habit of taking a fistful of peanuts and then offering them round. His enormous hand was now extended towards me, the nuts glistening in their own oil and some of his sweat. I was not obsessed by personal hygiene, but I spent a good deal of my day telling patients to wash their hands before eating anything. I hadn't washed when I arrived, but it would have seemed rude if I didn't accept Ranjit's offer. I took the nuts and squeezed them in my hand. When no one was looking I slipped them into an urn.

I looked around at the gathering, trying to stand back. The moon was full and had appeared above the front eaves of the house. A tandoor was heating up in one corner of the courtyard, its thin, blue smoke rising into the clear sky. There was a smell of sandalwood incense, too, mixed with the sweet scent of *Rath-ki-Rani*, Queen of the Night.

I felt happy here, particularly when Susie rejoined the group. She was in her forties with an aristocratic air that I had mistaken for snobbishness when I first met her. Now I had her down as an eccentric. She took all six of her female staff to Lodhi Gardens every morning to practice *Vipassana* meditation, much to the surprise of the locals out on their morning walk, according to Tapash, who had witnessed the spectacle. To look at, she was attractive in a natural, no-make-up way, and she had made a virtue of her hair greying early. It was long and shiny and made her skin look younger. She could be motherly, too, not just to Kashmir and their daughter, Jumila. When I first arrived, she had sent her driver round with my dinner every night in a stainless steel tiffin box, chilli chicken curries with brinjal and chapatis folded like napkins.

"And how is the new cook shaping up, Raj?" she asked, sitting down next to me. "Still stealing eggs?"

"I'm sorry, Susie, but you know the rules," Tapash said, interrupting. "You're not allowed to talk about servants."

"'Staff', please," Susie said. "You must call them staff. You don't have to listen."

Tapash turned to me and said, "I'm sure you've noticed, Raj, that when two or more expats gather in one place, all they can talk about is the lazy *mali*, the dangerous driver, the cheating cook and the awful ayah."

"It's the novelty," I said. "We're not used to this kind of thing in Britain."

His eyes lingered knowingly on me before he turned away. I couldn't be sure but it was as if, for a moment, he had forgotten that I was from Britain. I had only met Tapash once before, but he had never shown me any of the coldness that I had encountered with other Indians. Perhaps it was because he had been to Britain and considered himself cosmopolitan, able to mix easily with anyone. Or perhaps it was because he was without envy. He had been to the West, seen what he was meant to be missing and now he was back in India, contented.

"Actually," I continued, "I'm more worried about my neighbour's ayah. My Hindi teacher says she is too 'frank' with men, particularly my cook. And when I'm away she even climbs trees, which apparently confirms her lack of morals."

"Talking of ayahs," Susie continued, smiling at Tapash, who was shaking his head in despair, "I've written a letter of protest to the High Commissioner's wife complaining about them not being allowed to sit by the pool. It's outrageous, worse than the white suburbs of Johannesburg."

"Why do you still go there, then?" Tapash asked.

"The children need somewhere to swim, and until they clean up the Jamuna it's the only option."

Dinner turned out to be a feast – organic chicken from a French-run farm outside Delhi and cooked by Frank in their own tandoor oven. (Their Nepali chef had asked for, and been granted, special permission to visit the picture house to see Manisha Koirala in her new movie, the third film he had seen that week.) We squeezed fresh limes on the chicken and laughed at the funny shape of Frank's naan breads.

"They're like maps of India," Tapash said.

"Fresh cowpats, that's the secret," Frank replied. "I lined the tandoor myself."

I was thwarted by Ranjit in my attempt to sit next to Priyanka. He persisted in his questions about the High Commission, which led me to conclude that either he understood very little or he knew everything. I wanted to talk to Frank about it but I knew I couldn't. I couldn't talk to anyone. Susie glanced at me occasionally, nodding in Priyanka's direction when she was not looking. She could be indiscreet but at least her encouragement suggested that Priyanka and Tapash were not an item. Later she beckoned me to come into

31

the kitchen, waving her hands about with all the subtlety of a traffic policeman.

"How's it going?" she said, dipping her finger in a bowl of curd.

"How's what going?" I asked, knowing full well what she meant.

"You know, Priyanka. Beautiful girl, isn't she? Frank thinks she's a knockout."

"Is this a set-up or something?"

"Of course it's not. I just thought you might hit it off, that's all."

"It's a set-up. She's not with Tapash, then."

"Tapash!" she laughed, and then covered her mouth, looking at the door as he went past.

Outside in the courtyard I helped to hand round pieces of papaya and mango, ensuring this time that I was next to Priyanka when the music stopped. We talked quietly in a corner, unnoticed by the others, who were now slipping inside for coffee, no doubt at Susie's behest. Priyanka's eyes reflected the warm lights inside. It turned out she was from Kerala, which in a funny way didn't surprise me at all. I told her my family was from Kerala, too, which surprised her more. There was something so familiar about her that it scared me because I couldn't adequately explain what it was. Our conversation paused naturally, a moment free of all awkwardness, full of certainties, and then a crowd of people spilled back out into the night air and I was suddenly up and chatting with Frank, stealing glances across to our corner whenever I could.

Priyanka had stood up too and was now talking with Susie, calmly. She seemed so unhurried. We exchanged numbers before we left, but our parting was diminished by a change in her mood. It was like watching someone remembering a piece of bad news. The brightness vanished from her eyes as we talked, her words, so vibrant earlier, tailing off in mid-sentence. For a moment I mistook her manner for indifference.

I felt lonely that night as Ravi took me home, more than I had done for years. Loneliness was a much more potent emotion in India. If you couldn't find company in a country of one billion people, it was a sure sign that something was amiss. Whenever I dispatched Ravi on a task, he took a friend with him in the car, not wanting to spend time on his own. An advert for one of India's most popular vehicles, the Maruti, said, "You'll never drive alone." Every emotion was magnified here and loneliness, left to itself, could be more devastating than most. My feelings for Priyanka had also been magnified. They were quite irrational, way out of proportion to our brief encounter. In Britain I had taken time, too long perhaps, to decide if I liked someone.

Ravi was a man of little English, but he looked in the mirror as I stared out of the window.

"Problem, sir?" he asked.

"*Koi baat nay*," I replied, stretching what little Hindi I had learnt. As we approached the turning for Sainik Farms, we passed a line of cycle rickshaws parked in the middle of the road. Their drivers were asleep in the flatbed boxes behind the saddle, oblivious of the traffic passing inches either side of them. One man, legs tight to his chest, had his head twisted awkwardly against the box's wooden side as he slept. He had no fan, no mosquito net, not even a roof over his head. Just a wooden box, and he couldn't even fit into that.

CHAPTER FOUR

IT HAD BEEN a bad night in the republic. The neighbours across the road had decided to throw a party for two thousand close friends, most of whom finished dancing to Daler Mehndi at five thirty in the morning. *Tukatukatuk.* I was going off him. The mains electricity had failed earlier in the night. It was an illegal connection, like forty per cent of Delhi's power and all of Sainik Farms', so I couldn't ring anyone to complain. Jagu, the *mali*, had cranked up one of two generators in the storeroom, but a water pipe was broken and it soon overheated. The back-up was in bits on the floor. Sadly, the neighbour's party was being powered by a vast mobile generator outside our gate. Jagu had considered taking a feed from it but I told him not to bother. The republic might be a lawless place but residents stole from the state not from one another. So there I had lain, for most of the night, fair game for the mosquitos in the din and the heat.

I had risen at six, unable to bear any more, and was now standing on the balcony watching the sun rise, its nascent rays reflecting off the shards of glass that lined the top of a brick wall belonging to my immediate neighbours, the Bakshis, with whi I shared a driveway. The wall must have been over twelve feet high but Mrs Bakshi had explained to me when I first arrived that it could easily be breached by determined *goondas* from Haryana. "But it's like a fortress," I had told her. She had shaken her head and said that we must not take any risks. "We are very lonely out here." She rang the guardhouse throughout the night, she said, just to make sure that the *chowkidar* was not sleeping. Then she had added a strange word of warning: "There are insects and whatnots in the bushes at night."

Below me I could hear Chandar, my Nepali cook, grinding cardamom and cloves with a metal pestle and mortar in preparation for my morning pot of *massala chai*. The night guard, unaware that he was being watched, was holding a fragment of mirror close to his face, trimming his nasal hair with scissors as he listened to All India Radio on a crackling transistor. Life was stirring on the surrounding rooftops, accompanied by a muezzin from a mosque towards Qutab Minar. The call to prayer was quiet and insistent, barely amplified, a welcome change from earlier. Across the road, behind the top of a grand faux-Palladian façade, I glimpsed a body moving. It was a member of staff washing, naked, except for a thin brown cloth around his waist. He was busy scrubbing himself all over, occasionally dipping a jug into one of the house's large black-barrelled water tanks. Other similar scenes were unfolding on adjacent rooftops. I could see still forms sleeping, covered from head to foot by thin blankets, lying between vast, transparent satellite dishes. To the left, home of the sinister Dr Gupta, a more disturbing daily pageant was being played out.

The doctor's staff were feeding six large Great Danes that guarded the premises. But it wasn't the dogs that frightened me, it was the ghostly staff, two women in saris and a man, who walked slowly across the lawn, filling water bowls and emptying out plastic bags of bones on the lawn. The staff were albino white, their skin bleached by one of Dr Gupta's "fairing creams" which, so the republic rumour machine had it, he had tested on them before reducing the dose and going into commercial production. I was dreading the call to dinner.

At least the guard didn't salute me this time as the front gates stuttered open. Ravi drove me through Sainik Farms, past a young Nepali in uniform taking his employer's sweating St Bernard for a morning walk. The walls either side of the road were mostly topped with spiralling barbed wire, the exhaust pipes of diesel generators sticking out through holes in the brickwork like rusting trench guns. At the busy junction outside Sainik Farms, a woman was hanging out her husband's shirts to dry on the central reservation barrier. A barber hung up his mirror on a wall and dusted down a wooden chair, inches away from the smoking traffic. As we passed, his first customer of the day climbed into the chair. The barber rubbed his dirty hair, starting up a conversation as they both looked into the mirror. Ravi said he only charged fifteen rupees a cut. Two men, struggling to make ends meet, each trying to cling on to some self-respect.

The medical centre had its own entrance on the compound, complete with Gurkha guards and a large dented barrier, weighed down at one end with a basket full of rocks. As we waited while a guard checked underneath the car with a long-handled mirror, my eye was caught by a young man standing in the shadow of a laburnum tree, to the right of the entrance. He seemed nervous, looking around, making sure that the guards

36

hadn't seen him. This part of Delhi, known as Chana-kyapuri, was packed with embassies and patrolled by armed police who moved everybody on. He was holding a piece of card in his hand. Just as I looked away, the man lifted it up. The word "doctor" had been written in large black letters. I tapped Ravi on the shoulder, opened my door and told him to drive in.

"I'll be one minute," I said, smiling at the guard who had now spotted the man. "It's okay," I said. "He's come to see me." The guard, who was gesturing to the man to move and shouting, "*Challo, challo,*" looked confused and went back to his post on the gate.

I didn't know why I had got out of the car. A reflex action, a sense of duty, like standing up when somebody asked if there was a doctor in the house. I was also curious.

"I'm a doctor here," I said, nodding towards the medical centre. "Can I help?"

The man was in his thirties and wearing heavily pressed trousers and a clean striped shirt. Without any introduction he turned the card round to reveal four photos that had been crudely stuck down. At the bottom of the card was a piece of paper with some writing on it, one version in Hindi, the other in English. I had attended a couple of fairly gruesome post-mortems in England, but I had never seen anything so immediately shocking.

All four photos were of a child's bloated corpse, no older than two. The neck had been slit, many times, and there were numerous incisions above the heart. But it was the child's face that made me swallow hard. Both ears had been severed and the nose was gone. It wasn't immediately obvious, but it also seemed that the tongue had been cut out, to judge from the bruising and injuries inside and around the open mouth. The boy's eyes were open and intact, and the rest of the body, though distended, was unharmed.

The man let me absorb the photos before he started to speak in Hindi.

"I'm sorry, I don't speak any Hindi," I said, interrupting him. "I'm from London."

The man looked at me, surprised. *"Kya? Hindi nahi boltey ho?"* he said.

"Nay," I replied. It must have been confusing. I looked Indian, I was in India, but I didn't speak Hindi, or Urdu, or Punjabi. Unperturbed, he stabbed his finger at the bottom paragraph. The handwriting was good and the English understandable. The boy's name was Tinkoo and he had been abducted while playing outside his home in a village in Saharanpur district, northern Uttar Pradesh. His family had found his body a day later in the Ban Ganga river, a tributary of the Ganges. In his post-mortem report, the local doctor said he had drowned and his body had been attacked by fish. His family said he was offered as a sacrifice to Kali on the instructions of a local *tantrik* or witch doctor. He had been hung upside down and had his ears and nose slashed off, before his throat had been slit. Nobody had heard him scream because he was deaf and dumb. At the bottom of the card, underlined, was an appeal for an honest doctor: according to his family, the doctor who had conducted the post-mortem had been paid off by the *tantrik*, who had also bribed the local police.

"I can't do a post-mortem from a photo. It's not possible, nobody can," I said, regardless of whether the man could understand me. I was thinking aloud, trying

38

to order my thoughts. An image of Dutchie came and went. "I don't know when these photos were taken, the time of death. It doesn't look like fish – the eyes are still intact – and these injuries here, above the heart, are probably cuts, but I'm sorry, I couldn't say, I can't help you, I'm sorry."

We looked at each other for a moment before I handed back the card. It seemed so irreverent, but I glanced at my watch and then at the gates.

"I've got to go. I'm late. Here's my card," I said, handing him one.

He looked at it a moment and then said, *"Tantrik, angrez."*

"Angrez?" I queried, and he nodded.

As I walked in through the gates, I took a deep breath, thinking of the photos again. India had that ability to throw something at you that shattered all the parameters of normal, daily life: the deformed child suddenly at the car window, festering stumps for hands; a goods carrier on its side, steaming in your headlights; a fight between two cycle rickshaw drivers, one of them partially sighted, swinging wildly with a brick in his hand. I hoped the clinic was going to be straightforward.

The centre was so busy that I missed lunch, which was a good thing as I had little time to dwell on the photos and what, if anything, I could do about them. All I knew was that *angrez* meant Englishman in Hindi. After the last appointment cancelled, I decided to head up to Connaught Circus and have an icecream at Nirula's, an indigenous fast-food chain that Tapash had recommended in preference to McDonald's and its

Maharaja chicken burgers. I sat upstairs, above the icecream parlour. The place was packed with local families and single foreign travellers enjoying Western fast food, Indian style.

The post had been delivered just before I left the medical centre and I had brought a letter with me from home. My father had been delighted when I first told him that I had landed a job with the Foreign Office. When I explained that I was being posted to Delhi, he had visibly paled. Unlike my mother, he had cut off all contact with India when he left Kerala, his birthplace, to live in Britain. In its suddenness, his departure had been like an amputation, except that later on he never tried to reach out and touch what had been taken. India had been replaced comprehensively by a country that grew and grew in his affections.

After Independence, an event he never talked about, he studied to be a doctor. It was a late decision – he had previously been involved in politics – and he finally graduated as a mature student from the Trivandrum Medical College in 1956. Shortly afterwards he married my mother, also from Kerala, and they had moved in 1960 to Edinburgh. He had been part of a second wave of Indians who had migrated to Britain after the war and who were generally better off and more qualified than the earlier migrants, most of whom had come from the north and west.

He had never returned to India. When I had occasionally asked him why not, he told me his Indian relations were all dead and his home was now Britain, or Scotland, whenever he was talking with a Sassenach. He drank whisky, wore a kilt on New Year's Eve and could recite the whole of Burns's "For a' that and a' that". Almost all his friends were local Scots and he avoided the Asian community whenever he could.

From the day he had arrived in Edinburgh, where I was born, it was as if India had never existed. All traces of it were meticulously expunged from our family life. We were not the only family to suppress our Indianness to what now seemed a ludicrous degree. Perhaps it was a legitimate fear of racism (there had been race riots in Nottingham and London in 1958), but in those early years fitting in had meant being British – and, more importantly, being seen to be British, particularly in Scotland and Wales, where attitudes were more provincial than somewhere like London. At least, that had always been my father's line.

It was only now, with thousands of miles between us, that I was able to look objectively at my father. We were very close and I had, I supposed, adopted most of his prejudices, particularly about India, without ever really questioning them. In the past we had talked around the country, united in an unspoken pact that it was irrelevant to our lives. My posting to Delhi was the first thing that had ever threatened to come between us. At times I resented India for that, at others I felt an exhilarating, rebellious sense of freedom.

His letter was full of medical gossip. My father was retired, but he had carved out an illustrious career in the unglamorous world of occupational medicine, specialising in radiation exposure. He had worked first for the government and later as chief medical officer for a number of private companies. The university had asked him to teach, he had also been a senior lecturer at the Institute of Occupational Medicine, and he had undertaken occasional consultancy work for the UK Atomic

Energy Authority. He talked of a few heavy drinking sessions that I had thankfully missed, and hinted that he had started to use Viagra. As ever, he threw in a few interesting case studies, asking me what I would do (there was inevitably a trick of some sort), and quoted liberally from his latest letter to the *British Medical Journal*, in which he had brilliantly dismantled – yet again – the "Gardner hypothesis" which maintained that a radiation dose received by a father before his child was conceived might cause leukemia and non-Hodgkin's lymphoma in the child. It was a subject we regularly agreed to disagree on, and I knew he had included it to provoke me.

His comments on my life in Delhi were confined to my job, the medical centre, the international availability of certain vaccines. I think it was the only way he could begin to accommodate what I was doing. That I was in India was wholly irrelevant. I was a doctor working overseas. End of story.

There should have been some profound psychological reason for his almost anaphylactic reaction to India, some childhood scar that explained all, but I think he just preferred Scotland. It was as simple as that. He did once confide to me that he had spent some time as a student with the Muirs, a Glaswegian family of tea planters in Munnar, a hill station in Kerala. The experience had moved him greatly – he marvelled at their emphasis on health care, education, malt whisky – but it didn't completely explain the shutting off, the denial.

He signed off his letter with "Come home soon".

CHAPTER FIVE

LATER THAT DAY I sat at home trying to compose a reply
to my father's letter. Writing about India was much
harder than I thought, particularly when you were
addressing someone who had left it for good almost
forty years ago. Was I trying to justify the country or to
condemn it? There were the obvious points — the
expected poverty, the surprising wealth, dust, heat,
cows in the street, religion, pollution, sunsets and elections — and the way in which they were all taken to such
extremes, but my father knew that and had chosen to
reject it. Then there were the more unexpected things:
being given Boomer bubble gum instead of small
change, the man operating the automatic coffee
machine (he took your money, put it in the slot and
handed you your cup), finding your name, sex and age
(why age?) on a printed notice on the side of your train.

One aspect of Delhi life that particularly troubled
me was the proximity of abortion and ultrasound
clinics. I had even seen a clinic in Saket advertising
"Egg, Scan, Delivery, Abortion" all on one sign. It was a
sufficiently medical subject to grab my father's notori-
ously short attention span. In parts of the southern
state of Tamil Nadu, I told him, writing fast, in case
he got bored, the ratio of girls under ten compared
to boys was down to 850 to 1,000. The pregnant
wife of a first secretary had complained to me the other

day that she had had to insist on not being told the sex of her baby. She was having a scan at a private hospital and it had been assumed that she would want to know.

I decided not to mention Tinkoo and his defiled, bloated body. Not yet. It would have given Father too much satisfaction. We had always been competitive, and in my mind accepting the posting to India – accepting the existence of India – was a challenge to him. Unlike in other challenges, however, I expected to be proved wrong. My father had lived here for the first forty years of his life and his decision to leave must have been suitably informed. He had known the country better than I ever would. If I drew different conclusions, I feared it would feel like an act of betrayal. A part of me didn't want to question his judgment, to invalidate his life in Scotland, our life. But it was only a part of me.

A knock on the window disturbed me. It was the night guard, but I didn't recognise him as he had only started this morning. The old guard had been sacked after one of Mrs Bakshi's many alarms went off in the night and he had failed to rush to her rescue. He was the third night guard to be dismissed in a month. In his defence, he had said he thought it was a faulty car alarm, but Mrs Bakshi knew otherwise.

"You can't trust these people, they are so lazy, isn't it?" she had told me this morning. Far from being lazy, he was busy on the job with the Bakshi's ayah, but I didn't say anything.

"He was sleeping while a *goonda* might have been slitting our throats," she had continued. "Aren't you lonely at night?"

I had told her that it was hard to feel lonely when there were houses within yards of us on all sides, but she wouldn't have any of it.

"There could be anyone hiding in the bushes."

"Whatnots?" I offered, interrupting. "Insects?"

She looked at me with suspicion and then her face melted into an expression of warm solidarity, as if she had finally found an ally.

"Please turn on your garden lights at night."

The guard was now indicating that there was someone at the gate. I went over to the window and he handed me a card through the grill: it was Jamie's.

"It's like Fort Knox around here," Jamie was saying a few minutes later, as he strode around the empty, dimly lit hall. Something about his manner troubled me, the arrogance, his sureness of foot. Most of the house was empty, and his voice bounced off the polished marble floors. It had seemed silly to unpack. The High Commission had promised me every week since I arrived that I would soon be moving back onto the compound.

"I was told that *chowkidars* either let everyone in or no one at all," I said. "There's no halfway, no taking responsibility. Can I get you a drink?"

"Don't you have a bearer?" he asked, smiling.

I didn't smile back. "It's the cook's day off."

"I'm joking," he continued. "I'll have a whisky. You should get more staff, though," he said, looking around at the bare hall. "More furniture. A decent power supply. I hope you're complaining."

"I'm moving onto the compound any day now, so they say," I said.

"And tell any woolly liberals who make a fuss about servants that you're creating employment, which is true. It's the least we can do if we're living in their country. Mind if I smoke? I've been gagging for a stogie all day."

He didn't wait for an answer. I watched as he pulled out a large cigar and started to pick away at one end with a small penknife.

"Is there anywhere to sit around here?" he asked, looking hopefully through a glass door which led to the sitting room.

I opened the door, gesturing for him to enter, and then fixed us both a whisky in the kitchen. When I returned, he was sitting down on a sofa lent to me by Frank and Susie, his feet up on a *chucki*, a low circular grinding board. It had been converted into a glass-topped table by a furniture shop in Haus Khas village, where I had bought it on my second day in Delhi. I put the whisky down on it, next to his suede brogues, and then the bottle, which I had brought in from the kitchen on a small cane tray I had bought at the Assam State Emporium on the same day. I took the tray away again, feeling like a bearer, and sat down on the top of two marble steps that separated the sitting room from a dining area. Jamie continued to pick away at the cigar, humming to himself, occasionally pulling at the end with his teeth. He glanced up, catching me watching him.

"It's called a *coheba*," he said, holding the cigar like a paper dart. "After the CIA tried to kill Castro with an exploding cigar, he decided not to take any chances and employed his own roller. These are what he made. The best stogie money can't buy."

"I'm sure you haven't come all this way to talk about cigars," I said, suddenly resenting his presence, wishing he would remove his feet from the *chucki*.

"Oh, I don't know. I'd travel a long way if someone was really interested."

There was a pause in our conversation, a missed beat, which unsettled me more than it did Jamie. What was he doing here, anyway? Eight o'clock on a Sunday evening?

"Frank and Susie," he began, answering my question. "Friends of yours?"

"They've been very good to me," I said, taking a large sip of whisky.

"Completely troppo, aren't they?"

"Troppo?"

"Tropical. Gone native. Donned the turban."

"They're big fans of India," I said.

"That's one way of putting it. Not so keen on Britain, either."

"No?"

He shook his head, leant back and blew smoke high into the air. I watched it swirl under the central light, which was flickering faintly, underpowered by an overworked generator.

"Frank was a very active member of the Communist Party of Great Britain," Jamie said. "A long time ago, admittedly, but it's one of the reasons he left in the end. He was frustrated by their waning influence. I think the number of times the police brought him in also had something to do with it."

The police? Jamie wasn't describing the Frank I knew. I thought back hastily to our last meeting, his comments on the nuclear tests. Armchair CND, perhaps, but not the sort to bother the police.

"He seems harmless enough to me," I said, trying to process the implications of the whole conversation. "Is there a problem?"

"You tell me," Jamie said, switching his gaze suddenly from the ceiling to me. I turned away from his eyes, watching more smoke eddy in the dim light.

"I went round there for dinner on Friday," I said.

"I know."

How did he know? "His son had been very sick."

"Listen, Raj, being a doctor out here is meant to encourage others to drop their guard, not your own. He's a no-no, okay? A security risk, a neg-vet as the Americans say, just the sort of person you spend time with when you're working for me, only I didn't know. Not until I heard later."

"Who from?"

"Does it matter?" he said, pausing. It must have been Ranjit, all those questions about my job at the High Commission. "Did you know Frank's applying for Indian citizenship?"

"No, I didn't," I replied, getting up to pour myself another whisky. I glanced at Jamie's glass, which was empty. He held it up, rocking it from side to side as if he were ringing a bell, gesturing to a bearer.

"I'll be honest with you, Raj." He had sat back in the sofa, half lost in the smoke and weak lighting. "We have no idea where his sympathies lie. I just don't want you relaxing with people like him. Not now, not when we're about to embark on something so sensitive."

"What exactly are you saying? That I shouldn't see him again?" I asked, reluctantly filling his glass and taking my own back to the step.

"There are a lot of interesting expats in Delhi, that's all. I know it's tricky at the beginning, the first six months can be hell, but you'll meet a lot of good people out here. I'll see to it, personally."

Jamie let himself out shortly afterwards, taking his *coheba* with him, though not its smoke, which lingered long after he had gone. I hadn't told my father about my extracurricular duties in Delhi. If I could have picked up the phone there and then, talked to him, I would have told him that I regretted ever having got involved. It had been a decision taken with the best patriotic intentions, at a time when I was excited at the thought of working for the Foreign Office. Now I was wondering, too late, what my real motives had been. It was almost as if I had done it to shore myself up against India; another line of defence in case she had begun to pull in the night.

CHAPTER SIX

MONDAY MORNING AT the clinic was always depressing, but I felt more dejected than usual as I looked down the list of appointments. A name that would normally have made me smile instead left me resentful and angry. Susie was booked in at eleven o'clock with her daughter Jumila. I was not cross with her, but she reminded me of Jamie's visit the previous night. His cigar smoke had still been there at breakfast, hanging behind the curtains, lingering in the cupboards, much like his own influence, which I was finding increasingly difficult to shake off. I would be polite, of course, and as helpful as I could, but Susie would detect a change in my manner. She was too knowing to be deceived. And I wouldn't be able to confide, as I normally did, and she would feel hurt. I had been prepared for deceptions, but not so soon and with people so close.

"Raj, whatever is the matter?" she said, the moment she walked into my room. "You look terrible. Come, tell me."

"That's what I'm supposed to say," I replied, avoiding her look. Jumila came round the side of my desk with a toy umbrella.

"Raj, look what Daddy gave me," she said, opening it.

"It's bad luck you know," I said, "opening an umbrella inside." I clicked the umbrella shut and passed it back to her.

"Is it? Why?"

"Because it never rains indoors. But if you open your umbrella it will rain and rain, and we'll all get very wet."

She wasn't convinced by my explanation and opened the umbrella again, spinning it around on the floor. I knew Susie was scrutinising me.

"It's Priyanka, isn't it?" she said. "She hasn't returned your call."

"I haven't rung her," I replied, twisting on my seat at the mention of her name.

"Why ever not? She's a lovely girl. You seemed to be getting on so well."

"Is Jumila okay?" I asked, failing to change the subject with any tact. Susie looked at me again, realising she was making no progress.

"Well, since you ask, she's not, actually. I think she might be diabetic."

Susie was not one to make a fuss without good reason. Frank told a story of the time when she had refused to take Kashmir to the doctor's after he had fallen out of his treehouse and complained of a sore arm. "Stop fussing," she had said, giving him an aspirin. Three days later, she relented – Kashmir was still in some pain – and it turned out that he had broken his arm in two places. Ever since then, she had been a little more cautious, though not much.

I distracted Jumila with more stories about umbrellas and drew a sample of her blood, watched by Susie.

"Call her up again," she said. "And if she doesn't ring, I'll invite you both over to supper next week. Okay?"

"How's Frank?" I asked, desperately wanting this game to stop.

"He's fine. Busy as ever. Lots of meetings at the British Council today. It looks like they're finally going to sponsor his show."

"That's wonderful news."

"Did he ring you last night? He said he was going to."

"He might have done. I'm having trouble with my pager."

I was lying. He had left two messages, but I hadn't returned the calls. Jamie's smoke had still been turning in the light.

"He wants to invite you over on Saturday for some carrom. Boys' night in."

"I'll have to check. I think I'm on call."

"On Saturday?" she asked, suspiciously.

I told her I would ring Frank later and she left with Jumila and her umbrella, sensing, I knew, that all was not well.

Just before lunch the phone rang and it was Priyanka, soft and easy and confident. I suspected Susie's hands at work, but I was still pleased to hear her voice, scanning it for clues that we might pick up where we had left off. In my mind I hadn't included Priyanka in Frank and Susie's set. If Tapash had called, I would have made my excuses, but Priyanka was out of Jamie's range and I vowed to keep her that way, in the fresh air.

"Are you free for dinner?" I asked, far too hastily.

"When?" she said.

"Tonight?" I could hear the receiver moving against her ear.

"Actually I was ringing to say that I have to go out of town for a few weeks, maybe longer. My mother is sick and I must go home to care for her."

My heart sank.

"When are you going?" I asked, trying to keep my voice even.

"Tomorrow morning."

"Then you can still do supper tonight."

She paused. "If it was early, perhaps we could meet for a short while," she said.

"Great. I'll pick you up at six. Why don't we try Sagar?"

I was showing off but it worked. Sagar was a south Indian joint popular with south Indians, which was always an encouraging sign. Better still, she had heard about it but not been there. I should have rung Susie to thank her but all our calls were listed and Jamie wouldn't have been amused if he saw Frank's number showing up the day after our meeting.

"I can't wait to be out of Delhi, to be honest," Priyanka said, pushing a piece of *idli* around her plate. The restaurant had yet to become crowded. A few hours later and the queue would be round the block. It was even busier at lunchtimes.

"It's getting hot, isn't it?" I said. "42.5 yesterday."

I winced at my own words. Why was I talking about the weather? I was becoming a Delhiwallah. Everyone in the capital talked about the temperature as summer settled in, chronicling the smallest rise.

"It's not just the heat," she said, giving me the benefit of the doubt. "It's the people, the traffic, the selfish attitudes, that I don't like. There's no generosity, no cooperation."

"No civic sense," I added, looking at her eat the last bit of *idli*. A tiny crumb was resting on the corner of her mouth. She pushed it in gently, licking her finger.

"Not bad," she said. "Not bad at all."

"I told you it was a good place."

"Will you ever come to Kerala?" she asked.

"I don't know. If I am sent. I have no plans to go there. Why?"

"You could taste real *idli*, and *sambar*, and *vada*."

"Are you going to be there for long?" I asked.

She didn't answer. Something wasn't right. I feigned indifference but I could feel my jaw starting to collapse. We both tried to act as if I hadn't asked the question, as if the words hadn't left my mouth.

"How well do you know Frank?" I asked, managing to change the subject, trying to keep things together.

"Frank? I met him in Kerala, a couple of years ago. I was writing a story about foreigners who make India their home. He was on holiday at the time, staying with a British couple who live in Cochin. I sometimes think he understands India better than we do." She paused. "I suppose I'm closer to Susie."

"They were very good to me when I first arrived, very parental," I said, wondering why I was asking these things. She had to be kept pure, away from all the deception.

"They're like that, they hate seeing anyone unhappy here," she continued. "It's like you become their responsibility. Sometimes I think they feel responsible for the whole of India. God knows why. We don't."

"Is it true he's applying for Indian citizenship?" I asked.

"Why don't you ask him?" she said, mildly surprised, detecting for the first time, perhaps, a hidden agenda.

"Will you write when you're away, tell me all about the beautiful south?" I asked.

"I'm hopeless at letters. Writing all day at the office, I'm out of words by the evening."

"Call me, then. I'll ring you back."

She smiled, said nothing. Like me, she was probably aware, suddenly, that we were talking as if we had known each other for years. It was one of those early defining moments when a relationship was either acknowledged for the first time, or pushed away.

"I'm glad I met you, Raj," she said, looking into her empty glass of *lassi*.

"Me too," I said, hoping we were about to acknowledge. But she paused, too long for comfort, and then she pushed.

"My parents think they have found someone," she continued, not looking up. Her tone was subdued.

"Found someone?" I asked.

"A husband."

I tried to take in what she was saying. She was talking about an arranged marriage. This didn't happen any more, I told myself, not amongst sassy, cosmopolitan journalists. In the plains of rural Rajasthan, perhaps, but not in Delhi, not in Priyanka's world.

"I thought . . . " I trailed off, not knowing where to start.

"You thought I wouldn't approve of something like arranged marriages," she said.

"I didn't say that."

"But that's what you're thinking. They're backward, retrogressive, tribal."

55

Why were we suddenly cross with each other?

"Do you know who he is?" I asked, realising that I had been thinking all those things and worse.

"I know of him."

"And is he . . . " I paused, searching for the right word. "Is he nice?"

"What kind of a question is that?"

"I mean . . . " All I could think of was my English teacher at school who used to circle "nice" in red ink and say that the only nice things in life were biscuits. Priyanka was right. What I meant was that I hoped he was a bastard and it didn't work out.

"I trust my parents," she said, with an air of finality.

We had lost the intimacy of our earlier conversation. She talked about her work, I mentioned the clinic, but our exchanges were hollow, without conviction. The bill was brought to the table in a small dish made of woven banana leaves. We both seemed relieved that the meal was almost over.

"It's not how you imagine," she said. "It's arranged, not forced. There's no pressure or anything like that."

"Of course there is," I replied. Instead of getting angry, she turned her head away and wiped a tear from the corner of her eye. Last weekend I had watched couples in the open plazas of Dilli Haat, sitting in tears, inconsolable. I had imagined them to be wrestling with the realities of arranged marriages and dowry shortfalls and hilarious sexual problems. But what did I know?

"I'm sorry," I said, touching her forearm. My hand rested there for a while, stroking the soft, downy skin.

"There's no reason why you should understand," she said, slowly removing her arm.

"Yes there is. I should make a point of understanding. I'm sorry."

"We will meet a few times. If nothing clicks, that's it. Nobody gets hurt. The search will start all over again."

"Your parents won't mind?" I asked, grateful for any crumbs of comfort.

"The broker will. He's hired to find a suitable partner."

"We employ people, too. They're called divorce lawyers."

I was sounding like a bad comedian. I felt desperate and didn't know what to say so I said nothing, let her do the talking. She explained that her family were orthodox Nairs, very traditional when it came to marriage. If his *thalakuri*, or horoscope, didn't complement hers, the match was a non-starter. Once a boy had been found, she would only be able to meet him before the wedding in the presence of a family member. Most of the courting, she said, took place on the phone and bills could be enormous. She knew of one boy who had got engaged and then had to return to America for two months. It had cost him over 2,500 dollars to get to know the girl he was going to marry.

We were silent for a while as a young boy cleared our table. Both of us were unnaturally interested in him, watching as he wiped the table up and down, hoping that he might say something to help us out. His arms were short and he could only reach the far end of the table by lunging across, his bare feet almost leaving the floor.

"I've got some friends who had love marriages," Priyanka said.

"Are they still together?" I asked.

"Yes."

"But it's not something you'd ever consider."

She looked at me, smiling faintly before turning away.

"Love marriages don't have a particularly good track record in the West, do they?" she said.

"Oh, I don't know. Two out of three survive."

"Come, *challo*, let's go."

Ravi took us to her house in a leafy part of Defence Colony. I hated goodbyes and duly made a mess of our farewell. I leant forward to kiss her on the cheek as she offered a hand. We laughed nervously, caught between two customs and then she suddenly put her arms lightly round my shoulders and gave me a gentle hug. Before I had had a chance to respond she was gone, leaving me waving weakly at the door as it closed.

I thought about my mother on the way home, something I had done much more of since my arrival in India. I had never been close to her, even when she was dying. It must have been much harder for her than it was for my father to bury her Indian past. She had worn *salwar kameez* indoors, a sari on Sundays, but my father asked her to wear dresses and skirts if she went further afield. She had always obliged and if it hadn't been for the occasion when, as a child, I stumbled into the spare room and saw her doing *puja* in the corner, I would never have known there was any conflict. She had snapped the cupboard doors shut like a guilty child and told me to leave the room, but not before I had glimpsed the warm lights of forbidden gods, wrapped in twists of incense.

She had been a weak woman who had retreated into herself in Edinburgh the more my father grew in confidence and stature. She had never stood up to him, or challenged him, particularly about his other women, who were numerous, and I had often felt contempt rather than pity for her. On those occasions when we had all gone out together to cocktail parties or dinners, I had been embarrassed by her creased smiles and diminutive figure, always a step behind my father, as if being shielded from the world.

During the past few weeks, my feelings towards her had changed, a sadness replacing the anger. We had never talked about the *puja* incident, but when she lay dying, five years ago, I had asked her why she had been so secretive about her faith. "Promise me you will one day visit India," she had whispered.

CHAPTER SEVEN

WE WERE DRIVING down a quiet, private road in an expensive residential area of West Delhi, somewhere near the airport. Even Ravi, with thirteen years' experience of working for foreigners, as he never hesitated to remind me, was impressed. It was not possible to see much from the road, but when the guardhouses were bigger than the average person's home, it was a sure sign that a palace lurked somewhere behind the high walls.

The area was very green, too, which was a good barometer of wealth during Delhi's arid summers. How long the water table would survive was anyone's guess, but at least their lawns looked pretty. We pulled up outside a broad set of black gates, flanked on either side by two watchtowers reminiscent of Berlin during the Cold War. The intended air of menace was reduced, though, by a mass of red, white and orange bougainvillea cascading down the faded brick walls as far as the eye could see.

I had yet to come across genuine menace in Delhi. Despite the best efforts of *chowkidars*, the warnings about dogs and the razor-wire walls, most of the capital's posh colonies, try as they might, seldom possessed the belligerent paranoia of a smart suburb in somewhere like Johannesburg. In India there were too many loiterers for that level of deserted privacy, too many sweepers wandering down the roads, too many gardeners snoozing on the verges. Even here, the St George's Hill of Delhi, there was a busy *chai* stall on the corner, barely fifty yards away.

Perhaps it had something to do with the *chowkidars* themselves, who were not generally known for their imposing physical presence. Mrs Bakshi insisted that they were recruited solely for their ability to nod off in the afternoon heat while appearing vigilant. To be fair, *chowkidars* were not helped by the weapons supplied to them; most were equipped with sticks and whistles, which they blew at night, the sound carrying across the high walls to other guards, who whistled back, reassured that they were not alone in the wee hours, as the Indian newspapers called them. Outside the smarter houses and some of the bigger banks, the guards carried rifles, which looked impressive, but closer examination revealed them to be pre-Second World War Enfields with corks stuck on the end to keep the dirt out.

We were waved through the gates by two guards, who smiled and saluted before telling Ravi where to drive. Behind them, chatting over *chai* with another guard, was a policeman holding an altogether more serious weapon, a semi-automatic machine-gun, which usually signified the presence of a VIP, probably a politician, or his son, or an uncle.

Our hosts today were a wealthy Indian couple whom Jamie knew well. He had virtually insisted that I come along. I would have preferred to have been playing carrom and drinking Mr Tricky's Stemillion with Frank and his friends, but that was why Jamie had invited me. The couple whose lawns were unfolding before us had

61

family connections with a sheet steel conglomerate, but they themselves were arms dealers. It was becoming clear as we took the perimeter road around the estate that these weren't lawns but two, possibly three, cricket pitches, and we had yet to set eyes on the house. There were several summer follies dotted across the landscape, shaded by clusters of eucalyptus trees. Two more twists and turns, through a small forest, and there it was: a magnificently ugly blue castle, complete with parapets, a drawbridge and a moat. Even Ravi found it strange.

"English home?" he asked.

"I suppose so," I said. "We call it a castle."

We were directed towards some shade where there was a long row of glistening four-wheel-drives, the preferred expat vehicle: Tata Safaris and Sumos, Mitsubishi Pajeros, and a white Land-Rover, which I recognised as Jamie's. Four-wheel-drives seemed to provide expats with a sense of security, another layer to shield them from the realities of India, until they broke down and no one in the village, knew how to fix them.

It was only ten thirty but it appeared that I was late. I walked towards a large, pavilioned tent that had been erected to the left of the drawbridge and in which drinks were being served. A warm breeze was blowing across the adjacent cricket pitch, carrying the unmistakable scent of freshly cut grass. The sides of the white tent were billowing like untrimmed sails. Through the shimmering haze I could see some *malis* tending to the parched wicket, painting the crease lines and pulling up weeds. Beyond them two men were cutting the outfield with a manual lawnmower, one pushing, the other pulling on a tow-rope. They paused for a moment, passing a plastic bottle between them, pouring water into their mouths, careful not to touch the rim with their lips.

The roof of the tent was elaborately lined with cream silk, block printed with a blue family crest; the backs of the chairs, covered in white, were adorned with silver bows that looked like angels' wings. I recognised a few faces from the High Commission, glanced at the array of bottled spirits, all of them imported foreign brands, and took a glass of bucks fizz.

This was unashamed opulence as I had seldom seen it. I needed to step back from it all for a few moments and walked round to the far side of the house, where there was a paddling pool, some slides and a Mickey Mouse bouncy castle which looked considerably more authentic than the edifice behind it. A struggling generator was trying to keep Mickey upright but his face kept crumpling into a distorted, hideous frown that fascinated a small boy who was watching. Others were playing inside, occasionally disappearing in the plastic folds when the pressure dropped.

My eye was caught by a brightly patterned canopy flapping loose behind the bouncy castle. Two men were battling to tie down one of its corners in the wind. Half a dozen ayahs were sitting in a group underneath, one or two of them keeping an eye on the children. Beyond them, about twenty yards away, a young elephant was swaying from side to side in a pool of shade, a small howdah on its back. A mahout was spreading out leaves in front of the elephant on the grass and a seven-digit Delhi phone number had been written in white chalk between its eyes, which had been circled with brightly coloured patterns.

"He's opening the bowling," Jamie said behind me. I turned to meet his grinning face. "Glad you could make it," he continued, his arm round my shoulders. "I couldn't remember when you were off."

"It's been delayed a couple of days," I said. Part of my brief was to tour all the medical centres attached to British consulates around India. I had been due to leave that morning but the doctor in Madras, my first stop, had been taken ill.

"Some place," I said, walking back with Jamie to the front of the house. Two children were playing on the drawbridge, dropping sticks into the water.

"Do you know how many *malis* they employ?" Jamie asked.

"How many?"

"Guess."

"Twenty?"

"A hundred and ten. Can you believe that?"

"And they're into arms, is that right?"

"Steady," Jamie said, looking anxiously around him. "We only talk about the steel mills."

Kumar and Rita, our hosts, turned out to be a surprisingly modest couple, given that they employed a hundred and ten people just to mow their front lawn. Generous, too. There were tables and tables of food, most of it Western: hummus, caviare, scrambled eggs with smoked salmon, slices of rare beef, Mediterranean salads. Nothing out of the ordinary back in Britain, but out here in Delhi some extremely good contacts in INA market were needed for a spread of this sort. Kumar seemed most concerned that we all try his homemade "venison" sausages. A woman next to me giggled, knowingly.

64

"Black buck, isn't it?" she said.

Another young woman nudged her in the ribs. "Ssshhh," she said. "He's coming over."

"What's black buck?" I asked, trying to strike up a conversation.

Both women looked at me in disbelief and melted away, hands covering their mouths.

As I wondered what I had just said, Jamie leant across and whispered, "It's Salman Khan's favourite food."

"Who's Salman Khan?" I whispered back.

"He's a famous Bombay film star," Jamie said, still whispering. "He got caught shooting black buck in Rajasthan a few years back."

"And why are we whispering?"

"Because that's Salman Khan over there."

I looked up to see a well-built man wandering over to the drinks table accompanied by a woman in a mini-skirt who knew people were looking at them. One of her arms was in a plaster cast. It quickly became clear that they were the subject of discreet attention from almost all the assembled Indians, who made up about half the guests.

"Is he a good actor?" I asked Jamie.

"Not my cup of tea. But they say he's got a mean pelvic wiggle."

After a few minutes of consuming black buck and bucks fizz, we were all asked to change into our cricket whites. Ten minutes later we were standing in two groups. Jamie was captaining the expats, a mixture of British, South Africans and Australians, and Kumar was in charge of the local team.

"We're a man short," Kumar said, counting his men again.

"And we're one over," Jamie replied, double-checking.

For a split second, I experienced a feeling that I hadn't had since I was at prep school, when we used to stand in a line as two captains chose their teams, one by one. Perhaps it had been because I was the only Asian boy at the school, perhaps it was just my unorthodox batting stance, but I was always the last one to be picked. Even this far out, I knew what was about to happen. I noticed a few expats' eyes were already on me, discreetly, watching to see what I would do. I decided to hold my head up and managed a smile.

"Right," Jamie said, in a tone that suggested he had always been captain. "Who's going to be our mole on the other side?" I had that feeling again, butterflies mixed with a desire to be sick. It grew stronger, to the point where I thought I was actually going to throw up. As a way of stopping myself, I half raised my arm and said, "I'll go."

"Good man," Jamie said, a little too quickly.

I walked across to the Indian side and looked back at my old team, all eyes now on me. I might have been imagining it, but I heard someone, a British expat, say, "Makes sense, really, doesn't it?"

The match turned out to be a serious affair, far from the casual encounter that I had been expecting. For the record, I was put in to open and made a modest twenty, but the highlight came when Jamie was batting and I was asked to bowl. His eye was in, and he had been opening his shoulders, hitting a succession of boundaries.

"Are you sure?" I said to Kumar. "It's been a while."

"No problem," Kumar said, tossing me the ball. "Leg spin?" he asked.

"Right arm over," I replied. "You'd better push a few players back."

Kumar sent most of the fielders off to the boundary and I looked down the wicket to see Jamie, tapping at his wicket, concentrating. He didn't smile at me or crack any jokes about Shane Warne. He was nervous.

I bowled my first ball, which he prodded defensively back down the wicket to me. Again, I tried to make eye contact, to lighten the mood, but he wasn't having any of it. The next ball beat his bat, spinning up fiercely into the wicket keeper's gloves.

"Nice bowling," Kumar said, clapping in encouragement. It was a difficult situation I found myself in. Did I bowl a few short deliveries, let Jamie hit me all over the ground, or should I go in for the kill? I thought of Priyanka for a moment, adjusted my grip and let fly with a wrong 'un. Jamie was clean bowled. My team were ecstatic and I was congratulated with a hug from Kumar and high-fives from everyone else. Everyone except Jamie, of course, who threw me a withering look before heading back towards the castle.

"It's only a game," I said to him over tea. He grunted, taking a bite out of his sandwich. I couldn't believe how badly he was taking it.

"You were meant to be on our side," he said, softening. "Deep cover, remember?"

"What could I do? Bowl underarm? You just seemed to seize up."

"I hate playing spinners. Always have done. You never know which way they're going to turn."

He looked up at me with those unsettling eyes of his, timeless eyes that I was now convinced had witnessed acts of unspeakable cruelty. Then he suddenly relaxed, encouraged by the sight of a waiter coming round with a box of cigars.

"Ah, the stogie-wallah," he said, taking two cigars. He put one in his top pocket, the other he held up to examine. "Too dry," he said, sniffing it. "You know what you should do if you are without a humidor and your cigars are drying out?" I shook my head, knowing that he was about to tell me. "Put them in a plastic bag with a slice of apple." He patted me on the back and walked away in search of a light.

Not for the first time I sensed that I was being ignored by both sets of teams. I could understand the Delhiites' reservations – as Jamie said, emigration was hardly a compliment – but the coldness of most expats was unexpected. I had always been surprised by racism although I knew I should have been prepared for it. Living in Britain had involved little compromise for me; I was not consciously having to suppress my cultural identity, or trying to integrate myself into an alien land. My father had done that for me. I had been at peace, on a level with the land where I was born.

The cricketers' sudden hostility caught me off guard, pulling at my ankles like a hidden rip tide. Assuming it was just my imagination, I walked over to a group of English players, who were in the midst of a heated conversation about beggars.

"I have a simple rule," one of them was saying. "Five rupees for every limb. If it's a no-arms, no-legs situation—"

"—A bob, I call those ones bob," someone else interrupted.

"Right, if it's a bob situation, the bloke gets twenty rupees. The only snag is where to put the money." I slipped away to my car as they fell about laughing.

CHAPTER EIGHT

IF HE HAD been here now, Frank would have told me that this was a place that divided those who got India from those who didn't. It was an enthusiast's part of town, not exactly sight-seeing country, and known locally as Yusuf Sarai although the name rarely appeared on any maps. I was drinking *chai* with Ravi at a shack called the Haryana Tea Stall. Ravi had also asked for a glass of *lassi* and in a misguided attempt to get me to join him he had pulled back a muslin cloth on the counter to reveal a basin of curd buzzing with flies. I watched as he was served a stainless steel beaker of it, shaken with ice, and then I turned away as the man with the ladle carefully scraped off a layer of skin and smoothed it out on top of Ravi's helping, as if he were laying a table.

"Try, sir," Ravi offered, holding up his beaker.

"I'll stick to the *chai*," I said, sitting down. Without warning, there was a sudden swirl of smoke that curled round our table, engulfing us both. I turned to see a tandoor oven which had just been fired up behind us. A young boy was standing back, proudly, with an empty can in his hands.

"Kerosene," Ravi said, throwing both arms up in a surprisingly energetic gesture. "Whummph!" He was sitting on the edge of a bench, barely touching it, after I had insisted he didn't have to stand up all the time.

The tea stall was on one side of a small square at the far end of a narrow lane. On our left we were overlooked by the vast façade of the Uphaar cinema. According to Ravi, almost sixty people had died in there when a fire ripped through the building a few years ago. It had remained closed ever since, still displaying a hand-painted poster for *Border*, the film it had been showing at the time. Sunny Deol gazed down on us, his features betraying none of the tragedy that had unfolded a few feet away. Behind us there was another stall, serving simple *dal* and naan. Its tandoor was already glowing, and a man was pressing moist naan breads against the white-hot insides. After each one he took a pinch of flour and clapped his hands together, sending fine powder into the air.

But it was the small alley immediately opposite us, to the right of the cinema, that intrigued me most. I wandered down it after finishing my tea, carefully avoiding the dog turds and oil slicks. This was one of Frank's favourite haunts in Delhi. I was not getting it at all. I kept going, though, as there was a shop along here which was meant to be the best place in Delhi to take your computer. When it opened after lunch, I hoped they would be able to salvage something of my Apple Mac's hard disk, which had crashed the night before.

Towards the end of the alley I began to understand a little more of what Frank meant. I came across a small workshop with a yellow sign above it saying "Rashid's Enfields and Silverplus Explorers". Spilling out onto the road was a collection of Enfield motorbikes, 350cc and 500cc Bullets, most of them with their engines spread out in bits. Even in this dismantled state, the

71

bodywork shone through: the pregnant swell of the fuel tank, the sparkling spokes. I asked a mechanic if he knew of a computer shop and he nodded upwards. There was a sign on the second floor behind me saying "Anything Mac and some things IBM".

So this was it: Frank's India. One of the Enfields rumbled into life, its guttural roar drowning the noise of a nearby generator. I glanced up at the balconies overlooking the alley, wrapped in a tangle of telephone wires, and then noticed, for the first time, the entrance to a traditional *haveli*, its cusped arch crumbling, the old brickwork visible underneath the faded yellow plaster. I peered inside to a shaded courtyard, and saw a woman hanging a turquoise sari to dry on the timber railings; an old man sat on a charpoy bed reading a newspaper; next to him a girl was having her hair brushed by her mother. Apple Macs and Enfields and the humble pulse of domestic life – either you got India or you didn't.

Given the problems Frank had been having recently with his computer, I was not surprised when he walked into the shop five minutes after me. For an instant, I was delighted to see his sunburnt, rounded face, his swelling girth, until my own stomach tightened as I remembered Jamie's warnings.

"Raj, you found the place," Frank said, patting my back. "You're in safe hands with Arvind," he added, nodding towards a young engineer who was looking closely at a circuit board. "Where have you been, anyway? I've been trying to ring you for days."

I didn't know where to start but I knew then that I would confide in him, sooner rather than later, no matter how dangerous it might prove to be. I didn't need to give him the details, just a rough outline, like one of his sketches.

"Are you busy this evening?" I said, too abruptly, unable to disguise my unease.

"This evening?" Frank asked. A shiny new iBook was being unpacked on the table in front of us. "Aren't they wonderful?"

"I need to talk to you about something," I continued. "Not here, not now."

"No problem. Come round for something to eat, about eight? You missed a great game of carrom."

"I was playing cricket," I said.

"Very grand."

"I can't do dinner," I added quickly, "not at your place."

"No? Why ever not? It's not my cooking, is it?" His tone had become more concerned.

"How long will it take?" I asked Arvind, ignoring Frank.

"One, maybe two days," Arvind said, looking at me and then at Frank, sensing the tension. "It's not reading the disk, that's the problem."

"If anyone can sort it out, Arvind will," Frank said, giving Arvind's fragile shoulders a squeeze. "This is the story the West chooses not to hear about India. I bet you didn't know it was a bunch of Indians who invented the CD-ROM. Okay, they were living in America at the time, but the future of IT is right here. Believe me. These people have software in their DNA. Even Bill Gates thinks so. *Chai?*"

"I've just had one," I said. "Can you meet me in Hauz Khas village, by the reservoir, at seven? We can go for a walk."

73

"Okay," Frank said, more serious now, giving me a look, unconditional, unquestioning, that reassured me that I was doing the right thing, that my priorities were right. "The reservoir. I'll be down near the ruins, next to the tomb of Firoz Shah."

As I walked out of the alleyway and across towards the car, feeling immeasurably lighter at the prospect of sharing some of my worries, I noticed a Tata Safari parked in front of the cinema. It was on the other side of the square, partially covered by the branches of a neem tree, but I caught a clear glimpse of a foreigner sitting in the passenger seat, smoking, his elbow resting on the open window. He hadn't been there earlier, but I knew I had seen him somewhere before, around the High Commission compound, perhaps. As I got into the car, glancing across the square again, the Safari pulled out and drove off past us in a cloud of dust. The passenger window had been wound up and it was impossible to see through its tinted windows.

I climbed in alongside Ravi, careful not to bang the door against Frank's battered old Ambassador, which was parked next to ours. I told myself the Safari was just a coincidence, but this was not a regular part of town for expats.

I spotted Frank before he saw me, his squat silhouette wandering through the ruins in the dying sun. The remains of Firoz Shah's pillared *madrassa* looked warm and welcoming in the natural light; in a couple of hours they would be lit up by spotlights for the benefit of diners in the adjacent *recherché* restaurants of Hauz Khas village. I had a few moments to check if Frank had been followed. I hadn't seen a Safari in the car park and the village itself was too congested tonight to park amongst the chic boutiques and galleries. It looked as if he was alone.

Between us was a large expanse of empty reservoir, built by Alauddin in the fourteenth century and now used by walkers. In the middle of the open area there was a raised section where a pavilion had once stood. It was just a cluster of trees these days, ringing with the sound of birds. I made my way across the vast space dotted with leafy bushes which had pushed up through the uneven surface. Up ahead the dramatic ruins of the *madrassa* dominated the skyline. Much of the brickwork had crumbled, but it was still possible to imagine how it must have been when it was a thriving centre of learning. High up on one wall there was a series of arched windows, in one of which a courting couple sat opposite each other, chatting as they watched the walkers below. Once they would have been students, testing each other on their Arabic studies. Frank was sitting on a corner of a wall, lost in thought.

After a brief exchange we were soon into our stride, taking in a big loop of the reservoir, not talking at first. All around us there were people out walking, mostly women in saris and trainers, striding onwards with unnatural urgency. A man was whirling his arms round, one at a time, as he walked along. (It looked like he was trying to wind himself up.) Unlike in Britain, nobody was jogging. The heat of the day might have passed but it was still too warm for proper exercise.

"What's this all about, then?" Frank eventually said, shovelling his hands deep into his pockets and slowing.

I slowed down, too, until we were standing together, watching the sun slip behind the ruins.

"I'm not just a doctor, Frank," I began bluntly, avoiding his eyes as I kicked up some dust.

"Is that it?" Frank said, laughing out loud. "Is that bloody it?" His reaction threw me completely, his raucous laugh a reminder of the fun we had had together. I started laughing, too, for a moment, and then stopped awkwardly. "Tell me something I don't know," Frank continued. "Didn't you listen to Ranjit? Nobody at an embassy does only one job." His last words were said with a snobbish English accent, in perfect imitation of Ranjit.

"You knew, then," I replied uneasily, trying to adjust to our conversation's unexpected change of direction.

"I've been here long enough for it not to come as a complete surprise."

"I just wanted to tell you, that's all. I'm not comfortable with the deception, not with you and Susie."

"You know something, this reminds me so much of Tapash. He insisted on taking us out for a meal one day, said he had something important to tell us. When it came to the crunch, he couldn't understand why we weren't surprised."

"What was it?"

"He wanted to tell us he was gay. It was one of the worst-kept secrets in Delhi. Everyone had suspected for years."

"I'm not gay, in case you're wondering," I said, trying to lighten my mood, delighted that there was nothing between Tapash and Priyanka.

"You must be the only spook who isn't," he said.

"I'm not a spook, either. I just help out occasionally."

"Of course. Either way, you shouldn't be telling me, you know that."

"I know . . . " I paused, wondering if I should continue, but Frank interrupted me.

"So what have they told you?"

"About what?"

"About me. That's why you're telling me all this, isn't it?"

His presumption had caught me out again and my only option was to take his question seriously.

"They say you were involved with the Communist Party in Britain. And that you are applying for Indian citizenship."

"And?"

"And what?"

"Do you think any the worse of me?"

"Of course not."

We walked on in silence for a while.

"Find out what else they've got on me, would you?" Frank asked suddenly, his voice more pressing, more conspiratorial.

"On you?" I asked, looking up at him.

"Favour for an old friend, eh?" He put his arm round my shoulders.

"Frank, I can't . . ." I began.

"I'm kidding. Relax," he said, squeezing me. "I wouldn't ask you to do something like that. Just be careful, watch your own back. I've seen others get involved, just like you, on a so-called part-time basis. But it never is. Not once you're in."

We walked on in silence, sensing some people approaching.

"It was all very clear in my mind when they asked

me," I said, after a couple had passed us. "I was flattered. It was something I wanted to be involved in. Now I'm not so sure."

"How do you mean?'

"Expats can be who they want out here. There's no accountability. We all get on because we have to, but no one really knows the first thing about other people. Nobody asks any questions."

"Is that such a bad thing?"

"I just find it very disorientating. My feet can't find the bottom. You're invited round to dinner with complete strangers, spend a jolly evening together talking about servants and go home afterwards not knowing anything about them except where they last worked and how much harder it was to get a decent drink. These people are meant to represent the country I have chosen to serve."

"Serve? You make it sound like you've joined the army."

I laughed half-heartedly. "Sometimes they make me wonder whether it's worth it, that's all."

"I'd stick to medicine if I were you. A much better way to serve."

We stopped to watch the sun finally set, glowing, beyond the ruins.

"I'm off tomorrow, on a tour of the other medical centres," I said, as we walked on again. "I'll be gone for a couple of weeks. I can't wait to be out of Delhi, to be honest."

"Anywhere nice?"

"I start in Madras."

"And it's purely medical?" he asked, smiling.

"As far as I know."

Jamie hadn't talked much about my tour and I had assumed it would provide me with a couple of weeks' break from his world, a chance to breathe. As far as he was concerned it was an annoying hindrance, a delay to the real work that lay ahead, but he knew my cover had to be maintained.

Frank and I parted at the gate leading to the deer park. There was a distance between us as we agreed unconvincingly to meet soon, which saddened me. I had hoped to feel closer. But now we could no longer be whoever we wanted. We were suddenly accountable, tethered to two very different posts.

CHAPTER NINE

I KNEW IT was part of his job requirement to look pleased to see people, but Sir Ian, the new High Commissioner, appeared extremely interested as I caught his eye across the crowded terrace of his official residence. Too interested. He was hosting a party for a group of Labour MPs who were on a "fact-finding trip" to India. Over a hundred people must have been there, spilling out from the house's pillared verandah onto the lawn, where the trees had been strung with pea lights and paper lanterns. The residence, a colonial, Lutyens-style bungalow built by Baker, had also been lit, its whitewashed walls standing out against the clear night sky. Insects crashed against sunken spotlights hidden in the grass. Chefs were busily grilling skewers of chicken, mutton and *paneer* over glowing coals. The scented smoke drifted across towards the swimming pool, where a few people had wandered, watched by two Gurkha guards who were standing under a nearby tree.

It was a warm, sticky night and I was standing next to a large fan on a stand, almost tripping on the cable despite the brown, civil service tape that had been used to keep it flat against the patio's stone surface. It was one of several fans dotted around the terrace, each one attracting a group of people who were cooling themselves as they drank and talked. Sir Ian seemed eager to break away from the Labour MPs. He was tall, with a languorous manner that was exaggerated by the way the top half of his body leant back from his hips.

"I hear you're off tomorrow," he said, shaking my hand and putting a long arm round my shoulders at the same time. I felt myself arching backwards, as if to keep him company.

"I'm on the early flight to Madras," I told him, watching a bearer approach with a silver tray of drinks. He was wearing white gloves, and a *pugri* fanned like a cockerel's tail. Sir Ian stepped back to make way for the tray, encouraging me with the sweep of his lanky hand to take a drink.

"Chennai," he said in a quiet voice. "We call Madras Chennai now, don't we, Ruben?" He put a hand gently on the bearer's shoulder.

"Yes, sir," Ruben said, standing bolt upright.

"Chennai, Mumbai. Ruben's from Kolkata. The city of Kali. You will be going there, won't you?"

"Where?" I asked.

"Calcutta. Fabulous organ at St John's."

"Really?" I said, unconvincingly, as the bearer slipped away from Sir Ian's touch. "You play, then?"

"When I can."

"I'm going to Calcutta, Kolkata, after Mumbai. In a couple of months' time."

"Listen," Sir Ian said, his voice becoming suddenly more serious. "My son's with us on holiday at the moment. Their youngest has just taken a bit of a temperature. '*Chota* fever', as they say."

"Do you want me to take a look?" I asked, sensing that there was something more to the request. Sir Ian had been instrumental in my coming here but we had

81

only met once briefly in Delhi since he had interviewed me in London. He told me then not to expect too much contact with him, that Jamie would be running the show, but I was glad we were meeting again. He was more reassuring than Jamie, made me think I had made the right decision.

"Would you?" he said. I watched as his easy smile faded. His lips suddenly became pinched and his eyes widened into a brief moment of sternness, almost comical in its intensity.

"Now?" I asked.

"So kind." He glanced discreetly at his watch and then looked around him. "This lot should be going in a minute. Trouble is, they never take a hint."

He had relaxed again, leaning back as he popped a couple of cashew nuts into his mouth.

"Apparently the Queen goes around saying, 'It was a nice party, wasn't it?'" I said, repeating something I had once read.

He laughed loudly, throwing back his head. "About as subtle as my wife. Last week she turned all the lights out and told everyone it was a powercut, but nobody took a blind bit of notice. The journalists are the worst. They were still here when we got back from dinner."

Sir Ian's grandchildren were both in rude health, much as I had suspected. After a bearer had shown me through to the kitchen in the private wing an ayah walked in, accompanied by two young children who were pleading with her for some Swiss chocolate from the fridge.

"Got your hands full," I said, gesturing towards them.

"It was bedtime two hours ago," the ayah said, sighing. "Sir will be here in one minute."

I wondered if she realised the correctness of her respect, that her "sir" was a real Sir. It had taken two weeks for Jagu to stop calling me "Master". We had now reached a happy compromise with "Rajsahib", although I was hopeful we would one day lose the "sahib" bit.

I looked around the kitchen, thinking I could have been in the West Country back in England: flagstone floor, wooden worktops, onions dangling from a dresser, blue and white crockery, a copy of one of Rick Stein's cookery books. The only thing wrong was the absence of an Aga, too hot for Delhi's summers. The long-stalked ceiling fan would have looked a bit odd in Dorset, too. As I moved under it, I heard Sir Ian's voice approaching.

"Raj, so sorry to keep you waiting," he said, still outside the kitchen. "We must be brief. Dinner with Brajesh Mishra at nine."

He walked in, still chewing a nut, and closed the door behind him, which surprised me. He then grinned mischievously. "Come," he said. "Follow me."

I watched as he went past the kitchen table and through to a small back room where I could see a writing desk, some glass bookcases and an old gramophone. I followed him into the room, stooping through the low doorway. He gestured for me to step back as he closed the unexpectedly heavy door behind us. He then walked over to the gramophone, which had a large brass horn and a polished teak base. The bookcases were packed with big maroon books – W. H. Sleeman's *Rambles and Recollections of an Indian Official*, some old editions of Hansard – and there were two watercolours

83

on the walls. One of them was of Varanasi, painted by the Daniell brothers. The other was of Qutab Minar, which I could sometimes see from my balcony, before the smog gathered.

"Now, what shall it be?" he said, turning to a box of old 78s next to the turntable. They had been sorted into "Rare", "Very rare" and "Only known copies". "Bal Gandharva singing a Gujarati *garba*? He only sang one. The *thumri* queen of Calcutta?"

He threw a glance back at me as I looked round the small room, trying to work it out. It was a study of some sort but it seemed too contrived, too much like a period film set. There was even some blotting paper on the desk and a small brass inkwell.

"Used to be the dhobi room," he said, sifting through the heavy records. "No, I think it's got to be the great Vinayakrao Patwardhan from Madhur."

He held a record up to the light, blew some dust off it and placed it on the turntable. He then wound up the machine with a handle on the side of the box, lowered the needle gently onto the thick black vinyl and stood back. The hiss was deafening, drowning Patwardhan's voice and our own, which I suddenly realised was the point.

"Old-fashioned I know, but effective," he said, talking through a cupped hand close to my ear. "We've got a high-tech safe room on the compound, but nothing so sophisticated here, I'm afraid. Did you hear the Americans found a bug in Dick Celeste's mattress? Indian intelligence had rather fallen for his wife."

It was difficult to take in what Sir Ian was saying, not so much because of the noise as of the thought of British High Commissioners past and present holding high-level meetings in this musty little room listening to rare Indian 78s.

"Listen, I'll come straight to the point," he said, suddenly more businesslike, still close to my ear. "I want you to do something for me on your tour. Take a look at our man in Cochin, Martin Macaulay."

"Cochin?"

"Kochi, in Kerala. Gorgeous spot. The local Malayalis call it God's own country. Go there first and then fly across to Chennai. Not a big diversion."

I thought of Priyanka, who must be there by now, interviewing prospective husbands. The hissing worsened into a dense white noise until the needle stuck. Sir Ian knocked the wooden casing with a knuckle and the singer moved on.

"Does Jamie know I'm going?" I asked, trying not to shout.

Sir Ian shook his head. "Nobody does. I certainly don't and will deny all knowledge if anybody asks. That's a promise. Ring Chennai and say you are coming via Kochi. Then mention that you've heard Macaulay is ill."

"Is he?"

"Has been for years. Madras will be delighted – they're fed up with his moaning. He keeps asking them to send someone over."

"And what exactly will I be looking for?" I asked.

He paused for a moment before answering. "I can't tell you that, not yet."

Can't tell me? "I need something to go on, surely," I said, almost derisively. This is why I took this job, I told myself, for the secrecy, the hidden life, but it was suddenly losing its sheen.

"I know," Sir Ian said. He paused again, needlessly straightening some bindings in the bookcase, weighing up how much I needed to know. He leant back against the writing desk, careful not to knock the record player beside him.

"I'm not sure what you know about my job, but whatever you might hear to the contrary, we're basically salesmen these days, glorified reps in the global market." His voice was a projected, low shout now. We'd both worked out what could be heard above the singing without us standing too close, or Sir Ian having to cup his hands round his mouth. "Almost seventy per cent of my time is taken up with promoting bilateral trade. It wasn't always the case, of course, but that's the way these things are going. Still flying the flag, but for boardrooms rather than Buckingham Palace. Anyway, business has been booming in recent years. Billions of pounds of contracts are on the table, a large number of jobs, too, both here and in the UK. The balance sheet took a nosedive after the nuclear tests, but we're trying to keep that little episode in a box, as it were. We get it out occasionally during our chats with India but put it back again at the first sign of trouble, if it starts to affect the *relationship*." He exaggerated this last word, as if he were mocking an earnest counsellor. "In recent months, however, something else has started to cause us problems. Some people who are meant to be on our side appear to be batting for the opposition."

"Macaulay?" I asked, startled by the loudness of my own voice. Sir Ian didn't confirm or deny that he was talking about Macaulay, but carried on, leaning even further back against the front of the desk, occasionally glancing down at the noisy record player still spinning beside him.

"There's a feeling, how shall I put this" – he paused, fingers steepled together, rubbing against the front of his chin – "that our efforts here in Delhi are being undermined. What makes it more worrying for us, for me personally, is that there seems to be a degree of complicity in Whitehall. I shan't bother you with the politics of it all, but suffice it to say that not everyone back home is happy to see Britain and the old colony getting along so well, not as equals, anyway."

"And Macaulay? Where does he fit in?" I asked, resenting the lack of acknowledgment.

"Macaulay?" he boomed, as if it were the first time the name had been mentioned. Vinayakrao Patwardhan was winding proceedings up. "Let's just say that he's a historian, unpublished but influential."

"There could be worse crimes," I replied.

"A revisionist. When he looks back in his diary to 1947, he doesn't read the same entry as the rest of us. And, unfortunately, someone high up in Whitehall is listening to him."

I spent the journey home wondering what sort of audience it was that Macaulay commanded in London and why it mattered, given his lowly position, geographically and in the greater scheme of things. He was only an honorary consul, after all, a token presence of Her Majesty's government in India's deep south. I didn't want to entertain the possibility of seeing Priyanka again, not yet, and tried to banish her from my thoughts. All Sir Ian had added as the record scratched to its deafening finale was that Macaulay had been friendly with a number of previous British High Commissioners. He was also an internet devotee, an accomplished mahout and the longest serving consul anywhere in the former Empire. As I had suspected, Jamie was not involved, which both troubled and encouraged me. Did Jamie know Macaulay? He had been here almost four years, unlike Sir Ian, who had arrived in Delhi barely three months ago. Jamie and Sir Ian, I had been told, did not get on.

As Ravi turned the car into the driveway I sensed immediately that something was wrong. There was a yellow and black taxi parked outside the back door with its doors open like insect wings. Inside I could see a number of figures sleeping. Ravi slowed and hooted, his first reaction to anything. The taxi driver, an old Sikh man, stirred and turned to tap the people in the car, one of whom I now recognised as Frank.

I told Ravi to stop and I got out of the car. As I approached, I spotted Susie in the back with Kashmir and Jumila, who were both sleeping, clasped in her tight embrace. They looked like frightened refugees washed up on a foreign shore.

"Frank, what on earth are you doing here?" I asked.

"Is it such a problem?" Frank said, getting out of the front passenger seat.

"No, of course not," I said, cross at my own tone of voice. "Of course not," I repeated, noticing that he was dripping with sweat. I glanced at the car again. "What's happened? Are you all right? The children?"

"Can we go inside?" he said, looking back at his family. "It's a hot night."

"Of course, come in," I said, checking that the front gates had shut. I could almost inhale Jamie's presence, his disapproval.

I opened up the house, telling Jagu to crank up the main generator as we would need to run the air conditioning. Jagu was half asleep and was walking around with a wet towel wrapped round his head. I went back to find Frank, who was helping Susie out of the car. Kashmir was asleep on her shoulder. I offered to take Jumila, who was laid out on the back seat, but Frank picked her up, turning his back to me as he leant into the car.

"Can we have something to drink, Raj?" Frank asked quietly, as I followed him over to the house. Jumila woke momentarily on Frank's shoulder, her frightened eyes staring ahead.

"Water? Juice?" I offered.

"Something a little stronger?"

"Of course, of course." I patted Jumila's back gently but it was a futile gesture.

I showed them to the guest room, where they laid the children on a bed. Susie hadn't said anything to me yet, but as she curled up next to them she asked for a glass of water and managed the faintest of smiles. Her hair was unkempt, her eyes bloodshot. I said nothing as I went over to the window to turn on the air-conditioning unit. I walked past the listless figures again. I didn't know where to start. Susie was staring at the wall. Gently I let down the mosquito net, which tumbled all around them, and then I left, closing the door quietly behind me.

"Frank, will you please tell me what's going on, what's happened?" I asked, as we went into the sitting room.

"You tell me, Raj," he said, watching me pour a whisky. Sensing his attention, I kept pouring and handed him a large peg.

He walked around the room, taking big sips of whisky.

"I'll just take Susie some water," I said, leaving the room as Frank started to talk. Part of me didn't want to hear what he might have to say. Frank carried on regardless.

"We'd been at Karims for a meal out, we usually do on a Sunday, it's a fun place to be."

I could still hear him as I took the water to Susie. Her eyes were now closed and I left the glass on the bedside table.

"Go on," I said, by way of encouragement, coming back into the room.

"The first thing I noticed was the guard at the end of the road. He gave me an anxious look. Normally he's all smiles and we exchange a few words. But not tonight. By the time we got to the house it was obvious that something had happened. The front door was closed but it opened when I pushed it. The lock had been jemmied. Inside was like a bomb site. The whole place had been turned upside down, drawers emptied, pictures taken off the walls, books ripped open."

I knew as soon as he started that it had something to do with Jamie. As Frank continued to describe the mayhem, the defecation on the landing, the pile of Susie's underwear on the bed, ripped to shreds, I felt sick to the core. I also felt trapped, claustrophobic, unable to find a way out of it all.

I sat down on the sofa, watching Frank pace around. He was angry now, the first time I had seen him like this.

"Who did it?" I asked, with little curiosity.

"I was hoping you might know," he said, more quietly. "It wasn't the Indians, not their style. I thought I'd left this behind when we left Britain. I promised Susie."

"It's happened before?"

Frank laughed. "Our flat was turned over twice a week when we were living in London. We didn't bother keeping anything in it in the end."

"But why?"

"Why?" He laughed drily. "Why?"

He sat down next to me, patted my knee. "At least then we could blame the Tories, eh?"

"Frank, I don't know anything about this, I really don't. I told you today everything I knew. Jamie doesn't trust you, but he's got nothing to go on, nothing to justify this."

"Ah yes, Jamie. Shall I tell you something about your friend? I didn't want to mention it before."

I nodded, wondering what he was going to say, hoping it would justify my own reservations.

"We go back a long way."

"You and Jamie?"

"Our paths first crossed when I was still involved with CND. I was working on some research, compiling a list of the intelligence officers who had been assigned to keep an eye on us. We got hold of some pretty sensitive stuff, had a sympathiser on the inside. Jamie didn't seem to fit in anywhere. We knew he was working for MI6, but never figured out what his interest was in us."

I wanted to pick up the phone there and then and talk to Sir Ian, ask him why Frank's house had been ransacked, find out what Jamie was really doing in Delhi, but I had a horrible feeling that he didn't know.

"We did have one lead," Frank continued.

"What was it?" I asked.

"We intercepted a message to Jamie. It was signed with the initials IPI, printed rather than handwritten. It was the only time we ever saw it."

"IPI? What did the message say?"

"It was about someone who had recently joined us. A nice enough mole. His parents were from Gujarat. When we asked our man what it meant, he told us to back off, said we were getting into something too deep, too dangerous."

Part Two

CHAPTER TEN

A PATCHWORK OF water and land stretched out beneath me, green and innocent after the heat and dust of Delhi. Somewhere below was Cochin airport, although almost every strip of Kerala's lush soil appeared to be covered in coconut trees. To the aircraft's right was the Arabian Sea, whose glistening littoral we had followed ever since we had touched down briefly in Goa. It felt so good to be out of Delhi that I wondered how I had managed to stay there for two months. I had left behind the choking smoke of ITO junction, its morbid police sign recording how many people had died on the roads the day before, and the smog of Lutyens's Delhi, which was sometimes so thick it was impossible to see the President's Palace from halfway down Rajpath. But most importantly I had escaped from Jamie, whose twisting cigar fumes had proved far more constricting than the city's torpid traffic.

Frank and Susie had stayed the night but I hadn't seen them this morning. I felt terrible about what had happened and wasn't sure I could have coped with sharing breakfast with them, not yet. I suppose I hadn't expected my decision to work for MI6 to have such immediate and detrimental effects on the lives of those around me, particularly friends. I had prepared myself to live with what I knew might occasionally be uncertain consequences, but I never thought others would have to. To my shame, I had just left a note explaining that Ravi would run them home after he had dropped me off at the airport. I had also asked Jagu to give them a hand clearing their place up. I didn't care any more if Frank was under surveillance, if they traced my car back to me. Any loyalty to Jamie was fast evaporating. I also wanted to find out more about the initials "IPI", something that had kept me awake for most of the night.

The pleasure of acting now without Jamie's knowledge was considerable, given how much Jamie did behind the backs of others, but I was feeling something else as I sat there, looking idly at a map in the inflight magazine. Kerala was a reassuringly long way from Delhi, the same distance as Rangoon, Abu Dhabi, the Aral Sea. I felt a sharp sense of freedom, but I was also anxious. I looked at my palms, the moisture between my fingers, and closed them tightly.

Priyanka had given me a number in Kerala before she left and I knew I would ring her. At best she would be indifferent, more probably there would be quiet anger, disappointment. Either way I was prepared for it to be complicated, but I had to speak to her, to know where we stood. Sir Ian could have asked me to go anywhere, but he had sent me to Cochin. I owed it to myself, to whatever had determined that I was here.

I felt very neutral about my father, even though I was also journeying to the place where he had grown up, where his own parents had lived, and their parents before them. Kerala had been so thoroughly cleansed from our household that I could have been arriving anywhere in the world. I had no sense of pilgrimage because there had been no premeditation – I had never consciously meant to come here – but I felt a respect for the place, more out of duty than anything else. I was also curious to search for clues, to see if the same things provoked me as must have done him.

There were few immediate clues as I left my luggage at the Casino Hotel, near the airstrip on Willingdon Island, and took a cycle rickshaw down to the Malabar at the far end of the island for an early lunch. The swaying journey was slowed by the long chain of the rickshaw, which kept slipping, particularly when we rattled over several railway lines, but the young cyclist ignored my offers to dismount, flashing a brilliant white smile and telling me to relax. I had already asked him how much he wanted. "As you like," he had said, repeating words I had come to dread in Delhi, but I didn't protest. Already I sensed there was less hustling here, fewer people on the make.

Even the goods carriers lacked the menace of their northern counterparts. We passed a row of almost fifty of them parked neatly alongside the old railway terminus, which was painted in a municipal creamy orange, unlike the trucks themselves, which were decorated with blossoming vignettes of Ganesh, Shiva, even Jesus, surrounded by floral patterns and philosophical graffiti. One had "Not on our merits but on his grace". Another, more profoundly, said, "Love is sorrow of the mind". My favourite, though, was "Make Love Not War", written above the words "Use Dipper at Night".

We were greeted at the Malabar by a guard wearing white gaiters and gloves, who directed us into the drive as if we were a taxiing aircraft. He threw a disdainful look at the cyclist, whose taut legs were seesawing up and down as he struggled to pull me over the cobbled entrance. I had had enough and jumped out, telling him that I would walk the final few yards. He shook my hand after I gave him twenty rupees, and pushed his rickshaw back down the drive, watched closely by the guard.

As I sat on the terrace of the hotel overlooking the harbour, drinking a bottle of Kalyani Black Label, I wondered why anyone would want to live anywhere else. The fresh sea air was like pure oxygen (something the traffic police had started to be provided with as I was leaving Delhi), but it was the timelessness of the Mattancherry skyline across the water that made me want to raze Sainik Farms and its ersatz palaces to the ground. The clay-roofed warehouses, some with the pointed eaves of Chinese pagodas, couldn't have changed for centuries, storing cardamom and ginger and pepper inside their thick, cooling walls. Beyond them Cochin's famed Chinese fishing nets stood guard on either side of the harbour entrance, sparkling like dewy cobwebs.

Small dugout canoes with stitched, square-patterned sails bobbed about in the water in front of the warehouses. Fishing boats with high, arrogant bows chugged out to sea, *chugachugachug*, less intrusive than Delhi's diesel generators. The leading boats were escorted by a small school of porpoises, who occasionally broke off to turn circles amongst stray clumps of water hyacinth that were drifting out to sea. Even when a vast dredger hove into view, blocking out Mattancherry on its way to the main channel, its rusting hulk failed to jar. God, how I hoped Frank and Susie were all right.

As for Priyanka, she was probably engaged by now to an IT millionaire from Bangalore, but I would try to contact her tomorrow. I pressed my hands tightly together, clicking the joints in my fingers. First, though, I had to find Macaulay.

After finishing my beer, I climbed over a low wall and walked round to a rickety jetty where one of the waiters had explained I could catch a ferry to Fort Cochin. It was where Macaulay ran his internet café, according to Sir Ian, somewhere behind the fishing nets, near the Hotel Elite in Princess Street.

The harbour was a highway of ferries criss-crossing to and from everywhere except the Malabar jetty. When one eventually turned up, I cursed myself for having waited. Barely seaworthy, it was packed with people hanging off its splintered wooden sides and clinging to the corrugated iron roof, where there was a tangle of bicycles on their sides. I was already reading one of those short newspaper paragraphs that recounted how a ferry on the other side of the world had sunk between islands with the loss of hundreds.

I guessed there was bench seating inside for about fifty people, but over two hundred were on board. A taxi suddenly seemed a very sensible idea. The passengers came ashore, each one stretching across a yawning gap. I looked down at the water rushing past the jetty. The captain rang his bell and I took my chances. There was barely room to stand inside, but I pushed my way to the bow, where there was a small, open-air deck which was in the sun but cooled by a breeze rising off the sea. It seemed to offer the best chance of escape, if we began taking on water.

The internet café would have been easy enough to find even if I hadn't known it was near the Hotel Elite. I could have followed the steady stream of Western travellers who were making their way there. I wanted to get my bearings before introducing myself to Macaulay, and ordered a coffee at the Elite, from where I could see the café's entrance, halfway down on the opposite side of the small street. It was called the Cardamom Café and was on the ground floor of what looked like an old Dutch barn, with cane tables and chairs set outside. A couple of beach-blond Westerners were reading guidebooks and drinking milkshakes. Behind them in a darkened window a fluorescent orange poster with zigzag edges listed prices for internet surfing, emails, photocopying and word processing. There was also an address for the café's own website. I couldn't see who, if anyone, was inside.

The street itself, more of a sandy track, consisted of other Dutch colonial houses, most of which were still standing as they had been built over three hundred years ago, except for a few fading coats of deep yellow paint. One, almost immediately opposite, had been converted into a discreet shop. Hessian sacks of rice, cumin seeds, turmeric, nutmeg, dried red chillies and ginger were lined up outside, their open tops rolled down, small birds occasionally swooping down to peck for food.

After five minutes a foreigner appeared at the far end of the street, cycling purposefully towards the café. He partially dismounted with ten yards to go, both legs on one pedal, and then jumped off, swung his bicycle round and rested it against a lamppost next to one of the cane tables. He locked it with a chain, nodded briskly at the two travellers and walked into the café. Macaulay, I was sure of it. He was much more energetic than I had imagined, swifter in his actions, although he was unquestionably old, at least seventy. He was boney, too; tall with pointed shoulders and a slight stoop. His complexion was dark reddish, a trimmed mariner's beard slate grey. Both his trouser legs were tucked into thin yellow cotton socks. I paid for my coffee and walked across to the café.

A wall of cool air hit me as I pushed open the dark glass door and walked inside. There was a row of computer terminals down each side of the room, almost all of them occupied by Westerners. I paused for a moment, my eyes adjusting to the dimmed lighting. At the far end there was a counter and another terminal. Macaulay, if it was him, was punching impatiently at the keyboard with two fingers. He looked up for a second and then continued to type.

"Can I use one of the terminals?" I asked, losing my nerve as I walked towards him.

"That's what they're there for," he said waspishly, not looking up. His accent was Glaswegian, which unsettled me. I hesitated for a moment and then turned and walked across to the nearest terminal, trying to gauge whether his tone had been as dismissive as it sounded.

I sat down at the terminal, wiping my hands on my trousers, and stared at the screen. I realised at once that it had been a mistake not to declare who I was. It would only arouse suspicion later. But before I could say anything, a teenage boy was standing next to me, bent double at the waist so that his head was at the same height as his knees. I had only seen photos of polio victims. Even the mutilated lepers at the ring road flyover in Delhi were in better shape than this boy. His legs were thin and bandied and his hands had withered, clutched in front of his chest like a kangaroo's paws. He had enough movement, though, to lean forward, head pulled up to look at me, and click the cursor with his hand. He smiled as the modem started to dial and then he retreated.

"Actually, I was looking for someone called Martin Macaulay," I called out, getting up from my seat. I had managed to sound almost as uninterested as he had.

"Uh huh," he said, still looking at his own screen. It was definitely Macaulay.

I approached his desk, keen to end the charade.

"I'm sorry, I should have introduced myself first," I continued, sliding my card across the counter. I was conscious of the polio boy standing in the shadows, glancing from me to my screen and back again. "I'm a doctor from the High Commission medical centre in Delhi. I was told that Mr Macaulay was unwell."

I looked at the boy and managed to return his smile. Macaulay tapped on the keyboard with a final flurry and then swivelled round on his chair to face me. He had pale, watery eyes and the skin on his face was rippled with tiny broken blood vessels.

"If I wanted a *desi* Indian doctor I could have got one around here," he snapped, ignoring my card. I noticed one of the Westerners at a keyboard to my right glance round and then return to his screen, smirking to himself.

"I'm not Indian," I said, struggling with the words, which suddenly felt heavy in my mouth. "I was born in Edinburgh."

102

"It gets worse," he said, looking at a pile of letters lying on the counter. I noticed the top one, which was addressed to "Dutchie Reason, c/o The Cardamom Café, Fort Cochin, Kerala, SOUTH INDIA". He gathered the letters up – had he seen me looking at them? – and tucked them away under the counter. There can't have been many Dutchies travelling around India. I tried to think back to the clinic, the man's mumbled words, Jamie's eagerness to get him out of the country.

"Well I'm Macaulay," he said, holding out his hand to shake. Without warning his demeanour had changed, as if the storm inside him had blown itself out. Perhaps he had made a mistake and now realised that I was someone else. "I wish I could say your presence makes me feel better, but it doesn't," he said. "You've come a long way, which means I must be closer to death's door than I thought."

"I was just passing through," I replied, trying to making light of my visit. "I got a message that you had requested a doctor so I thought I would drop by."

"You must be Foreign Office, then," he said, glancing at my card. "Many Asians working there these days?"

"Not many," I said, wondering if he was about to revert to his previous tone.

"But plenty of you in the health service, I gather," he added. The Westerner to my right looked round again. I glanced over at him and he turned back to his screen, shaking his head in what appeared to be disbelief.

"A few. Why?" I said, turning back to Macaulay.

"Just curious. It's easy to lose touch. PC still means a computer around here. You'd better come through," he said, gesturing towards a door beside the counter. I followed him into a surprisingly spacious, high-ceilinged room, thanking the boy who kept the door open for us.

There was a single bed in the corner, with a wooden frame and a mosquito net, and a small table with a laptop computer on it. I noticed he was limping, something that hadn't been evident in the sprightly way he had leapt off his bike. Spread out across a narrow sideboard were a gas cooking stove, a Sumit mixer, some papayas, mangos and a few fresh coconuts, together with a box of Taj Mahal teabags and a foil packet of coffee beans.

A planter's chair with extendable armrests had been positioned under the fan in the middle of the room, a few old copies of the *Spectator* scattered across its cream canvas seat. On the wall next to the bed there were two black-and-white photos showing a group of men standing in front of a slain tiger, and a small shiny picture, almost like a hologram, of a Hindu deity, the identity of whom I couldn't be certain.

Macaulay gathered up the copies of the *Spectator* and gestured for me to sit on the planter's chair, while he turned on the fan and sat down on the corner of the bed.

"Edinburgh, you say," he began, snapping shut the laptop.

"My father moved there in the Sixties," I replied, sitting back much further than I thought in the chair. I looked more relaxed than I felt. "He was a doctor as well."

"Was he from Kerala?" Macaulay asked. "Nair's a very common name around here."

"Yes, he was. A place called Perunna, I think. It's near Changanacherry?"

"I know it well."

"You do?" The words sounded so alien to me, a feeling made stronger by Macaulay's apparent familiarity with them.

"Of course. I've been there many times. Have you?"

"No. This is my first visit to India."

"A sort of homecoming," he said, grinning.

I hadn't expected our conversation to take this turn. Without realising it, he was asking the questions, drawing up his own diagnosis.

"I don't have any family here," I said. "They all left years ago."

"Really? What's your father's name?"

"Ramachandran," I said. "Ram, he's known as Ram back home."

"Back home," he said, smirking, but not in an unpleasant way.

"What's funny?" I asked.

"I suppose Kerala's become my home. And there's your father calling Scotland his." He paused. "Ram Nair, it could almost be Scottish – Ramsay Nair. You know, he probably had another name, the name of his house. Most Nairs do."

"I didn't know," I said.

There was a natural break in the conversation and he popped his head round the door to talk with the boy. I looked round the room again, and then I noticed something on the mantelpiece, hidden behind a stack of paperbacks. It looked like a human head, only shrunken, its eyes and lips neatly stitched together. Macaulay was now facing me again. I tried not to look over at the mantelpiece but he caught me and followed my glance.

"It's not a real one," he said, smiling at my uneasiness. "You can tell by the nasal hair – there isn't any. And the ears are a dead giveaway. It's very difficult to duplicate a shrunken human ear."

"What is it, then? A monkey's?" I asked, watching as he moved it forward to the front of the mantelpiece, blowing some dust off and straightening it fondly, as if he were adjusting a relative's photo.

"Yes. Unfortunately. It would be worth a lot more if it was genuine. My grandfather bought it, thinking it was an authentic head trophy. But the Jivaro used very coarse stitching. Sadly, this is a counterfeit, the work of a very accomplished London taxidermist."

Macaulay sat down again, just as the boy came limping into the room, clutching a fax. He gave it to Macaulay, caught my eye and shuffled out again.

"That boy, he's not well is he?" I said, glad of the interruption.

"Paul? I took him on to make me feel better."

"Madras mentioned you've got problems with your health," I said, relieved at last to be steering the conversation. "It's only to be expected, you know, as the body gets older, matures."

Half an hour later I regretted having raised the subject. Macaulay believed he was suffering from at least fifty ailments including malaria, migraines, a suspected ruptured hernia, septic verrucas, mouth ulcers, excessive wind, incontinence, penile dysfunction (hilarious) and, most degenerative of all, a virulent and increasingly rare strain of racism that left me marvelling that he had not been lynched by the Keralites he had chosen to live amongst.

106

His initial hostility to me failed, oddly, to resurface in our discussion. In fact, it seemed to have been replaced by warmth and a genuine interest in my job, background and family that made me think schizophrenia should have been added to his list of complaints. I listened patiently as he described the agony of urinating with a gall stone the size of a golf ball in his bladder, and the graphic details of his recent prostate operation. "They sliced right up, right up the side," he said, slashing at his crotch. "These Malayali doctors, they don't muck about, you know." But my concentration wavered every time I thought about the letter to Dutchie, the head on the mantelpiece.

Macaulay sensed he had lost his audience. He rose slowly from his bed, went over to the sideboard and pulled out a rusty chopping knife he kept in a drawer. For a brief, disturbing moment, I wasn't sure what he was about to do next. Then he picked up two fresh coconuts, scalped them with the knife, passed one to me, and we drank their milk through straws, sucking in silence. After we had finished, he cut the coconuts open, each one with a single, sickening chop, the halves rolling apart on the sideboard. I watched him scoop out the jellied flesh with a spoon cut from the outer husk, but declined to join him, feeling increasingly queasy.

After he had finished, Macaulay invited me to dinner at his home in the evening. I made my excuses, saying I had to look up an old friend, but he insisted, telling me to bring my friend along. He gave me a number to call if I was coming. His house, he said, was on an island in the middle of Cochin harbour and he would need to send someone he called "fatman row-row" in a boat to fetch me from the Dutch Palace jetty in Mattancherry. As I left the café, passing through rows of flickering computer terminals, I knew that I would take up his offer. I just had to persuade Priyanka to come, too.

CHAPTER ELEVEN

THE ABSURDITY OF asking Priyanka to dinner with a stranger on an island became increasingly apparent as I walked down the road away from the café. I turned a corner and headed across the Parade Ground, an English village green complete with its own church and cricket pitch. A group of children were sitting in the shade of a vast rain tree, known locally as a cow tamarind, some slumped between its webbed roots, others leaning on the handlebars of their bikes. I strolled past them towards the church, taking in the scene. I could almost have been in Shamley Green or Abinger Hammer, had it not been for the brown Brahminy kites circling above.

I wanted to get as far away from Macaulay as possible before I rang Priyanka. I carried on walking, past the old Customs House and on round to the fishing nets. Macaulay had touched something deep inside. The sudden switch in manner had left me feeling particularly uneasy. It wasn't just the glimpses of an unreconstructed racist that disturbed me – that was almost to be expected in ageing expats – more the sense of a hidden agenda, a burying of differences for the sake of another plan. He had asked too many questions.

I watched the fishermen operate their cantilevered nets for a while, rolling their shoulders as they pulled on ropes weighed down with small boulders. The crows stole what few fish were caught and it soon became clear that the fishermen were too drunk to care. It was time to ring Priyanka. There was an ISD/STD phone booth just beyond the nets, next to the ticket office for the Vypeen car ferry. I waited for the line to connect, watching the ferry head out across the harbour, absurdly angled against the strong incoming tide. The phone rang, once, twice, three times. I could feel my pulse across the top half of my body.

"Hello," a female voice said. It was not Priyanka's.

"Can I speak to Priyanka, please?" I said, wondering if I was talking to a sister. The tone sounded similar but her accent was stronger.

"Who is calling?" she said, her voice more hesitant, suspicious.

"My name's Raj. I'm calling from the British High Commission," I said. For the first time it dawned on me how selfish I was being by ringing her. Of course she would be angry, accusing me of not respecting her family, their customs. I contemplated hanging up but decided to hold on. I could hear muffled voices in the background and then a man came on the line.

"Can I help?" he said. It was an older voice, probably her father's. I felt like a teenager trying to secure parental permission for a date. I managed to suppress a nervous laugh. Part of me wanted to weep, too, as I knew her reluctance to come to the phone meant only one thing.

"I just wanted to have a word with Priyanka, if that's okay," I continued, businesslike. "I'm calling from the British High Commission. I've got some medical data she wanted for a magazine story she's writing. About foreigners and the illnesses they get in India."

110

I paused, taken aback by my own improvised persistence. Should I go on? "You know, Delhi belly, bubonic plague, the routine sort of thing," I added, allowing a small laugh, wondering whether I should add hilarious sexual problems.

"Would you hold on for a moment?" the man interrupted, ignoring everything that I had said.

I heard some more talking in the background, and then Priyanka came to the phone.

"Raj, is that you?" Her voice was strained, unnatural.

"I'm sorry for ringing you. I'm in Cochin," I said.

"I thought you were . . . " Her voice tailed off. "We can't talk Raj, not now," she said, almost whispering. I could hear the sound of her hand shielding the receiver, as if she were turning Around, checking to see if anyone was listening. "Please, remember what I said."

"I'm here for a couple of days," I continued, trying not to believe that she had already found a husband. "I wondered if we could meet. If, that is, you're not . . . "

"I am."

"Already?"

"Next month – the article's due out next month," she added, covering herself. And then, more formally, she said, "What information have you got for me? My father said you have some data on sick foreigners."

I could hear someone in the background, possibly her sister again.

"Yes," I said, equally formally, digesting her news. *She was getting married next month.* I suddenly felt protective of her, worried that our conversation, its breach of family protocol, would place her in danger. But I also desperately wanted to see her.

111

"I'm meeting someone for dinner tonight," I continued. "A patient of mine. He's British, has lived in Cochin for over forty years."

"Is that sort of information relevant to the article?" she asked.

"He's called Macaulay," I continued, going through the motions. It was an increasingly lost cause. "He has a house on an island in the harbour. I think he would make a great article."

"I know all about him," she said, her voice gaining in enthusiasm. Almost by chance I had appealed to the journalist in her. "*Seven Days* has been trying to interview him for years but he refuses to talk to anyone. You know the state government have accused him of spying?"

"Really?" I asked, wondering why I hadn't been told, praying that Macaulay would be a big enough draw.

"Do you have any other information?" she asked.

"I think he would give you an interview," I said, entering the realms of fantasy. "He's asked me to bring someone along tonight for dinner. Can you come?"

There was a long pause. Go on, I thought. Forget all about me, think of the story, the glory.

"Can you come?" I repeated. "We have to be at the Dutch Palace jetty at seven. Someone will pick us up from there."

"I'll need to talk to the office," she said.

"I'll see you at seven, then, on the jetty. Dutch Palace."

I hung up, wondering what I had done. Her father sounded so straight, decent, his suspicion so unnatural. I had never even asked her what he did for a living, how many sisters and brothers she had. We knew so little about each other. For a moment I thought about walking away, pretending that we had never met in Delhi. But I knew something had happened the night when we first saw each other at Frank's house, something so unforced and natural that I felt I had been carrying the memory of her around with me all my life. And that hug when I had dropped her off after our awkward meal at the restaurant. It had been too long for a goodbye, hadn't it?

But it all counted for nothing now. She was getting married. My only comfort was her professional interest in Macaulay, her journalistic ambition. At least that might lure her out, allow us to meet one more time. There was something else, though, that kept me going. I didn't know who Priyanka was engaged to, but I did know that everyone should be allowed one chance in life to get out of the water. And if I could just see Priyanka, even for five minutes, I would understand from those honest, pellucid eyes of hers whether she was swimming or if the tide was carrying her out to sea.

I had a few hours to kill before I needed to be at the jetty so I decided to take an auto rickshaw down to Mattancherry and look around the old spice warehouses that I had admired from across the water. Most of them were antiques shops now, crammed to the ceiling with dusty rosewood fourposter beds, faded court fans, teak temple pillars, colonial clocks, Belgian glass lanterns and splintered statues of the Virgin Mary. The smell of ginger and cardamom was still strong, though, particularly in the narrow lanes around the noisy Pepper Exchange. And I discovered one or two old clay jars, vast, swollen urns inscribed with dragons, that had once

113

brought cooking oils from China and returned laden with spices.

There was an ancient Jewish synagogue here, too, where a dwindling community of white Jews still worshipped. According to one local shop owner, the synagogue was lucky to be standing. Another one, in a suburb outside Ernakulam, had been secretly dismantled and exported stone by stone to Israel, despite numerous rules drawn up by the Archaeological Survey of India to prevent such cultural pillage. The scam had only been unearthed when an astute Kerala minister, on holiday in Israel, thought that the synagogue looked vaguely familiar.

I reached the jetty a little early. There was nobody around who fitted the description of "fatman rowrow", just a few people sleeping on the ground with handkerchiefs covering their faces, shielding them from the sun. I had convinced myself that Priyanka would show up, and when a small boat came into view, rowed by a man with an overhanging stomach, I looked up the street towards the Dutch Palace, expecting her to appear. When nobody came, I strolled over to a stall selling panama hats and checked the street down towards the Pepper Exchange. There was still no sign of her. It was only after the rowing boat had arrived that I conceded, for the first time, that I might have exaggerated our brief encounter in Delhi. My conversation with her earlier in the day suddenly seemed embarrassing, childish.

I decided to ring Frank. I knew it was risky but it was eating me up not knowing how he was. There was a booth across the street, from where a few minutes later I was listening to the sound of his phone ringing. An

Indian voice answered. I hesitated, wondering if the line was tapped, and then asked for Frank.

"London," the man said. "Gone to London."

"Susie? Madam?" I asked, not sure whether I was worried or relieved that they had left Delhi.

"London."

I asked for a number and after a long pause and much rustling of paper I was given one. What were they doing there? Had they gone from choice, or had they been forced out? On balance, I felt they were probably better off out of Delhi. I would ring Frank tomorrow; it was too late in London.

Increasingly disconsolate, I went over to the boatman and asked if he had been sent by Macaulay, pointing at the harbour as I said the name. I couldn't bring myself to ask whether he was "fatman row-row" but it seemed not entirely impossible in the circumstances. His many chins were unshaven, the whiskers grey, and he wore a tight white vest, which failed to cover his stomach.

"Macaulay?" he said, nodding as he looked me up and down.

"Macaulay," I repeated, encouragingly.

"*Shari*," he said, nodding his head from side to side. It was hard to tell whether he was saying yes or no.

I persevered, despite his lack of English, asking him whether he had seen a young woman called Priyanka. It was a desperate question, made worse by having to repeat her name slowly, syllable by syllable. But when I said her name in full again, rolling the 'r' for good measure, his eyes lit up like an Italian icecream seller.

"Ah, Priyanka," he said, nodding towards the harbour. "Five," he added, beaming as he tapped a finger on his watch. If my arms had been long enough I would have hugged him. Instead I settled for a tentative pat on his hairy shoulder and we made our way down to his boat.

The water was choppy in the middle of the main channel and our progress was painfully slow. I watched as the oars twisted in the rusty rollocks, glancing up occasionally at fatman, willing him to row-row faster. But his pace had the steadiness of habit, fast enough to beat the tide but sufficiently slow to avoid breaking into a sweat. I wondered why Macaulay didn't provide him with an outboard engine.

It was not immediately obvious where we were heading. Already we had rounded Willingdon Island, passed the terrace where I had been drinking beer a few hours earlier, and we were now drifting out towards an island on the far side of the harbour entrance which I assumed was Vypeen. I could see a smaller island in the foreground and another one behind that. I pointed towards it, gesturing beyond the first one, and he nodded. It was covered in thick vegetation but I caught a brief glimpse of some white pillars and a grand, box-like porch through a gap in the coconut trees.

Had fatman, whose hairline was finally beginning to bead with sweat, really understood what I had said? Was it a desire to please? Or had those three syllables, Priy – ank – a, broken through the language barrier to mean the same as they did to me?

We were almost at the island now but our progress was slowed still further by a bed of water hyacinth, its roots sticking to the oars like glutinous noodles. A man had appeared on a small jetty, waiting to take our bow rope. There were no other boats around, and when I looked back to where we had just come from I realised that we were much more tucked away than I had originally thought.

I began to doubt whether Priyanka could really be here and felt foolish again. But then I saw her sitting on a cane chair on a lawn in front of the main building, her white *salwar kameez* clearly visible through the trees. Her posture was unmistakable, upright, in control. She was talking with Macaulay, who was also wearing white, having changed into a *kurta pyjama*. There was a tape recorder on the table between them. Behind it, squatting on the grass close to Macaulay was a photographer, whose flash suddenly brightened the dimming light.

I jumped off the boat, trying not to run, and walked round a curved gravel path. There were some rhododendron bushes between the jetty and the lawn, but I managed to catch a few more glimpses, her head tilting back with that light, unselfconscious laugh of hers. Her presence here meant one of two things. Either she was a career journalist who had been presented with an irresistible scoop. Or she wanted to see me. If the latter was the case, she might just wish to tell me to back off, a final plea to show some respect. I was hanging on, by a single spinning thread, to something else.

"Raj," Macaulay said, in a booming, friendly voice as I stepped onto the lawn and approached them. "Glad you could make it." We were clearly picking up from where we had left off.

I glanced at Priyanka, who looked away, abashed rather than cross. I wondered if the pulse beating in my temples was noticeable. Priyanka ran a hand through her long, healthy hair and glanced down at her note-book. *She wasn't swimming.*

"How could I turn down such an offer?" I said, still a few yards away, looking around at the incongruously grand setting. The lawn, dotted with painted croquet hoops, had been recently mown with precise diagonal stripes. There were rosebeds in full bloom at each corner, and the gravel path swept on round the lawn to the house, which appeared to be an original white Lutyens bungalow, although it looked more recently built. A square porch worthy of a viceroy dominated the entire setting, offset by Lutyens's trademark pillars that ran along the front of the house on either side. A Union Jack was fluttering from the flat roof, and there were rows of solar-heating panels just visible through some *jali* lattice set further back.

"I think you know Priyanka," Macaulay said, as I drew level with them. I shook Macaulay's hand and then turned to Priyanka, who surprised me by standing up and kissing me briefly on both cheeks. There was no intimacy in the gesture, just a calculated setting of tone: a breezy Western friendship, nothing more.

"How was your journey?" she asked, neutrally. *The tide was carrying her out to sea.* As she sat down again, the sweet smell of coconut hair oil still lingering, I caught her eye, acknowledged the new rules of engagement.

"Not bad," I said. "A two-hour delay in Goa."

"I meant the boat trip," she said, smiling for the first time. "Did it make you seasick?"

"No," I replied, annoyed at myself. "We met in Delhi," I said, turning to Macaulay. "I've been helping her with one or two articles."

118

"Including this one," Macaulay said, gesturing to a *mali* to bring up another seat. "I don't normally do this sort of thing — it always lands me in trouble — but I relented when she said she was a friend of yours."

"Really?" I said, genuinely curious. I checked myself, wary of revealing my own suspicions about him, his earlier sudden change of heart towards me.

"Are we nearly finished?" he said to Priyanka. "I have a little work to do before dinner." Macaulay took out a packet of Wills cigarettes, offered me one, which I declined, and then lit one himself with a plastic lighter. He inhaled through one end of his bunched fist, between his curled thumb and forefinger, the cigarette itself pointing upwards, perpendicular to the normal angle, like an improvised hookah.

"Do you have enough, Thomas?" Priyanka asked, turning to the photographer, who was still squatting, apparently taking a picture of the Union Jack.

"I'm done," he said. "Although I wouldn't mind one more with the elephant." Thomas glanced over to the far end of the garden, where, for the first time, I noticed a large tusker standing quite still in the shade of a jacaranda tree. I was amazed that something so big could be so discreet.

"I think we've done the mahout bit, don't you?" Macaulay said, sounding bored.

"Okay," said the photographer. "The light's dying, anyway."

I watched Priyanka as they talked. She was sitting upright, despite the temptations of the garden chair, writing tidy words with a carefully sharpened pencil.

"I might need a little more on your news agency," she said.

119

"You make it sound so grand," Macaulay replied. "It's just a hobby, nothing more. I collect stories from the Indian press and send them to friends overseas. That's all there is to it. 'Three die in bogey mishap', that sort of thing."

He caught my eye and winked, trying to bind me into his circle of foreign friends. I looked away.

"Perhaps we could discuss it over dinner," Priyanka suggested, leaning forward to turn off her tape recorder.

"If we must," he said. "I have to leave you for a while. I suggest you go inside, have a drink. The mosquitos are appalling here, even worse than Vypeen, which is saying something."

CHAPTER TWELVE

THE SOLITARY LIGHTBULB on the verandah where we were talking was not very bright and neither of us was surprised when it flickered a couple of times and died. "Dim-dum", as Jagu, my *mali* in Delhi, had called it. For a few moments Priyanka and I sat in the darkness, watching the beam from the nearby Vypeen lighthouse sweep across the tops of the palm trees and out to sea, before coming round to the house again, lighting up the mosquito nets draped between the verandah pillars. The moon had yet to rise but the sky above us was already a matrix of stars and smudged galaxies. The noise of cicadas in the garden had grown louder in the humid darkness, no longer a background accompaniment to our stilted words.

Priyanka was all artifice tonight, and I had so far spent the precious fifteen minutes we had been left on our own swapping facts about Kerala, its high levels of literacy and graduate unemployment, recent threats to its secular tradition, the south-west monsoon. We had been unable to talk about Macaulay, a subject that would have broken the impasse, because we were both aware of him moving around behind us in the drawing room. Perhaps the powercut – "load-shedding", Macaulay called it – would help, let us start again.

"Are you angry with me for calling?" I asked, still looking out towards the lighthouse. I could hear her sipping her *nimbu pani*, the ice cubes knocking against the glass. Then we both turned as Paul, the boy from the café, came round the corner of the house and up the verandah steps, clutching two gas lamps. I winced as he managed to untwist his contorted body and hang one from a hook on a pillar; the other he placed on the table between us, catching my eye and smiling. Priyanka waited for him to go and then looked back at the sitting room.

"Raj, Cochin is a very small place," she began, less falsely than before. "We have met once before in Delhi, professionally, that's all. You are here because of work, seeing one of your patients, and I'm researching a story."

"Is that what you told Macaulay?" I asked.

"It's also what I told my family," she said, looking round again.

"And is that why you're really here? For work?"

"I'm getting married next month," she said, flatly.

"So you said," I replied.

"You almost embarrassed my father today. I know it must all seem very provincial, but when a woman in Kerala is engaged to someone, the father doesn't really expect her to receive phone calls from other men."

"So why did you come here tonight, then?" I asked, trying in vain not to sound annoyed.

"Because the management at *Seven Days* has been trying to secure an interview with Macaulay for over two years."

"And that's it," I said, smirking. "Well I'm glad if I've helped to further your career. They might even let you go on honeymoon now, you never know."

"And because I wanted to see you," she added, more softly, ignoring my petulance. "To explain to you in person."

We both sat in silence again, watching a moth circle the lamp on the pillar. Behind it a bat flitted low over the lawn and disappeared into the darkness. Her change of tone was encouraging.

"I wanted to see you as well," I said, tentatively.

"Why?" she asked.

"Why? Because when we met in Delhi I thought there was something between us."

"But you can see that's irrelevant now," she said, frustration creeping back into her voice again. "We met twice. It was fun."

"Fun," I replied, mockingly. "Clearly not fun enough."

"It's not like that, Raj," she said, despairing. "I've met a few guys who were fun to be with, at school, college, work. But I always knew I would eventually end up with someone my parents had chosen. I'm sorry it worked out like this, that we happened to meet just before they started looking. It must all seem very callous."

"And now that they have found someone?" I said.

"I would ask that you respect their choice, respect me."

I contemplated asking about the new man in her life, but decided against it. She probably couldn't have told me much about him, anyway.

"I was cross when you rang," she continued. "You knew why I had come back to Kerala. It was so . . . presumptuous."

I knew as she chose the word that it was probably the best of a bad bunch. She was right, it had been presumptious, but I owed it to our brief time together in Delhi, to the serendipity that had brought me to Cochin. At least she acknowledged that something had happened. But now that I had seen her again, it was clear that I must leave her to get on with her life.

A moment later my resolve weakened as I noticed her wiping a finger across one eyelid. "I'm sorry," she said, getting up. "I must go to the bathroom."

Dinner turned out to be a surprisingly mundane affair, given the extravagant surrounds. Macaulay explained that he had built the house – it was an almost exact copy of a Lutyens bungalow – after hearing about an expatriate in Delhi who had constructed one in the depths of the Haryana countryside.

"Of course, Lutyens didn't actually build all the bungalows in New Delhi," Macaulay was saying, as we tucked into a bland moussaka. The first course had been tinned tomato soup. "Only four were his own work and they are in the grounds of Rasthrapati Bhavan. The rest were Baker's."

"But why did you look back for inspiration, rather than forward?" Priyanka asked, jotting something down in a notebook beside her plate. She had requested permission earlier to record the dinner but Macaulay had objected. He had, however, agreed to her "taking minutes", if she must, during the meal. She was sitting opposite me near one end of a large dining-room table. Macaulay was at the head, in between us. We were all surprisingly close, bunched up with our plates and chairs, leaving three-quarters of the polished rosewood table empty.

124

"The simple answer is that I cannot bear air conditioning," he said. "Lutyens didn't have that luxury, if you can call it that, in his day. Instead he devised a brilliant solution to living in hot climates. His bungalows were spacious with high ceilings and always ventilated by cross breezes. That's the important point. Nobody to my knowledge has managed to come up with anything better."

It was certainly cool in the dining room, the air stirred by two long-stalked fans as it passed from the verandah through to a central courtyard, where a fountain was playing. The downward current from the fans occasionally disturbed thin strands of hair on the top of Macaulay's balding head. He flipped them back as if he were closing a lid. As we talked, he struck me as an increasingly lonely figure, confident and busy, but perhaps out of fear he was also adept at keeping others at arm's length, turning attention away from himself. My report for Sir Ian was going to be unacceptably thin unless the guard dropped.

I looked around the room for more clues about the man, his rumoured influence. The furniture was colonial and the pictures were mostly Daniell prints. The only sign of a past, of a family, was a collection of silver-framed photos on an Edwardian half-moon table.

"Can you tell me a bit more about your views on the British Raj" Priyanka was asking.

"I thought we went through this on the lawn," Macaulay said, and then turned to me, grinning. "This is the bit that always lands me in hot water." I smiled but didn't like the conspiracy between us, the exclusion of Priyanka.

"You said earlier that there was no justice in India

any more for the common man," Priyanka continued. "What do you mean exactly? That there was more justice before Independence?"

"Of course. Under British rule, the District Collector was, generally speaking, an honest man. We had one or two scoundrels, but he could be counted on to be fair. He also provided moral leadership, a civilising influence. Can you see any evidence of that today in Bihar? Take a close look at this," he said, gesturing towards a print behind him which I hadn't noticed before. "*Suttee*, or *sati* – a grotesque practice outlawed by Lord Bentinck in 1829." Macaulay stood up to look at the picture more closely. In it, a woman, her arms raised and breasts bare, was about to throw herself onto a raging fire. Priyanka stayed seated but I pushed my chair back and joined Macaulay.

"An eighteenth-century Dutchman called Baltazard Solvyns," he said, as we moved along to the next picture. "He saw it all with his own eyes. They're etchings. He did this one as well." I shuffled behind him, pushing a chair in to make room. A woman with a bowl on her head had her hands clasped together in prayer. Next to her a bamboo ladder disappeared into a small, circular hole in the ground.

"Buried alive, wretched woman. The *Joogee* caste of weavers from Orissa. One of the few Hindus who bury their dead. And the living. The woman climbs down into the hole, usually about eight feet deep, and the ladder is quickly withdrawn. Her dead husband has already been lowered inside. She places his head on her knee, lights a lamp and then a priest on the surface says some prayers while friends and family walk round the hole, throwing in sandalwood, flowers and a few new clothes. Then they start chucking in the earth, gently at first. When it reaches the wife's neck, they pause, before covering her up as quickly as possible, treading down the mud to ensure a speedy end. It usually takes five minutes for the woman to die, but at least her cries are muffled."

I stared at the picture, listening to Macaulay's words, noticing that he had slipped into the present tense.

"Sometimes they give the woman dried saffron pistils. It makes her laugh hysterically. Either that or opium. Anything to preserve the wife's dutiful smile. It's coming back, you know," Macaulay said, sitting down at the table again. "Roop Kanwar was the turning point. Beautiful lass, barely nineteen, burnt to death in Rajasthan, 1987. The authorities were scared witless by the international scandal it provoked, the revival it sparked off. They've been covering up ever since. Have to. Nobody would ever visit India again if they knew how many *satis* were taking place, here in modern India, in the twenty-first century."

I lingered in front of the picture, half listening to Macaulay, to Priyanka's replies, her profound scepticism about a revival of *sati*, and then I spotted someone in the background, standing under the shade of an umbrella that was being held for him. It was not a local *Joogee*, or a priest. He was a Westerner, wearing a long tailed jacket, breeches, a white wig. An East India Company official, perhaps. Whoever he might have been, he was watching the burial from a discreet distance, choosing not to interfere.

"Was it a mistake, then, for the British to hand over rule?" Priyanka asked, catching my eye and raising her eyebrows as I sat down again. Macaulay sighed at the question.

"I don't think it should be seen solely in terms of that one moment," he said. "Mistakes started to be made two hundred years earlier. All I am saying – and I would be grateful if you could quote me accurately on this – is that things could have been done differently. The British Empire in India presented a unique opportunity for something new, a cultural synthesis that could have benefited the whole world, not just India and Britain. But we mocked Indians who took up our Western ways, and the British who adopted local customs were cruelly ridiculed, too. You just have to look at Tagore, a Bengali who only blossomed when he came into contact with European thought. Independence, for me, was final confirmation of a missed opportunity, the denial of a rare synergy that existed between two very different cultures. Can we leave it at that?"

"But you do think India should have been given its Independence?" Priyanka persisted.

"Another soda, anyone?" Macaulay said, pointedly ignoring her. He stood up and strode over to a revolving cylinder next to the drinks table. His "gammy leg", as he called it, seemed to have dramatically improved. I glanced at Priyanka, who rolled her eyes upwards in despair. We both declined, but were intrigued by the machine. Macaulay took an old soda bottle and placed it neck first in a central drum and then turned a handle on the side, like an organ grinder. The drum spun round, clunking. Then Macaulay took out the bottle, picked up a screwdriver from the drinks table, and hammered it with the palm of his hand into the bottle's neck, dislodging the glass marble cork. There was a sudden whoosh and he poured the soda into a glass, mixing it with a generous measure of chilled vodka before sitting down again.

"My grandfather's," he said, looking at me. The vodka he had been drinking all evening was beginning to glaze his eyes. I was increasingly convinced his catalogue of health problems was nothing more complicated than alcohol poisoning.

"Talking of family," he continued, clumsily squeezing half a lime into his glass with his thumb and forefinger, "I've been finding out a bit more about your father."

"Mine?" I said, taken aback. Once again he was turning the tables.

"Yes, Ram Nair of Changanacherry." He said the words with an air of theatrical triumph, as if he were introducing a famous music-hall act.

"I didn't know your family were from there," Priyanka said, looking at me with surprise.

"A long time ago," I said, already resenting whatever Macaulay was about to reveal.

"1960," Macaulay stated matter-of-factly. "June 15th. The day your father left for Britain. After travelling by bus and train from Perunna outside Changanacherry to Bombay, he caught a boat to Portsmouth."

I could feel my hands turning cold. I was shocked that he knew such detailed information, ashamed that I wasn't aware of it myself. He could have been bluffing, of course, but why? The dates approximated to what little I had ever bothered to ask my father. I was conscious of Priyanka's eyes upon me. We hadn't been alone since our discussion on the verandah and her abrupt departure, but I sensed that she was with me now, that she had picked up on my discomfort.

129

"How do you know these things?" Priyanka asked.

"I happened to come across him in my notes. For the book I was telling you about. He was really quite militant. Young but very committed."

"My father?" I asked, laughing nervously, without conviction.

"Of course," Macaulay said, his tone still rigorous. "The freedom struggle wasn't all it could have been in what we now call Kerala. Cochin and Malabar were more active than Travancore. The local Malayalis were generally more concerned with ousting a Tamil Diwan than with the British. Your father, though, was very active in politics, inclined to the socialist wing of Congress. As a youth, it seems, he hated the English with a passion, ran several local Quit India campaigns. He was even involved in the famous Keezhariyur bomb case. I'm still checking, but I think he was one of twenty-seven people who were charge-sheeted."

Macaulay helped himself to another portion of cold moussaka, and I scrabbled to process what he had just said, tried to equate it with the man I knew. The only time I had heard my father talk against the English was when we had once discussed Scottish devolution.

"I'm surprised they let you anywhere near the Foreign Office," Macaulay continued; he was the only one who was having seconds. "Not exactly Eton and Oxford, was he?"

"It really doesn't sound like my father," I said, still conscious of Priyanka, grateful for her company. "I can't think of anyone less suitable to be a freedom fighter."

"If he had been so anti-British, why did the government in London let him settle there?" Priyanka asked.

130

"Why indeed?" Macaulay said.

"I'm sorry, it just doesn't add up." I stood up from the table and walked over towards the verandah, feeling a warmth spreading across my face. I needed to get away from Macaulay for a few minutes.

"Come on, Raj, it was a long time ago," he continued, calling after me. "I'm sure he's since sworn loyalty to Queen and country, flies the Union Jack at home, just like me."

"The rampant lion, in fact," I said, my back still to the table.

"Well, there you go," Macaulay continued. "A brave-heart Scot."

"How did you manage to find out this sort of information?" Priyanka asked.

"By over forty years of hard legwork, that's bloody how," Macaulay said.

"In India?" she asked.

Macaulay hesitated before answering, as if he were momentarily thrown by the question. Either that or he was weighing up how much to reveal.

"And London," Macaulay said, finishing his drink. "Immigration records, Home Office." He stopped, clearly checking himself, and rose from the table.

"Now," he said, putting an arm round me as I stared out into the darkness of the garden. "A frame of snooker before the steamed pudding?"

I declined the offer, removing myself from his touch and leaving Priyanka to ask him a few more formal questions over coffee. I sat outside on the verandah again, thinking back over what he had said and why he had told me, wondering whether there was a shred of truth in any of it. Sir Ian had spoken about

Macaulay's influence in Whitehall, his credentials as a historian. I needed to talk with Priyanka but we hadn't been allowed a moment to ourselves. I knew already that she had discovered far more about Macaulay than I ever would. We had to compare notes, however difficult it might prove. I was meant to be sounding Macaulay out. Instead he had spent the evening talking to me about my past, and to her about his own.

"Doesn't he give you the creeps?" Priyanka asked, suddenly at my side. I turned to see her putting a note-pad away in her shoulder bag. I looked behind us and could see Macaulay in his study, off from the main room, talking on the phone. Behind him a young man wearing only a *lunghi* round his waist walked into the room. He was a Westerner, barely out of his teens, his chest pale and smooth.

"Who's that with him?" I asked.

She turned round to look. "I've no idea."

"I thought journalists were supposed to pry," I said. The man disappeared out of sight again.

"I've got enough material to fill the magazine twice."

"Is he a spy, then?"

"He didn't tell me that. Anyway, I thought you were interested in his health."

"I am. I'm examining him tomorrow. Tonight is purely social."

We looked at each other for a moment.

"He did hint on the lawn that he has friends in high places," she said, turning away.

"In London?" I asked. Priyanka nodded. "What kind of friends?"

"He didn't elaborate." She paused. "I imagine people

who can pass on the sort of information he told you about your father."

I smirked, checking that Macaulay was still on the phone.

"You didn't believe any of that, did you?" I asked.

"The places sounded right. I had no idea you were from Perunna. It's where my family are from." She paused again. "I can get it checked, if you want me to."

"I wouldn't bother," I said. "You haven't met my father."

"It doesn't ring true, then?"

"No, it doesn't."

I wished I could be at home with him now, drinking a malt in front of the open fire. He would have liked Priyanka, might even have overlooked the fact that she was from India.

"I have to be getting back," Priyanka said. "Macaulay said the boat was waiting. Are you staying here the night?"

"No," I replied. "Not if I can help it." I wondered if Macaulay had intended me to stay. I turned round and he had disappeared. "I'll come back on your boat. If that's allowed."

"Sure," she said, for the first time looking at me in the way she had in Delhi.

"I'd better go and find Macaulay, say goodbye."

I walked back over to the house, climbed up the steps and went into the dining room, but Macaulay was not around. I looked in his study and the sitting room. Both were empty. Then I heard something in the kitchen, a smacking noise, like a clap, or two pieces of flat wood being hit together. I walked down the corridor and stood outside the kitchen door, which was closed. I could hear Macaulay's voice talking quietly, insistently, but the words were not clear. Checking behind me, I knelt down and looked through the keyhole. Standing near the stove, at the far end of the kitchen, was the boy in the *lunghi*. Macaulay was in front of him, prodding a finger aggressively into the boy's bare chest, pushing him across the kitchen. When the boy backed into the stove and could retreat no further, Macaulay slapped him hard across the mouth, quickly following up with another, harder stroke, this time with the back of the hand. The boy winced, catching his breath, and then hung his head as blood gathered between his split lips. Macaulay grabbed the boy's chin with his thumb and forefinger, lifted it and kissed him hard on his bruised mouth. After a few seconds Macaulay tossed the boy away and looked over towards the door, his lips smudged with red. It didn't seem an appropriate moment to say goodbye.

I suspected fatman row-row's steady pace suited me more than it did Priyanka as we made our way slowly across the harbour towards Willingdon Island. I longed for him to take his time, to wipe his brow, lose an oar, let us drift all night with the hidden currents below. The water lapped at the sides of the boat, glistening in the stark light of the moon, which was almost full and now high above us. We were both sitting in the bow, behind fatman, who had his back to us. Priyanka was staring out across the water to the left, in the direction of the Ernakulam shoreline, which was lit up like a Parisian boulevard.

"What's the headline going to be, then?" I asked. "Relic of the Raj?"

"It's more complicated than that. Did you notice the picture in the bathroom?"

"No."

"Kali with an infant Shiva, dancing in a cemetery. People used to hang it in their houses in Calcutta to keep away cholera."

"He's a hypochondriac," I said. I didn't want to tell her about the boy in the *lunghi*, not yet. For the moment, as sole witness, I could deny it had happened. It was easier that way, less frightening.

"He upset you, didn't he?" she asked, more quietly. "Those comments he made about your father."

I watched her put one hand into the water, letting it trail through her long fingers. "He had no right to talk about him like that," she continued, cupping some water in her hand and letting it go. "Are you a close family?"

"There's only the two of us. My mother died a few years back." I paused, guiltily, knowing that she hadn't expected an intimate revelation. "We've never really talked about India."

"Not even when you were posted here?" she asked, passing respectfully round my mother.

"A bit, I suppose," I said, lying, thinking back to how my father had greeted the news with complete indifference. I had been speaking on the phone to him from London, after my second interview at the Foreign Office. The news had gone in, to be processed later, but at the time all he had done was pause, like someone waiting for a cyclist to pass before crossing the street. A moment later he was asking if I had read in the

135

newspapers that day about a colleague of his who had been charged with embezzlement.

The recollection made me smile. Sometimes his ability to shut something out could be infuriating, but there was a certain phlegm, a British stoicism, to the approach, too. In that one brief moment on the phone, he knew and had accepted the enormous implications of what I was saying, that I would soon be travelling to India, a chapter of his life that he had chosen to keep from me. His ability to continue the conversation, as if nothing had happened, was a measure of his confidence in himself, in the decisions he had made all those years ago, and in our own relationship, that nothing would change. Thinking of it now, it gave me strength, renewed my belief that Macaulay was wrong, that there were no skeletons.

"I find that very hard to understand," Priyanka was saying. "If my father had originally come from England and I was suddenly posted to London, I would want to know everything about his time there, what it was like, why he left."

"You would probably know already, that's the difference," I replied. "In our family India has been taboo ever since I can remember."

Our boat continued on its blissfully slow progress, the peace briefly disturbed by the dramatic appearance, from behind Willingdon Island, of the dredger I had seen at lunchtime. Rusting chains were rattling against its stained hull as a vacuum boom was lowered down one side into the water. A foghorn sounded six times and a searchlight danced across the surrounding water, pausing on a fisherman's dugout fifty yards to the stern, and then on us. We both shielded our eyes from the beam, worried that we were too close. Fatman looked briefly over his shoulder and kept on rowing.

Priyanka talked with him in Malayalam and then said to me, "He used to work on the dredger."

"That's all right then," I replied, noticing that we were drawing near to Willingdon Island. My time was running out with each pull on the oars.

"Can we meet up again, professionally, to talk about Macaulay?" I asked, watching the dredger inch slowly forwards against the skyline. Some fishing boats were heading down the main channel, their engines idling as the tide carried them out to sea.

"I'll send you the article as soon as I have written it," she said. "And my notes."

At least it was a gentle way of saying no. I could see one side of her face in the moonlight. Her cheek was smooth and dry. She swept a defiant hand through her hair, refusing to say anything else. Part of me felt angry: without me she wouldn't have secured an interview with Macaulay. But the feeling subsided as quickly as it had come, replaced by a heaviness of heart that I had seldom felt before. In this light her beauty was ephemeral, so out of reach.

"We can't see each other again, Raj," she was saying, her hair rippling in the salty breeze. She turned her head further away from me. "We mustn't."

"Why?" I asked quietly, hoping she wouldn't answer. I didn't want to hear her say it.

"I don't trust myself," Priyanka said, her voice wavering. Our words were slowing down, mesmerised by the oars, the lapping water. "That's why."

I put an arm round her shoulders, glancing at fatman, who was lost in his own world. She turned and put both arms round me, burying her head in my shoulder to stop the crying. I held her tightly and then she had lifted her head and we were kissing.

"Malabar Jetty?" fatman said, his voice separating us like an electric shock. The boat rocked precariously as we moved to either side. Fatman turned round, but all he saw were two people sitting primly. We both suppressed a giggle as Priyanka dried her eyes. And then her features hardened.

"Malabar," she said, looking at the shore and then directly at me. There was no reproach in her eyes, just a frightened appeal. I wondered what she meant and then I turned towards the shore, barely fifty yards ahead, and saw an old man waiting for us.

CHAPTER THIRTEEN

THE MAN ON the jetty was Priyanka's father. He bent down to take our rope and helped Priyanka to step ashore. I was left to disembark on my own but I didn't sense any coldness towards me.

"This is Raj, the doctor who has been helping me with a couple of stories in Delhi," Priyanka said to him, with impressive composure. "And this is my father," she said, turning to me.

Her father nodded as we shook hands. "Raj Nair," I said, looking at him for a moment, conscious of how the name resonated in Kerala. His face looked creased and tired with worry.

"Raj was the one who arranged the interview with Macaulay," Priyanka said, stepping in. We were both waiting to see his reaction, wondering if he had seen us in the dark. But he had not come here to chastise us, or to pass judgment. His worries lay elsewhere.

"Priya, your mother has been taken ill," he said quietly. "You must come quickly. We have been trying to contact you all afternoon."

"What's the matter with her?" Priyanka asked anxiously. The whole tone of the conversation had shifted.

"She's had a stroke."

"Mummy?" Priyanka said, bewildered.

"A minor one but she's not well."

139

"Can I be of any help?" I asked. "I'm a doctor in Britain."

"We're not short of good doctors in Kerala," he said, opening the door of a white Maruti for Priyanka. She climbed in without looking at me, trying to hide the tears that were welling.

"Ring me at the Casino if there's anything I can do," I said as she pulled the door closed. A moment later and they had gone, leaving me alone on the jetty.

I looked out across the water and watched the dredger, which was turning around slowly in the harbour mouth. The Chinese fishing nets, still now and silhouetted in its arc lights, were like petrified limbs, clawing at the night sky. Fatman row-row was standing next to his boat, fiddling unnecessarily with the bow rope. I went over to him and gave him a tip, fifty rupees, which he slipped into the top of his *lunghi* with the deftness of a street magician.

"I tell nobody," he said, grinning in the direction of the car, which was far away now, turning onto the main road, its headlights sweeping briefly across the water.

I wished I had someone to tell as I tried in vain to go to sleep in my hotel room. Instead I decided to look at the internet, see what was on the Cardamom Café's website. It took a few minutes to unplug the phone and wire up the computer to the exchange, but I was soon scrolling down the café's home page – "a small corner of India that is for ever England."

The site appeared to be a forum where people could air trenchant views on the British Empire that was, and speculate why India was worse off fifty years after Independence than it had been fifty years before.

Vintage Macaulay. His name didn't appear anywhere on the site, but the tone was unmistakably his.

One section, "The Arrogance of Hindutva", began: "India has always operated best when she is in partnership with others, whether it's the Mughals or the British. To strike out these chapters of India's history with a saffron pen is to miss the point about India, which is ultimately too hospitable, too welcoming to stand on her own. The British did not subjugate her, rather they allowed her to blossom, much like the support a rubber tree gives to the twisting pepper vine that grows in its shadow."

Another link, called "Bombast and the Bomb", started: "Imagine a country where girls as young as five work in firework factories and women are encouraged to throw themselves onto their husband's funeral pyres. If this is how they treat their own people in times of peace, what cruelties can we expect them to mete out to other nations in the full madness of nuclear war?"

After skimming through these and a number of other tracts, I was not surprised that Macaulay, if he was the author, remained unpublished as a historian. The only passage that read well was called "An Indian Writes – a short extract from *The Autobiography of an Unknown Indian* by Nirad C. Chaudhuri, complete with its dedication to "the memory of the British Empire in India . . . because all that was good and living within us was made, shaped and quickened by the same British rule", an acknowledgment which someone explained in a footnote had been removed "in suspicious circumstances" from a recent British edition.

Of more surprise was that Macaulay had an audience, let alone one over which he had any influence. The site

141

had registered 312 hits, which was hardly a cyber scramble.

It was only when I clicked on "Cardamom News", a small link at the bottom of the site, that I began to understand, for the first time, why Sir Ian might have reason to be worried about Macaulay's activities in India.

I was denied access to the link, which provided a "comprehensive news wire service", but a pop-up window explained that for a small fee, payable by foreign credit card only, I could receive twice daily bulletins, via email, on India's most "exotic" stories, the contents of which may be used "in their entirety without acknowledgment". It appeared to be a lot more professional than the amateur email service Macaulay had described to Priyanka. A banner along the top of the window said: "Join over two hundred other foreign media organisations and subscribe today for the stories the world wants to read about India."

"Exotic" could have meant anything, but the animated logo that pulsated in the corner of the window was of a cobra emerging from a wicker basket. I considered signing up there and then but decided to wait, in case members were screened. It would only have aroused Macaulay's suspicion.

As I clicked back to the previous page, there was a knock on the door. I stood up to open it, expecting to find room service. Instead a man I recognised from reception was standing there with a note in his hand.

"Sir, we have been trying to connect a call to your room for the past one hour," he said.

I took the note from his outstretched hand. It read, "Please call Priyanka on 66822". The man was looking over my shoulder at the computer on my bed. I glanced back at the tangle of wires connecting it to the phone line.

"I've been on-line," I said. "Thanks."

I closed the door and rushed over to the bed, disconnected the modem from the wall and reconnected the telephone. I tried to slow myself down as I dialled, but I pressed a wrong digit and had to start again.

"Tripunithura hospital," a lady's voice answered.

"Can I speak to Priyanka Pillai, daughter of Mrs Pillai, a patient of yours," I said.

There was a long, crackly pause and then Priyanka was on the line.

"Raj, I've been trying to ring you," she said.

"Is everything okay?" I asked, pleased to hear her voice again, even though it was freighted with anxiety.

"She's not well," Priyanka said.

"Do you want me to come over?" I asked.

"No, I don't think that would be a good idea. She just looks so . . . changed. I hardly recognise her."

"What treatment are they giving her?"

"Ayurveda."

"Ayurveda? Priyanka, she needs proper medicine, immediate anti-platelet therapy, a scan, maybe even some cortizoids. She can have a herbal massage later."

"The doctors know what they are doing here, we've come before. They saved my father last year."

"I'm sure they did."

There was a long pause.

"Perhaps you should come over. Only, my father, he asked me in the car all about you. He wasn't angry, but—"

143

"—What did you tell him?" I asked, interrupting her. "That we'd only met once in Delhi?"

"Yes."

"I'll say the same. Nothing more. I promise."

The hospital was five miles outside Cochin and I decided to take a hotel taxi. Although it was late, the roads were still busy, the Ernakulam waterfront ablaze with boulevard lights and bustling with young lovers, beggars and nutsellers rattling their metal roasting pans to intricate rhythms. Perhaps it was the heat and humidity, but night-time in India was not reserved for sleeping. There was nothing sacred about it, no culture of do not disturb. If I hadn't made my preferences known to the hotel, I would have been interrupted throughout the night with polite knocks on the door and offers of bed sweets, drinking water, clean towels.

According to the sign at the main gates, the hospital was also an ayurvedic college, which did little to restore my confidence. I told the taxi driver to wait and I walked inside, carrying my medical bag. I had put together a few things before I left, including some aspirin, an effective and practical anti-platelet drug in cases of minor strokes. A bleary-eyed receptionist sitting at a wooden table looked up at me as I approached her and then glanced to her right. Priyanka appeared from the shadows. She looked wan and pale.

"Where is she?" I asked, relieved that we were exempted, at least for a while, from confronting what had happened earlier that evening on the boat.

"I'll show you to her," Priyanka said. I followed her down a dimly lit corridor, conscious that my black medical briefcase was being scrutinised by the receptionist. There was a thin smell in the warm air, like camomile.

Priyanka's mother was sitting up in bed in a room on her own, her hand held by a younger woman whom I took to be Priyanka's sister. She was less attractive than Priyanka, her hair tied back tightly, her features more severe. Mr Pillai was sitting on a bedside chair with his head in his hands. He smoothed back his hair when I walked in and stood up to greet me, politely rather than warmly.

"Thank you for coming," Mr Pillai said.

"I came as quickly as I could," I replied, glancing at his wife. My first impression was that she was not as ill as Priyanka had suggested: a minor stroke, ischaemic rather than haemorrhagic.

"She's improved a lot in the past hour," Mr Pillai said. "I've discussed it with my daughters and I don't want anything else done to her, not yet."

"But *accha*," Priyanka said, protesting quietly.

I glanced at Priyanka for an explanation but she turned away and walked over to her sister. I looked at Mrs Pillai again and at some dark brown bottles of medicine on the table next to her.

"A stroke can be very serious," I said. "Even if it's only a mild one. It's important to reduce the risk of a more dangerous recurrence. Is she on any medication? You should at least be giving her aspirin."

Mr Pillai held up his hands, as if to say "stop".

"My life was saved here last year," he said, pausing longer than I expected. "If she doesn't improve, I'll ask you to do all you can to help her."

As he finished, a man, presumably the doctor, breezed into the room looking at some notes. He glanced up, taking in the number of people now assembled. He was young, barely thirty, and had a lean, smooth face, with high cheek-bones and calming eyes.

"This is Dr Gopalakrishnan," said Mr Pillai. "Our family doctor. He came in specially when I rang him."

I shook his hand and he smiled briefly, knowingly, at me. His complexion was pure and his head barely moved as he talked.

I smiled back at him, shaking his hand. "Raj Nair."

He acknowledged the name, and then walked straight over to Priyanka's mother.

"He's a doctor in Britain," Mr Pillai said, following him over to the bed.

Dr Gopalakrishnan was too busy to reply. I watched him as he spoke quietly to Mrs Pillai, appearing to find her pulse at several points on her wrist and then administering some medicine from one of the bottles on the bedside table. I was beginning to feel surplus to requirements and wondered why I had come. The whole family was listening to the doctor, who was explaining something to them in Malayalam.

After a few moments he turned and came over to me.

"You may talk to her now if you wish," he said. "She's had what you call a transient ischaemic attack. She should make a full recovery. I'm giving her an internal detoxification, *panchakarma* therapy, to clear any obstructions in the nerve pathways."

"What she needs is a full neurological assessment and a brain scan," I said bullishly. "And she should be checked for dysphagia."

"There's nothing wrong with her swallowing," he replied, still smiling benignly. "We always check before embarking on *panchakarma*."

146

"At least some anti-platelet therapy," I said, less hostile, disarmed by his uncombative manner.

"We're not against Western medicine here, Mr Nair," he said. "We like to work with it. But in the case of strokes, it's far from clear that all drugs are safe. Some thrombolytic treatments can cause catastrophic haemorrhaging."

There was a pause as he let the words gently rest his case. He was referring to what American doctors called "clot-busting drugs", recent therapies such as Tissue Plasminogen Activator or TPA, which were used to treat severe strokes. We both knew that I had no similar knowledge of ayurveda.

"If it was a more serious stroke I would have admitted her to the main hospital at once," he added quietly, without any smugness.

"Three hundred grammes of aspirin a day – that's all I'm saying," I continued, almost talking to myself. "Studies in Scotland have shown it can reduce further attacks by up to a quarter."

"She's responding well to our herbal preparations," he replied. "Please, she is happy for you to see her."

I walked over to the bed, Priyanka and her sister parting to let me through. Mrs Pillai looked much older up close, more frightened. I listened to her breathing and took her pulse, and then asked a few questions about what she could and couldn't feel. Her eyes were kind, just like Priyanka's. There was no paralysis and it was hard to disagree with Dr Gopalakrishnan's overall diagnosis. I was not going to win my argument about aspirin and decided to let the matter drop.

"I think she's okay," I said to Priyanka. "She's not in bad hands."

"Thanks for coming," she said, standing next to her watchful sister. Her voice was betraying nothing of our earlier encounter. Neither of us knew when we would see each other again but the formal circumstances had drained us of all emotion. If we met again, this empty moment wouldn't matter; if this was it, the last few days would seem even more unreal than they already did.

Mr Pillai showed me out of the nursing home, walking down the corridor with me in silence until we reached the outside, where he slowed down, seemingly less eager to get rid of me. He had the introspective air of a reconciled thinker, his measured conversation paced with lengthy intervals.

"Priyanka's friends in Delhi, Frank and Susie, spoke very highly of you as a doctor," he said, after a particularly long pause. "They said you worked wonders with Kashmir when he was sick."

I was taken aback by the sound of Frank and Susie's names but glad to hear them again, happy for the excuse to talk about them.

"Do you know them?" I asked.

"I've met them a couple of times when we've been staying with Priyanka," he said. "They've been very good to her."

We were standing by my taxi now, but he appeared to be in no hurry to get back to his family.

"I think she'll be okay," I said, nodding towards the building.

He didn't speak, letting the silence determine the direction of our conversation. Perhaps he was going to say something about Priyanka, her marriage. I couldn't bear the silence any longer.

"Has Priyanka mentioned my father to you?" I asked.

"No. Should she have done?"

"I just wondered if you ever came across each other. He grew up here, studied medicine before leaving for Britain."

"What was his name?" he asked.

"Ramachandran Nair," I said. "He lived in Perunna. Ram Nair."

He paused as he searched back over the long years, running through the memories like fingers across files. I could only begin to guess at what images he was pulling out: his childhood, perhaps, playing on the leafy rubber plantations I had seen in photos of Kerala, or his days at school in Cochin, clinging to the outside of a bus with ten others on the morning run, a scene I had witnessed yesterday near the fishing nets. They must have been so different from my own memories and yet they could have been so similar if the man whose face he was now searching for had remained in Kerala.

"I knew someone by that name," he said, neutrally, "but then it's very common here. Did he study at the Medical College in Thiruvananthapuram?"

"Yes," I said, guessing he meant Trivandrum. I was impressed by the agility of his mind. "He was a mature student."

"Organised a big Quit India student rally, shortly before Independence," he said, his voice growing more confident with the recollection. "Was he involved in the Keezhariyur bomb case? I think he might have been."

"I don't know about that," I said, closing my eyes, my heart sinking.

"If I've got the right man, he had the world at his feet. Passed his IAS, fêted by Congress leaders in Delhi, then decided to drop it all and study medicine. I'm sure it's him because I never heard anything else, which is strange. If he settled in Britain, that would explain it."

I told him I would keep in touch and then stepped slowly into the waiting taxi. My limbs felt weak and I was grateful to be driven.

CHAPTER FOURTEEN

THE NEXT MORNING I was up early, determined to see more of Fort Cochin before I was sapped by the debilitating heat. I also wanted to ring Frank. I was leaving in the afternoon for Madras and I had to administer some formal treatment to Macaulay before I went, if only to maintain my cover. There was nothing very much wrong with his physical health but I would present him with a shiny bottle of big white Western pills with a good seal on it. I had thought about telling him his *doshas* were out of balance but he would probably have hit me.

I took a motorboat across the harbour rather than one of the rowing boats. It would have been too painful a reminder of our return trip from Macaulay's island. Several times since I had caught the scent of coconut oil in the warm wind and felt my mouth drying.

Fort Cochin was a different place in the cool before breakfast, bustling with activity that would have been inconceivable a few hours later. Around the corner from the nets, in the dunes behind an untidy stretch of sand known as Mahatma Gandhi beach, a hundred people or more were stretching, doing their morning exercises, playing badminton, practising gymnastics. I watched as a group of boys took it in turns to somersault in the air, landing in giggling heaps on the soft sand. Behind them a man was throwing his arms in all directions and rolling his neck at the same time. For a moment I thought he was having a seizure but it was just a bit of energetic limb-loosening.

A path along the back of the beach was clearly reserved for business class. Executives in tight white tennis shorts, Adidas shirts, trainers and white socks pulled up to their knees were walking briskly in twos or threes. I recalled my meeting with Frank in Haus Khaz and the walkers we had passed as we strolled round the old tank. It was time to call him. I knew he hadn't blamed me for what happened, but I was still dreading the call, in case he had been forced out of Delhi by further harassment.

"Raj, should you be ringing me?" he asked cautiously. There was a long echo on the line.

"It's okay. How are you Frank?"

"Coping." He didn't sound it. His voice was subdued. "And you?"

"Listen, I'm sorry about what happened in Delhi. It was my fault, I'm sure of it."

"Whatever. These things happen. Christ, they used to happen all the time."

"You're all okay, though? Susie and the kids?"

"We're fine."

"That's good. Very good."

An awkward silence, broken only by a sudden hiss. For some reason I expected Frank to have bounced back, as if nothing was wrong. But he sounded tired, defeated.

"We thought we'd let things blow over in Delhi," he continued, sounding marginally more upbeat. "Catch up with friends back here for a while."

"Good idea. There have been no more problems, then?" I asked.

"Not yet," he added, managing the faintest of laughs. "Watch yourself with Jamie, won't you?"

I promised him I would, adding that I would call again soon, although I wasn't sure when. It depressed me hearing him talk like that. In the past I had always come away from Frank's company feeling stronger, better able to cope with the world. Ravi had once described him as "easy-go-happy", which just about summed Frank up.

After breakfast at Brunton's Boatyard, overlooking the harbour entrance, I walked across to the Cardamom Café. I found Macaulay busily lifting a new computer terminal out of a box. He visibly slowed up when he saw me, one hand reaching for the small of his back.

"Could you help me with this a moment, Raj?" he asked, his voice strained. "I think my disc's prolapsing again."

I dropped my bag and took hold of the terminal, which was surprisingly light, as Macaulay slumped into a cane chair next to me. I thought of the boy he had hit in the mouth.

"I hope you've got something for me," he said. "I feel terrible."

After putting the computer down, helped by Paul, who adjusted it on the table as best he could with his shrunken hands, I went over to Macaulay.

"I've got some medicine which I brought out from London," I said, opening my case and removing a bottle of pills. "A sort of Viagra for the whole body."

"Uh huh," he said, taking the bottle from me and examining the seal, as I knew he would. "It's not a duplicate, is it?"

"As I say, I brought it out with me from London," I reassured him, although I didn't tell him that it consisted of painkillers so mild that a local copy from the medicine market in Old Delhi would have been twice as effective. "Take two morning and night after you have eaten."

I glanced up to find Macaulay looking at me more seriously. "You didn't come all this way just to give me a bottle of pills," he said, his watery eyes scrutinising me, floating from side to side.

I closed the case on my lap, trying not to betray any unease. I was finding it hard to shake off the images of the previous night.

"How do you mean?" I asked, glancing at his lips.

"I've been thinking about it," he continued. "The Medical Centre in Delhi sending someone all the way down here just to see me. It doesn't add up."

"I'm on a tour," I said, my mouth drying. "Next week I'm due to see one person in Tashkent who's been waiting two years for a visit."

"What was her name, Priyanka? It's her, isn't it?"

I smiled with relief.

"Sonsy girl," he continued. "Did you meet her in Delhi?"

"A friend introduced us," I said, wary of dragging Frank and Susie's names into our conversation.

"And you've been working out a way of coming to see her ever since," he said, laughing. "Let me know if I can be of any other assistance."

"It's not like that."

He paused and then looked at me again.

"You know who her father is?" he asked, his head suddenly still, except for his eyes, which were blinking. I felt my stomach tightening. I didn't think I could bear another revelation about the freedom struggle. But

154

before I had time to reply, Macaulay had leant forward and was patting me on my leg.

"I jest," he said, smiling in a way that left me unconvinced. His breath smelt of whisky.

I wanted to move on, conscious that this was my last chance to gather information about Macaulay before I reported back to Sir Ian. His inscrutable manner discouraged personal questions, but I couldn't just rely on Priyanka's notes.

"I had a patient in Delhi last month," I said, watching another terminal being carried in through the door. Macaulay stood up to oversee its installation opposite where I was sitting.

"He'd fallen ill in Cochin," I continued, but he wasn't listening any more. His demeanour had shifted. "I presume you were involved in sending him up to us?"

Macaulay ripped open the top of the box with surprising strength, almost menace. We had fallen back into the old ways again but I had to persist, hoping that something might make him drop his guard. The stand-off was broken by two Westerners who came up to the door outside and knocked on the glass.

"Sorry, we're closed for half an hour," Macaulay explained, walking over and turning round a sign in the window. "Dotcom land's expanding."

"Were you involved?" I asked again, watching him return to the new terminal.

"With what?" he asked, plainly annoyed. He plugged in the keyboard lead.

"With the patient. He was a backpacker called Dutchie, Dutchie Reason."

I watched his face closely for a reaction as he sat down at the new terminal and moved the keyboard into

155

a favoured position, inching it slightly to the left and then to the right.

"What do you want to know?" he eventually asked, looking at the screen, which had flickered into life.

"We're reviewing our procedures," I said, still watching him. "Too many drugs cases, particularly in Goa."

Macaulay tested the modem connection as he spoke, tapping hard on the keyboard.

"He hung around the café for a few days, said he was expecting a letter. We run a poste restante service here as well. Then I heard he'd been found at Ernakulam Junction, face down on platform two."

"Why wasn't he sent to Madras?" I asked.

"Ask them," he said, the first hint of defence creeping into his voice.

"I have," I said, lying, taking a gamble. "They knew nothing about him."

Macaulay turned round to look at me. "He needed to get home."

"He was talking deliriously by the time I saw him. Kept on mentioning something about Kali."

Macaulay stood up and leant over the top of the terminal, fiddling with some leads at the back of the screen, his body language suggesting the matter was closed.

"Mr Nair, I have work to do," he said, his head out of sight. "I'm grateful for the medicine you have given me, doubly so if it actually works, but I must now ask you to let me get on with my day."

"Did the letter ever arrive?" I asked. Macaulay ignored me. I turned to leave and noticed Paul, who had been listening to us talk. He watched me closely as I walked out of the door, his face full of unclear meaning.

"Oh, Mr Nair," Macaulay called from behind me. I was already on the other side of the street. I looked back to see him holding out a sheet of paper. "I almost forgot. There was a call for you. From a Jamie Grade. Delhi numbers." I walked back over to him and took the piece of paper, checking his eyes for something to tell me that he knew Jamie, but he wasn't letting on.

The note asked me to call Jamie as soon as possible, giving his office and residence numbers. My first thought was how Jamie had known that I was in Cochin; my second was what he thought about me being here. He obviously knew I had been visiting Macaulay and for the moment, at least, I had to assume that he had rung Madras to try and contact me there. They would have told him I was here. Still, it didn't look good, given that Sir Ian had gone out of his way to keep Jamie in the dark.

I walked round to the parade ground and decided to go inside St Francis Church, but as I turned the corner by the post office I was conscious of someone coming up behind me. I turned to see Paul, trying his best to run. I walked quickly towards him, reducing the distance he had to cover. He was carrying a large padded envelope in one hand, clutching it close to his chest. He stopped a few yards from me, panting hard and wiping sweat from his forehead. He held the package towards me, as best as he could.

"Please, take this," he said, in surprisingly rounded English. "Dutchie was my friend."

I took it from him, recognising it as the package Macaulay had put under his desk when I had first arrived at the café.

"Did you know him well?" I asked, gently squeezing the padded envelope. It felt like documents of some sort.

Paul smiled fondly. "We played Game Boy together, at the café. I always beat him."

"What was he doing here?" I asked.

"Running away, so he said."

"Did he know Macaulay well?"

"Mr Macaulay hated him."

"Why did he hang around, then?"

"Because Mr Macaulay loved his body," Paul said, laughing. "Perfectly formed, like mine. It drove him crazy. So he let Dutchie stay on his island. He had no money."

"Where can I contact you? Do you live at the café?" I thought again about the boy in his *lunghi*.

He shook his head. "Mattancherry. I'm at the café from nine to nine. It's best you find me there."

We looked at each other for a moment, each sensing that the other had much more to say.

"Are you really a doctor?" Paul asked, after a pause.

"Yes, I am."

"Mr Macaulay doesn't think so."

"No?" I said, trying to make light of his words. "What does he think I am, then?"

"Are you British?"

"Yes. I was born in Edinburgh. My parents were from Kerala."

"Mr Macaulay thinks you are Indian."

"He's entitled to his opinion. What do you think? Do you think I am Indian?"

He ignored my question. "And he thinks all Indians who live in Britain are . . ."

"Are what?" I asked.

"He has many files," Paul said, his voice trailing off. "Indians who shifted to Britain. He has information on them all. He's been waiting for you, someone like you, for many years. What happened to Dutchie?"

"He's okay," I said. "He's back in Britain now."

"He saw the files. It was a mistake. Macaulay caught him," he said, more distracted.

"What did you mean when you said he's been waiting for someone like me?" I asked, trying to sift through everything he was telling me. Paul was getting nervous, looking around to see if anyone was coming.

"You've made all his work worthwhile," he said.

"How? What was in the files?"

He looked around again and spotted someone on the other side of the parade ground.

"Please, be careful," he said. He twisted awkwardly on his deformed feet, and set off down the road.

"Wait," I called after him, but he was picking up speed, his dragging feet kicking up dust as they went.

I decided to let him go and turned to see who it was that had frightened him off, but the parade ground was empty. I walked over to the shade of the rain tree, where the children had gathered the last time I was here, and sat down, leaning against the bark. The package had been sent from Delhi but there was no sender's address. I tore it open and pulled out a sheaf of photocopied A4 documents, old typewritten records of some kind. There must have been a hundred pages, the first of which was headed: "India Office – Public and Judicial Department." Across one corner of the page someone had stamped: "Declassified 1997". I flicked through the pages, each one containing passages

159

marked with black biro in the margin. The first section that caught my eye read as follows:

"Strong arguments can be adduced in favour of the retention of IPI as a self-contained unit for some time to come. Admittedly, if it is so retained by the Security Service it will be performing some functions which are outside the Security Service charter – but this would seem to be justifiable until the situation is clarified."

"IPI". I glanced up for a moment, saying the initials quietly, the same letters that had appeared at the end of the intercepted letter to Jamie. I looked down at the paper again to check that I had read them correctly. Trying to remain calm, I flicked back to the first page, where the words "Indian Political Intelligence (IPI)" had been underlined.

According to Frank, the intercepted message had been about an Indian, someone from Gujarat, who had joined CND.

I put the documents down for a moment and rested my head against the tree behind me. There was no indication who had sent them to Dutchie, no covering note, just the Delhi postmark. Breathing in deeply, I glanced at my watch, looked around and set to work, reading through the pages as quickly as I could, skipping from one marked-up section to the next.

Set up shortly before World War I, IPI had been a highly secret branch of Britain's intelligence services with a remit to preserve the internal and external security of British India. It had operated out of London, sharing an office with MI5, and had monitored the activities of a large number of Indian revolutionaries, subversives, communists and freedom fighters on the subcontinent, as well as those who were domiciled in Britain and Europe. It had expanded under the leadership of someone called Philip Vickery to become an extensive intelligence-gathering operation, the existence of which had never formally been acknowledged and was only known to a select few. Vickery's field officers had kept under surveillance a large number of Congress activists, communist extremists and, latterly, anyone who had even marginal connections with the rise of Indian nationalism. The activities of British citizens who were thought to be sympathetic to their cause had also been monitored.

All communications between Vickery and MI5 and MI6, with whom it had reluctantly shared information, had been signed simply IPI. Only once, when IPI was finally closed down after Independence, had Vickery signed a valedictory communication with his own name. The organisation's cessation was particularly intriguing, given that Frank's intercepted message must have been in the 1980s, over thirty years after the department had formally been wound up. IPI's official assets, worth £3,000, had been handed over to India after Independence, but there was a strong sense from one heavily censored passage (whole sentences had been blacked out) that more sensitive data had either been destroyed or withheld. IPI itself had become part of MI5, merging with a department known as OS4. As for Vickery, who had favoured "the retention of IPI as a self-contained unit for some time to come", he continued to be an important player in the intelligence community, eventually dying in 1987, aged ninety-six.

There was one page, near the end, that I kept returning to. The type was of poorer quality, as if it was a copy of a copy, and a number of names, mostly field agents, had been removed. But there was still a sub-heading which referred to the minutes of a high-level meeting in 1946, off Parliament Square, where the fate of IPI had been decided by a group of security chiefs. The following four paragraphs were completely blacked out, and someone had written in the margin: "Retained under the provisions of Section 3(4) of the Public Records Act 1958." Whatever IPI's fate might have been, it was clearly too sensitive for public consumption.

I turned to the last few pages, which were mostly about Vickery. In amongst them was a grainy, photocopied photograph of him, a tweed-suited man standing in front of some palm trees, holding a white pith helmet in one hand. He was smiling, his head tilted slightly to one side. I had seen his face somewhere before.

I put the documents down, my eyes tired after reading so much dense, dirty type. The sun had set, but the air was still warm and moist and the back of my shirt was sticking to the bark of the tree. If my father had been a militant in the freedom struggle, IPI would have known about him. But I knew he wasn't. Macaulay clearly had access to data of some sort, however ill-informed it might have been. Paul's talk of files on the island seemed to confirm that. But what was Macaulay's link, if any, to IPI? Had he once worked for the organisation? It might explain the rumours of him being a spy.

The photo on Macaulay's desk: it had been of Vickery.

I looked again at the photocopied image and thought back to our dinner on the island, to the half-moon table behind Macaulay's chair. The photo had been framed

162

and was much smaller, like a cameo, but the tilted head and smile were the same.

I tried to slow my thoughts down, follow the most plausible links. IPI had been disbanded. Macaulay was a historian, unpublished but with influential friends in Whitehall. He used them to gain access to some old IPI files, and even kept at his island retreat some of the more sensitive assets, perhaps, that were supposedly handed over to the Indian government in 1947.

But why keep files specifically on Indians who had emigrated to Britain? And what was the connection, if any, with Jamie? IPI. Jamie had received a confidential communication about an Indian working for CND, signed with the initials IPI. When Frank had made his own inquiries, his mole had told him to back off, said it was too dangerous. Jamie, Macaulay, IPI – what was it that linked them?

At least one thing had become clear: Dutchie was more than just a traveller, or Jamie would not have gone to such lengths to get him out of the country without a fuss. If he had been sent to Cochin, by whom? Sir Ian? Dutchie hadn't stumbled on the files by accident. He had been looking for them.

None of this would have mattered if Jamie's involvement could have been ruled out, but it couldn't, and that worried me. Macaulay the historian with access to a few dusty archives was one thing, but if he was working with Jamie, a senior station head at MI6, IPI, one of the least-known, most shadowy arms of Britain's intelligence services, might conceivably still be wielding some posthumous influence over fifty years after its supposed demise.

I needed to talk to Frank.

CHAPTER FIFTEEN

FRANK SEEMED GENUINELY alarmed when I told him about the IPI files, but excited, too. It was as if he were finally confronting something in his past that he knew he had been avoiding for years.

"If you say these files are declassified, a copy should be with the Oriental and India Office Collections by now," Frank was saying on a better line than last time. "I'll ring the British Library, see if I can have a read of them myself."

At last he was beginning to sound like the old, reassuring Frank again. He used to spend a good deal of time as a student at the British Library, partly researching Indian miniatures, mainly because of the surprisingly large number of women he managed to seduce there. ("It's the pheromones," he had once joked. "Libraries are awash with them.") That was what most upset me about the night I had found him and his family on my drive. Frank had been visibly distraught and he wasn't meant to be like that. But it had reminded me that everyone had their limits and I knew that what I was about to ask Frank might test them again.

"Frank, you remember when you first told me about IPI, the message you intercepted," I began.

"Yes," he said, the first hint of suspicion creeping into his voice.

"You said then that you had a sympathiser, someone on the inside. Do you think they might still be sympathetic?"

"Raj, it was a long time ago – almost twenty years."

"I know, but he still might be able to help. We need to establish a link between Macaulay and IPI."

"We?"

"Macaulay, IPI and Jamie," I added. Frank had never met Macaulay, but I knew the mention of Jamie would stir something, although I wasn't quite sure what. It seemed that Jamie had been an irritant in Frank's life for longer than he cared to remember.

"It's a long shot – I don't even know if he's still alive," Frank was protesting, but I knew already that he would look up his old contact.

I rang Priyanka next, at her office. It was a risk, but I had already considered my approach and began by telling her that I had some potentially sensational news about Macaulay. She was writing her article, wrestling with an angle, she said, and I could hear the mixture of relief and excitement in her voice when I told her that Macaulay might be a spy after all.

We agreed to meet at an icecream parlour across the road from her office in Panampilly Nagar, where I waited for her to appear, reading the files again and inhaling the sweet smell of honeybee, blackcurrant and "hold me tight" icecreams.

It was hard to concentrate, the tone of her voice on the phone lingering, teasing. After an initial, formal exchange of words, an unmistakable quickening had crept into both our voices. In my case it was the knowledge that we had a legitimate reason for seeing each other again, an alibi that would exempt her from family reproach. Of course, it didn't make any difference – we were still committing the crime of seeing each other on our own – but I felt much better, as if our imminent encounter was entirely due to outside professional elements beyond our control rather than because of our own feelings. Did she feel the same? Or was it just the journalist who had agreed so promptly to another meeting? Her manner last night as I had left the nursing home, accompanied by her father, had been hard to read: if there had been any emotion on her face it was fear.

There was only openness when she walked into the parlour, her face melting into a gratifying smile when she spotted me in the corner. She gave me a small wave, her smile lasting all the way to the table. Something about her had changed.

"Sorry I'm late," she said, sitting down opposite me. She gave my forearm a small squeeze.

"No problem," I said, thinking that I would have waited for forty days if I had known she would breeze in with such radiance. I assumed it must be her mother. "Any news from the hospital? I was going to ring them."

"I just had a call from my father," she said, looking briefly at the plastic menu. "She's much better today."

"Excellent. Must be the herbs."

She glanced up at me again, a look of childish anticipation in her eyes, as if she were about to impart a secret.

"He also said something else," she said. "Our *thalakuris* are not compatible."

"Our what?"

"The match is off."

I looked at her for a moment and then realised she was referring to her future husband. I tried to find something in her face to corroborate what she was saying, a small crease of sadness, a welling up of despair, but all I could see was happiness.

"The broker's been with him all morning. They've got an astrologer there as well. My horoscope is very problematic. I have *chovva dosham* – Mars, the ruiner of many girls. With great difficulty they found a boy who also had *chovva dosham*, but now it seems something else has cropped up in the *thalakuri*. My father's very upset. *Pura niranju nilkunna pennu* – 'the girl who is so grown she fills the house'."

"You must be devastated, too," I said, risking a smile to match her own.

"He was too fat," she said, laughing.

"Too fat?" I said, subconsciously breathing in. "I thought you said you liked him."

"I did. I do. He's very sweet, but . . . "

"But?" I said, teasing.

She looked around the room and then leant forward. "His breath smelt of *veluthulli*."

It sounded pretty horrible, whatever it was. "*Veluthulli*?" I asked out of the side of my mouth, in case my own breath smelt of the two Nilgiri coffees I had drunk while waiting for her.

"Garlic. We never use it in our family. Never."

"No, of course not." Annoyingly, I felt a touch of sympathy for the man as I made a mental note never to order garlic bread again. "What did he do, anyway? You never said."

"He was very rich," she sighed. "That's my only regret. He ran a dotcom company."

He did?" I asked, tickled by my own prescience. "In Bangalore?"

"No, here, in Ernakulam."

"These cyber CEOs, you can't trust them. Really, they're fly-by-nights. One click and they're gone. Here today, crashed tomorrow. E-money, no substance. What you want is the son of an industrialist, a solid fortune like steel or marble, something that hurts when you drop it on your foot, not this ephemeral net nonsense."

She looked slightly taken aback by my outburst. "I didn't realise you felt so strongly," she said.

"I don't. I'm just jealous."

My words hung between us in the cool, scented air.

"There's no need to be," she said quietly. "Not any more."

"I'm going back to Delhi this afternoon," I said, unable to draw my eyes away from hers.

"So soon?"

"I got a message yesterday. Will you be staying in Cochin?"

"I've told my father I want to leave it for a while. The broker's desperate for me to stay. I'll be here for a few more days, until Mummy's settled back at home."

"Then Delhi?"

She nodded, her eyes fixed on mine, limpid, full of promise.

Then I remembered Macaulay, his words about my father, IPI, Jamie, each recollection chipping away at a moment that I wanted to last. I had to discuss these things with Priyanka before I returned to Delhi, share them with someone, to have them validated by a third party, in the hope that they might become more real. At the moment I couldn't process the potential implications.

"I've come across some new information about Macaulay," I begun.

"I need something." She gestured to one of the waiters for a coffee. "When we talked he seemed such good copy but then I played it back and I realised he'd actually said nothing."

"He's clever like that. Gets people to reveal far more of themselves than he ever discloses of himself."

"So what have you got?"

"Did I ever tell you about a person called Dutchie? He was English, a backpacker." She shook her head. "He turned up half dead in the clinic one day. Anyway, it turns out he stayed here in Cochin, with Macaulay."

"On the island?"

"One of the select few. You saw that guy walking around half naked the other day? According to Paul, the boy with polio, Dutchie came across a whole load of files at Macaulay's house. It seems he shouldn't have seen them. A few days later he was found unconscious on a platform at Ernakulam Junction."

"What sort of files were they?"

"You didn't see any, then?"

"No. And being a good journalist, I had a snoop around when I went to the bathroom."

"According to Paul, the files contained information on Indians who had settled in Britain."

"What sort of information?"

"He didn't elaborate. But you heard what Macaulay had to say about my father." I held up the sheaf of papers. "This morning Paul gave me these. Somebody sent them to Dutchie at the café but he never received the package."

"And? What are they?"

"Recently declassified files. Certain sections were marked. This bit, for example," I said, handing her a page. As she read, I told her a bit more about IPI, its secret remit to follow anyone suspected of being a revolutionary, its supposed closure after Independence. For a moment I thought that she was not interested, but she read carefully, moving to other pages that I had marked. I watched her gently bite her lower lip as she concentrated, drawing her teeth slowly across the soft inside.

"I still don't get it," she said, five minutes later. "How's Macaulay involved?"

"Remember what he said about my father, his supposed role in the Quit India movement? It's just the sort of information IPI would have compiled."

"You think Macaulay might have once worked for IPI?"

"Yes," I said, showing her the first paragraph. "Have a look at this bit again. It was said by Vickery, the man who ran IPI for thirty years: 'Strong arguments can be adduced in favour of the retention of IPI as a self-contained unit for some time to come.'"

She looked at me for a moment, holding my stare. "It was closed down," she said flatly, putting the pages on the table.

"Possibly." I picked the papers up and found her the section about the meeting off Parliament Square, the page that had been heavily edited. "Did Frank ever tell you about his life in England?"

"Frank?" she said, clearly surprised by the introduction of his name. "Not really, why?"

"He didn't ever tell you about his days with CND or with the Communist Party of Great Britain?"

170

"No," she said, laughing. "But then nothing about Frank surprises me."

"He was having a bad time of it when I left Delhi," I said, thinking back to the pitiful sight of his family on my driveway. It was a relief to be sharing it. "The British authorities were getting suspicious, didn't like him applying for Indian citizenship."

"Is he all right?"

"He's okay." I paused, weighing up whether I could continue without revealing anything of my other role in Delhi, wondering whether I cared any more. I carried on, before the resentment built, knowing I would soon tell her, in the same way that I had known I would tell Frank. "Frank told me something about a man who works at the High Commission. Jamie Grade. He's meant to be head of spooks."

"Spooks?"

"Spies. MI6. Frank crossed swords with him in the late 1980s, when he was working for CND. He says they intercepted a communication to Jamie. It had the initials 'IPI' at the end of the message."

"What did it say?"

"It was about a British Asian, originally from Gujarat, who had recently become involved with CND."

"My God," she said quietly.

She paused for a moment and then looked at me, her face suddenly colder. "Why are you interested in all this? I thought you were just a doctor."

"I am," I said, turning away, hating the deception. Then I faced her again. "But I'm also British and I feel uncomfortable when I read about organisations such as IPI. Offended."

171

Despite my falseness of tone, she temporarily bought the story, which upset me more than having to keep the truth from her.

"But I don't understand," she said. "Why sign something 'IPI' fifty years after it was officially disbanded?"

"I don't know. I'm more worried about Macaulay. He claimed to know a lot about my father."

"But you don't think it's true."

"Your father said he remembered him."

"My father? When?"

"Last night, when I was leaving. He said he remembered a Ramachandran Nair, thought he had been involved with politics."

"Did you talk to him for long?"

"For a while. Why?"

"He didn't mention it." She looked at her watch. "I must get back to the office. I'll tell them to hold it over."

Our eyes searched each other's faces. There was so much to come that the inevitability of it was almost overwhelming, like an approaching storm over Delhi, humid, unstoppable, just a matter of when.

"If I find out some more about Macaulay, shall I email it to you?" I asked.

"Please. The biggest problem is going to be proving any of this. We need to see those files."

"He's got a website, too. Ostensibly for his café."

"I'll take a look."

"You must be careful about Macaulay. Dutchie was a jibbering wreck when I saw him. Muttering something about Kali."

"That would follow. Who was that boy, then, in the *lunghi*?"

"Just another traveller. Handpicked by Macaulay from the hundreds who pass through the café. He has a weakness for young men."

"He was rather gorgeous."

"Was he?" I was about to tell her what I had seen in the kitchen, but she wrong-footed me.

"In a sort of Hrithik Roshan sort of way," she continued. "Muscly. Just like you."

She leant forward and squeezed what passed for my biceps. Her hand lingered for a moment and I took it in my own. Instinctively she looked around the parlour but there was no one watching. I held her hand tight. "He split the boy's lip," I said.

"Who did?" she asked, looking at me for an explanation.

"Macaulay. When I went back to say goodbye, I found him in the kitchen, smacking the boy. It was hard, not just a slap. And when his mouth started to bleed, Macaulay kissed him."

"You saw this?" she asked, appalled, withdrawing her hand. I suddenly felt guilty for sharing it, for puncturing her happy mood.

"They didn't see me," I said, looking out of the window.

"That's awful," she said after a pause. "Awful."

"Can't you come away, just for a while?" I asked, turning to her again, trying to lighten the mood with a smile.

"Raj, please, you mustn't," she said, getting ready to go.

"Why not?"

"It's unfair. You know it is. This is my home town, where my parents live. Where I grew up. It's not like in Britain, or Delhi. I'm accountable."

173

She wasn't angry, just a little strident. We were both pleased to have moved away from Macaulay.

"Delhi, then?" I asked, fiddling with my empty coffee cup, our bill tucked underneath the saucer. She didn't answer. I looked up after a few moments and saw her eyes were moistening.

"I'm sorry," I said, touching her forearm. "I didn't mean—"

"It's okay," she said, interrupting me, regaining her composure. "I should be thanking you."

"Thanking me? For what? Being pushy and insensitive to your family?"

"You know perfectly well what for."

"I don't," I protested, relieved at the change in direction.

"For your timing."

Everyone should be allowed one chance in life to get out of the water.

"That was the easy part. It was all in the stars."

I stood up and gave the bill to a waiter, together with a hundred-rupee note. Outside on the street the hot air blew into our faces like a hair-dryer. We crossed the busy Manorama Junction, heading back towards her office. To the left was one of Panampilly Nagar's wide, leafy avenues, straight ahead was a bridge leading back towards the congested M. G. Road.

"There's my editor," Priyanka said, nodding at a group of men who were drinking coffee and smoking at a stall across from the office, in the shade of some trees. They hadn't seen us yet. Priyanka stopped, pulling me back out of sight. I suddenly wanted to tell her about Sir Ian, why I was really here, but it was too late.

"Ring me when you get to Delhi," she said, our faces close.

I leant forward to kiss her mouth but she moved her head discreetly away.

"Not here," she said. "We're very provincial in Cochin, remember?"

Back at the hotel I asked for my bill to be prepared and then took a lift to the second floor, where I walked along what looked like a ship's corridor, sloping gently upwards towards the bow and my room at the end. It was still being cleaned and I couldn't keep my eyes off the two young women as they made my bed, folded back the top sheet, changed the towels. They were both college students, bright with brilliant smiles and fluent in English. I was relieved when they finally went, their presence had been too unsettling.

My flight to Delhi left in two hours and once my case had been packed I sank into one of those unproductive hotel dazes, alternating between TV, minibar, and bathroom. I ordered a club sandwich from room service and then took a long shower, which only ended when a metal bell rattled on the tiles above the taps. I stepped out of the spray, wrapping a towel around my waist. For a moment I considered not putting anything else on, in case it was one of the women back to turn another sheet, but I checked myself and slipped on a T-shirt.

I opened the door and Priyanka was standing there, smiling, nervously or with quiet confidence – it was impossible to tell. She stepped quickly into the room, checked the corridor in either direction, and closed the door.

Afterwards we lay there for a few minutes, on our backs, next to each other. I looked across at her breasts, dark and swollen, rising gently up and down. She was completely relaxed, her legs slightly apart, arms above her head. We hadn't said a word since she had arrived and I wanted to keep it that way, hoping that it might prolong the exquisite feeling. I half expected some tricky remorse or regret, anger even at what we had done, but when Priyanka finally spoke, her voice was bright, full of poise.

"This goes against all my upbringing, everything I was taught at school, all that my parents told me at home, the world that I believe in." She paused. "And do you know something?"

"What?" I said, stretching my hand out to find hers.

"I never want it to end."

Part Three

CHAPTER SIXTEEN

IT FELT STRANGELY reassuring to be back in the republic. The road outside my house had been resurfaced in anticipation of the approaching monsoon, which last year had apparently turned Sainik Farms into a nouveau Venice, its tiny lanes transformed into fast-flowing canals. The road had also been raised by three feet, something I only realised when Ravi turned off into our drive and the car plunged downwards. The front wall, which I shared with the Bakshis and which had once stood the height of a prison perimeter fence, was now barely four feet high. Mrs Bakshi can't have slept for days.

As I climbed out of the air-cooled car into the hot wind, acknowledging a salute from the guard, I looked back at the wall again, pleased at how disempowered it now was. The once hidden activities of the busy road behind it had taken centre stage: a clay pot bobbed past on a hidden head, followed by the upright torsos of two gliding cyclists and the board of an icecream wallah selling *kulfi*. I felt less isolated, a little closer to India.

My only worry was the sky, which seemed darker than it should have been for a forty-two-degree day in late April. The brutal sun had been weakened in some way. Then I saw them, thousands of tiny pieces of black paper, floating down to earth like charred confetti. I looked down at the driveway, which was littered with the same small pieces, and noticed a plume of smoke rising in the distance, beyond Dr Gupta's house, too far away to smell the burning. Someone was incinerating reams of paper: court evidence, tax returns, forged five-hundred-rupee notes. It could have been anything in the republic.

The atmosphere inside the house was decidedly tense as Chandar, my cook, opened the doors, turned on the fans, and began sweeping up the thick layer of dust that had blown in from the rocky outcrops of Haryana. It was clear that he had been away rather than looking after the house. As I worked my way through the mail over a cup of *massala chai*, I wondered whom I should ring first: Sir Ian or Jamie, who had left several neutral-sounding messages on my answerphone. I had spent most of the flight back trying to work out how Jamie was involved with Macaulay. For the moment I had to assume that IPI not only existed but was the link between them. In which case, Macaulay would have told Jamie about my visit, my questions, my father. What I didn't know was how Jamie would respond, if at all, to the information. I had an overwhelming desire to see Sir Ian first, to share what little I had discovered.

I rang him at his office, even though he had warned me against making any direct contact. His secretary took the call.

"I'm afraid Sir Ian's very busy at the moment," she said, when I told her my name. I could hear Sir Ian's voice in the background, talking on another phone.

"Please, just let him know one thing," I insisted, sensing she was close to hanging up. "Tell Sir Ian that I have a rare recording from Kerala that would be a worthy addition to his collection of 78s. Please, just tell him that."

180

His secretary must have detected the urgency in my voice, noticed it was at odds with the innocent contents of my message. She put me on hold for a minute and then came back on the line.

"Could you be ready with the records in half an hour?" she asked. "He'll have them picked up outside the Mughal Gate."

The line went dead before I had a chance to ask for more time. It normally took me forty minutes to reach Chanakyapuri. I downed my tea, rushed outside and found Ravi, who was chatting in the shade of the guardhouse with Chandar. Two minutes later, we were weaving our way through Sainik Farms again, faster than was safe, and on into South Delhi, past the lychee sellers who had suddenly appeared on Lala Lajpat Rai Marg, their flat-back rickshaws decked out in vermilion plastic. I didn't tell Ravi to slow down.

By the time we reached the British High Commission, the evening light had turned a vivid yellow, tinged at the edges by dark storm clouds. Ravi dropped me on the main road and waited at a discreet distance. I walked down a quiet slip road to the Mughal Gate, the Commission's main entrance. The unusual light was enriched by the brief beauty of Chanakyapuri's laburnum trees, which were in full bloom, overflowing with brilliant yellow. In two weeks they would be green again.

In truth, I didn't know what to expect, whether I would be ushered into the compound or picked up by a car. A few moments later I had my answer. The heavy double gates opened and the High Commissioner's electric-blue Rolls-Royce swung round the corner, bumped through the entrance, where it was

181

saluted by Gurkha guards, and drove out into the open, manicured spaces of Chanakyapuri. I spotted Sir Ian's wife through the rear window, but the car didn't stop. Behind it, however, another car, a white Ambassador with darkened windows, drew up alongside me. The back door opened and I could see a figure inside, sitting on the back seat, one hand gesturing. I glanced at the Gurkha guards, who were now closing the gates, seemingly uninterested in me, and then stepped inside the car.

"Keep your head away from the window and listen to me very carefully," Sir Ian said. He was wearing a polka-dot blue bow tie and a black dinner jacket. There was no welcome, no introduction. His tone was cold, phlegmatic.

"I saw Macaulay—" I began.

"I know. Please, we haven't got long."

Sir Ian leant forward and tapped the thick glass that separated the back seat from the driver, who looked British. He nodded and flashed his headlights at the Rolls-Royce, which was thirty yards ahead of us. I hadn't seen a glass partition in an Ambassador before. Then I noticed a compact fax machine between the driver and the front passenger seat and realised that this was no ordinary car. There was a two-way radio unit under the dashboard, where there would normally have been a cassette player, and a mobile phone charging on either side. The back of the car was no less sophisticated, with a small foldaway desk behind the front passenger seat, complete with a pinpoint reading light, and a closed laptop computer.

"I have just received a copy of an intelligence report from London," Sir Ian continued. "It's about your father. He was picked up this morning by Special Branch and is being interrogated about his consultancy work at the UK Atomic Energy Authority. They're also asking questions about his early career at Dounreay. The implications are very serious: basically, they are questioning his loyalty. The report also casts doubt on your own suitability to be working here with Jamie and recommends that you should be brought in for questioning, too."

"Me?" I said, thinking about my father, how Special Branch's visit would knock at the very foundations of his life in Scotland, undermine all that he believed in and loved. I could picture him in his tartan pyjamas, insisting that there must have been a mistake, offering them all tea and oatcakes.

"The message was sent to Jamie and it will be up to him how to proceed," Sir Ian was saying. "A copy was routinely circulated to me. It's strictly a security matter and I cannot be seen to be involved. Jamie needs more evidence before he will act. Behave as if you know nothing, do whatever he asks. It will buy you time. Remember, he doesn't know you are aware of this report. You must try to hang on to that."

"This is about IPI, isn't it?" I said quietly. Sir Ian's staccato words were ringing in my ears. *They thought my father was a traitor.* "Why didn't you tell me before?" Sir Ian looked at me for a moment, the first time our eyes had properly met since I had got into the car. He was tired. "At least warn me?"

"I know how it must seem," he said, turning away. "It was important you knew nothing. I couldn't afford for you to say anything that might have alerted Macaulay. It would have jeopardised everything."

183

"Does it still exist?" I asked.

"IPI? Not as such." He paused. "Have you ever heard of something called the Cardamom Club?"

"The Cardamom Café," I said. "And Macaulay's email service, Cardamom News."

"They're all connected. The Cardamom Club is best understood as a particularly invidious mindset," he continued. "A group of like-minded individuals in the intelligence community who keep the old IPI fires burning."

My father would not begin to understand what was happening. I thought of him in a cold cell, emptying his pockets, his old hands shaking, exaggerating his Scottish accent.

"And these people sent the report, about my father?" I continued, hesitantly.

"Yes. They've got members in Five, Six, a few at Cheltenham."

"But why?" I asked, raising my voice. "Why? What conceivable threat can my father, a seventy-year-old, dying man, pose to anyone?"

I hadn't openly spoken of his deteriorating health before, not since I had been in India, and it felt weak and cheap to do so now.

"I know," Sir Ian said, sighing. "The fact remains that these people believe that our national security is being compromised by warmer ties with India, whether it's increased bilateral trade or from people closer to home, certain immigrants whose loyalties, they claim, can be called into question."

"You mean people who fail the Cricket Test."

"It's a little bit more serious than cheering for the wrong side. You must understand that there were certain British intelligence officers who never really recovered from the shock of losing India. They had fought and lost their own very personal cold war. The arrival of large numbers of immigrants a few years later rubbed salt into their wounds, particularly when they started to do well. Ex-IPI officers, who had reluctantly taken up desk jobs in MI5, were convinced – deluded – that some of these people were former Congress activists, subversives, communists, revolutionaries, you name it – basically the old enemy. Never mind we'd invited them. They were especially alarmed by the later wave of much better qualified arrivals in the early Sixties. They watched them work their way slowly into sensitive jobs in the civil service, the armed forces and, in the case of your father, even the nuclear industry. The more extreme among them believed that some of these people, the deep sleepers, would wake up one day and start reporting back twenty, thirty, forty years later to a country that now had ambitions to become a superpower."

"Did anyone really believe that?" I asked. "Anyone?"

"Someone must have done. Because the Club's still going, welcoming new, younger members every day."

"Can't you stop them?"

Sir Ian managed a dry laugh. "Not until we know how far up the line this thing goes. Macaulay and Jamie report to someone higher. Much higher. Out here, on the ground, different camps are clearly identifiable. The boundaries become more blurred in Whitehall. I can't blow the whistle, not yet, not until I can be sure who will be listening. I could be recalled to London tomorrow if the wrong people find out that I sent you to Macaulay. That's how high this thing goes."

"It was a calculated decision, then, to send me?"

"Yes. It was."

"I was bait, in effect." I was beginning to comprehend just how much I had been used. Sir Ian didn't answer. "How much did you know about my father?" I continued.

"Nothing, and I doubt whether any of it is true. As I said before, Macaulay is a revisionist."

"But you knew that he would be interested in a British Asian working for the Foreign Office."

"I knew Macaulay, a fully paid-up Club member, would come up with something when he saw you, yes. In the event he excelled himself. You confirmed his worst fears. Even if you were just a doctor, you were living proof that the Club has good reason to be concerned. The 'threat' could live on, buried deep in the second generation."

I thought back to Paul's words again. *He's been waiting for you, someone like you, for many years.*

"But you didn't think that sending me would lead to my father's arrest, and possibly my own," I said, trying to justify Sir Ian's decision to send me, to find something that might exonerate him from an increasingly obvious charge of callousness. Sir Ian hadn't given a second thought to my own interests or safety. He had made a cold decision that he would ultimately be able to count on my support, the colour of my anger, once I had discovered the existence of something as noxious as the Cardamom Club.

"Of course not," Sir Ian said. His voice was conciliatory. "But, as I said, I knew Macaulay would find something and I needed to see which Whitehall hands the security report passed through."

"Was there any mention of IPI, even just the initials?"

"No. In fact, it was impossible to establish which desks the report had crossed."

"None of this would ever have happened if I had gone to Madras," I said, sitting back, unable to hide my growing frustration. "If I had stuck to my original brief. If I had stayed working as a doctor."

The back of the car suddenly felt hot and cramped.

"Wouldn't it? Working for Jamie?" Sir Ian's voice was also getting louder. "Come on, you know he never really took to you. Now we know why. He was waiting to pull you down, sooner or later."

Sir Ian put a hand on the car door as we cornered sharply. He was right, of course. Jamie had always been suspicious of me. It hadn't been his idea to employ a British Asian. He had even told me so, said such things caused problems at the MEA. My promotion had been exactly the sort that the Club opposed. It was Sir Ian, not Jamie, who had lobbied for me. And then there was Jamie's anger at my friendship with Frank. My days had been numbered from the moment I set foot in India.

"On whose authority were you acting, anyway?" I asked. "Sending me to Cochin."

"On behalf of all decent thinking people in both countries. Not a big mandate, I admit, but enough to fight for." Sir Ian's tone was more resigned than before, a hint of world-weariness creeping into his voice. "My belief, for what it's worth, is that the Club is involved in something far more pernicious than just keeping track of immigrants. The forces of globalisation are very attractive, initially. But when those we trade with

187

threaten to become equals, or even superior, not everyone feels comfortable. The Cardamom Club can't cope with the notion of a strong and independent India."

"A nuclear India?"

Sir Ian nodded. "They're big boys' toys. Not for the likes of Delhi. The Club's doing what IPI used to do best: spreading lies, propaganda, spinning a dark subcontinent to the Western world." Sir Ian was twisting his hands as he spoke, as if he were turning a globe. "I see its fingerprints everywhere, in the morning newspaper cuttings that are laid on my desk. 'PM's astrologer has finger on the nuclear button', 'Indian rope trick rises again'. I can sense its exotic influence on CNN, see it on the BBC. It's nothing new, of course. Krishna Menon protested to *The Times* about its Indian coverage – that was the 1950s. The spirit of IPI is far more pervasive than you imagine, has been for a long while."

He sat back and looked out of his window, signalling that the lesson was over.

"And what if I do come up with some evidence?" I asked, thinking of Macaulay's website, the news service.

"Take it back to the media. Complete the loop. I look forward to reading about it. Now, if you will excuse me, I have a dinner engagement at Rashtrapati Bhavan."

Leaning forward, Sir Ian tapped on the glass with the back of his fingers, his wedding ring clicking against it, and then he opened a panel to the side of his headrest, and adjusted his bow tie in a small mirror. The driver slowed, looking in his own mirror.

"Just tell me one other thing," I continued, trying to ignore the fact that we were about to stop. "Did you send Dutchie?"

Sir Ian's hands fell motionless for a moment, and then, still looking in the mirror, he flicked some hair back at the side of his head, just above his ears.

"His uncle, Walter, was a good friend of mine," he said, tweaking the wings of his tie. The driver glanced at us again as we came to a halt. The Rolls-Royce carried on ahead, towards a roundabout. "Dutchie was once involved in an unorthodox, extremely successful intelligence operation. A one-off. He proved surprisingly good. I fear this time it didn't go so well."

"Where is he now?"

"Back in England. Recovering with his father. Macaulay did something to his mind. Fortunately, he never made the connection, never suspected Dutchie might have been sent. He was a drifter, a traveller who accidently stumbled into a room full of files. After that, Jamie just wanted him out of the country."

"But he was onto something."

"He did well."

"But why send someone like him?" I asked, thinking back to his shaved head, his nose stud, the no-hope demeanour.

For the first time Sir Ian cut a lonely figure as he looked out into the darkness.

"At that stage I didn't know what I was looking for," he said. "Actually, he blended in very well to the internet café culture down there. Christ, I couldn't exactly ask Six to investigate Macaulay. He was too close to Jamie, to previous high commissioners."

"So once Dutchie's brains had been scrambled, you turned to me."

"I thought it might matter more to you. It should. Now, if you will excuse me, you must get out. Please,

189

be careful with Jamie. I won't be able to interfere in his decisions."

He rapped the glass again and then turned his face abruptly away from me, his arms folded like a sulking tenor's. The Rolls-Royce slid past us again, having completed a circuit, and stopped a few feet in front. I opened the door and stepped out onto the street, watching the two cars speed off down Rajpath towards Sir Ian's dinner engagement at the president's palace. On either side of the road icecream vendors were packing up their Mother Dairy trolleys, each one illuminated by green fluorescent tubes. India Gate was behind me, spotlit against the stormy night sky. Lightning was rippling beneath the surface of the clouds, brightening them from within, searching restlessly for fissures to escape through. A warm wind blew dust up into my face. I turned to walk away from it, in search of a taxi or rickshaw, and then I heard a familiar horn as Ravi drew up alongside me.

CHAPTER SEVENTEEN

I KNEW IT was a risk, but I needed to call my father, ask him how he was, find out what sort of questions he had been asked. I wouldn't be able to sleep tonight unless I had at least tried his home. His phone was probably tapped but I had to take my chances, try to talk in a way that didn't suggest I knew about his visit from Special Branch, or the security report that Sir Ian showed me. If the Club established a link between myself and Sir Ian, if it concluded that I had been sent to Cochin to investigate Macaulay rather than to cure him, they would act fast, knowing that someone was onto them.

I told Ravi to stop in Saket, by the Anupam cinema. He parked nervously along one side of the busy square next to the cinema, nodding at a pick-up truck fifty yards ahead. There was a ripped red flag billowing from its battered bonnet and behind it a white Maruti was being towed away into the darkness. At least six men, crimson bandanas tied round their heads, were clinging onto the crane, one of them with his foot on the Maruti's front bumper, half-heartedly trying to stop it banging against the lorry. They were the city's pirates, triumphantly displaying their urban spoil.

We agreed that Ravi would drive around the block while I made the call. I headed for the nearest STD/ISD sign and asked for an international line. I was ushered into a booth, from where I could look out onto the square. It was milling with students, a few couples on dates, but mostly groups, chatting in the warm evening air, files clutched to their chests. In the centre of the square there was a circular, pink stone fountain, the centrepiece of which was a four-foot-high Coca-Cola bottle. Behind it a queue was snaking round to the front of the cinema, past booksellers who had laid out their wares, much of it soft porn, on the pavement.

The cinema defined Saket, gave the square its fizz (more so than the Coke statue) and was in the process of being refurbished. The Marilyn Monroe figure had gone, replaced by a shower of expensive gold stars, stuck onto a brilliant yellow and blue façade. It was not quite Leicester Square but this was not the India I had expected to see when I first came here. The multi-screen complex was flanked by a busy McDonald's on one side, and a Domino's Pizza on the other. All around the square there were fresh-juice shacks and snack bars serving *chaat*, their awnings covered with adverts for Magic and Speed cash cards for cellular phones. A big hand-painted billboard promoted "Cybernuts" internet access. Others were advertising Indya.com, 123India.com and indiainfo.com, unashamedly patriotic portals.

I tapped in my father's home number and watched the red digits on the display panel shuffling along like the back row of a family photo. It took a few seconds to connect and then the familiar phone was ringing. We had spoken only occasionally since I had been in Delhi, both of us preferring to correspond less personally by email and letters.

Someone picked up the phone but there was only silence.

"Dad?"

I imagined the receiver being moved from one shaking hand to the other.

"Dad?" I said again.

"Is that you, Raj?"

It was my father's voice, tentative, trembling. I wanted to tell him I was sorry, explain why they had asked him so many questions.

"Are you all right, Dad? You don't sound yourself."

"I thought you might be someone else."

"I'm just ringing to see how you are. Did you get my last letter?"

"Something's happened, Raj." His voice was faltering, as if he were in pain.

"What? Tell me."

"Are you coming home soon?"

"I haven't got any leave until the autumn. You know that. What's wrong? Are you sick?"

Tell me what happened, how many of them came in the night. Were they brutal with you? It sounds as if your teeth have been knocked out.

"The police have been here." He was more composed now.

"The police? Have you been burgled?"

"I thought it only happened to other people. The shopkeepers."

"What are you talking about?" I tried frantically to think how I would react if I hadn't known about Special Branch's visit. He said the police had paid him a visit, that was all. What could have happened?

"Have you been drink-driving again?" I asked. It didn't ring true.

"They were asking so many questions."

193

"About what?"

"Can you come home soon?"

"I'll try. I promise."

"They asked me about Dounreay. If I had ever broken the Official Secrets Act. Asked me – of all the people." He had been requested to sign the Act on a number of occasions. That was the nature of his work, a measure of its importance, his standing. "I told them I would rather die than break my word."

"Of course you did, Dad," I said, trying to encourage him. "Did they say why they were asking? Why now? After all these years?"

"No. They weren't like the local bobbies around here, Raj. Two were from London. So aggressive."

"Did they hurt you?"

"No respect. Only anger. It was like being a Catholic at Ibrox Park." For the first time, he managed the faintest of laughs, which stopped suddenly, when he became breathless, and turned into a cough.

"Did they hurt you, Dad? You must complain."

"And at my age in life. I told them I had been retired for over fifteen years."

The inconsistencies in his conversation suggested that he had given himself some sort of medication. I could only assume he had been injured, but that he was too proud to tell me.

"I'll be back soon," I said. "Just tell them the truth. You can't do any more than that."

"And then they asked for my passport."

"I'll ring again," I said, and I paused for a second before I replaced the receiver.

I could smell the *coheba* from the moment I opened the

194

back door and stepped inside the kitchen. Ravi handed me the car keys and headed off to bed. I suddenly felt very afraid and wanted him to hang around, but I didn't know how to ask. Chandar was off duty and the *chowkidar* had already returned to his slumber in the gatehouse. I closed the kitchen door silently, wondering if Jamie was still here or had left his smoke behind him. There were no other cars in the driveway.

I slipped off my shoes and made my way into the unlit hall, deciding not to announce my arrival. The house was uncharacteristically silent. I could hear blood pumping in my chest as I tried to keep still. The glass doors separating the hall from the sitting room were closed, the distinct blue light of the television flickering across the ceiling inside. Jamie was sitting in an armchair, his back to the door, watching a lingerie show on Fashion TV. He drew on his cigar and then exhaled, his head tilted upwards.

I stood there for a moment, watching him, wondering whether to walk quietly out of the house again or challenge him about my father, insist that he was innocent, tell him to call off the dogs and leave an old man alone. The fact that he had broken into my house seemed almost irrelevant, but then it started to scare the hell out of me as he sat there, shrouded in smoke. His confidence was frightening, too calculated to be dismissed as arrogance. I opened the door, loud enough for him to hear, but he didn't turn round. Immediately he was seizing the initiative, letting me do the running.

"What are you doing in my house?" I asked, neither angry or conciliatory.

"What were you doing in Cochin?" he said, his eyes still on the screen.

"My job," I replied. A moment later, the television image disappeared and we were plunged into darkness, a dying glow emanating from the screen. I couldn't help but smile: India the great leveller. A powercut wasn't in Jamie's script and the advantage had swung back to me.

"Haven't you got your bloody power supply sorted?" Jamie said, annoyed. He sat up in his seat, less at ease in the dark. The desire to challenge him about the Club became almost overwhelming, but I knew Sir Ian was right. It was better, for the moment, to keep those cards close to my chest. Jamie did not know that I was aware of his hand – my father's visit from Special Branch, the report recommending my own questioning – and I had to maintain the pretence. It was my only chance.

I walked back into the hall and over to the stairs, under which there was a locally made inverter (two car batteries in a rusting metal box that provided enough power to run the lights and fans for a few hours). A red light was glowing on a side panel, indicating that the inverter had overloaded. I flicked a switch next to it, off and then on again, and the television came back to life. I went back to the sitting room. Jamie was standing, the TV remote pointing idly at the screen, which was now showing men modelling swimwear.

"I thought you were going to Madras," he said, turning the television off. He lobbed the remote onto the sofa and fixed me straight in the eyes. I was standing by the door, eight feet away from him, but it was still too close, his gaze too piercing. I walked over to the windows, pushed the wire mesh mosquito panels and opened the glass behind them.

"I was seeing our consular rep in Cochin, Martin Macaulay." The pretence was easier to maintain than I thought. "Do you know him?" I asked.

"What do you think? It's my job to know everyone, particularly someone who has been with the High Commission for over forty years. I thought you were meant to be in Madras."

"Macaulay's been pestering them for a visit. Madras was delighted. I also wanted to see a bit of Kerala."

"You told me it was a tour, not a holiday. I need to know where you are, who you are seeing, all the time. It's important."

"You didn't make that clear."

"I didn't think I had to. How was Martin, anyway?"

"To be honest, I couldn't find much wrong with him."

"That sounds like Macaulay. I couldn't find a drink."

I suppressed more anger at the thought of him rummaging – he was only trying to provoke – and I asked him casually what he wanted. A few minutes later, we were sitting at either end of the sofa drinking local Aristocrat whisky from a supply I kept locked in a bedroom cupboard. There was a bottle of Talisker in there, too, given to me by my father, but I was damned if I was going to waste it on Jamie.

"I'm glad you're back," he said, his voice less hostile. "We've got work to do. Do you remember your dinner with Frank?"

"Yes." I tried not to flinch at the name.

"There was a girl there called Priyanka."

The glass was at my lips as he rolled out the syllables – polluting them – and it was only by an enormous act of will that I continued the action uninterrupted. I knocked back a larger measure than I had intended but otherwise my hand remained steady, the whisky unspilt. It burnt against my throat as I looked at Jamie.

"I remember her," I managed to say.

"I am sure you do." He paused. "She's a pretty woman. Well connected, too. Her father was a senior officer in RAW, based in Bombay. I want you to get to know her better. Not a tough first job, it has to be said."

He was trying to lighten the mood but I kept the tone quiet, businesslike. It was the only way I could cope with the exchange. RAW stood for Research and Analysis Wing, India's equivalent to MI6.

"Is she a client at the medical centre?" I asked, spinning two lumps of ice round my glass. The energy had to be dissipated somewhere.

"Not as far as I know. Why?"

"I thought that's what I'm here for."

"Is there a problem?"

His gaze was upon me now, scanning up and down, searching for a sign, something to tell him the game was up. Macaulay would have told him about our dinner together on the island. He was bluffing, I was bluffing, but I had to believe I still held the better hand. Macaulay didn't know how close we were. He had probably just told Jamie that he saw us together. I hung on to Sir Ian's words: *Jamie needs more evidence*. My only chance was to delay him, play along, put off my own arrest, give myself time to gather evidence against him, Macaulay, IPI, before their case against me became unanswerable.

"There's no problem," I said coldly. "Where's her father?"

Jamie didn't blink.

"That's for you to find out," he said. "He worked in Bombay so I should try there first. You are due to pay a visit to the medical centre there."

"And what's so special about him?"

"He once stole some information from us and we want to know why."

"What sort of information?"

"A few nuclear secrets, the sort of thing we prefer to give to our friends. I know it's not what you came out here to do, Raj, but that's how this game often works out. Get your hands up her sari, bit of jiggy-jiggy, meet the family. You're both from Kerala, aren't you? It could be the perfect match."

Was it a chance comment? How much did he really know? The phone was ringing in the hall. I stood up to answer it, my legs weakened by the thought of breaking the whisky bottle across Jamie's head, sticking the razored shards into those eyes.

"Can I speak with Raj Nair, please?" The voice on the phone was distant but familiar.

"Who is this?" I asked, glancing back at the sitting room. Jamie had switched on the television again, volume turned down.

"It's Paul, from Cochin."

"Paul?" I said, too loudly. Paul from the Cardamom Café. I looked over towards Jamie again. "Where are you?"

"Raj?" Paul said.

"London? If it's any consolation, it's forty-two degrees here."

"Raj? Is that you? Can you hear me?" Paul said, obviously confused.

"Yes . . . the line's a bit faint."

"Dutchie's come back," Paul said, persisting. "I just got an email from him."

"Great," I said. Drops of sweat were beginning to form on my forehead. I glanced at Jamie again, who I knew was listening. "What's he doing these days?"

"He's in Dharamsala. You can meet him at the Shambhala café. He has lunch there every day."

"Do come and stay if you're heading out this way," I said, scribbling down the name of the café on a scrap of paper.

"What? Raj, I told him about you. The documents. He wants to meet up."

"No problem. Any time. It's about nine o'clock here. Yes, four and a half hours ahead," I said, folding the paper up and putting it into my trouser pocket.

"Raj?"

"I'll do that. Thanks."

I put the receiver down, wiped my forehead with a handkerchief and returned to the sitting room.

"Do you get a lot of visitors from England?" I asked.

"Not in the middle of summer," Jamie said, flicking restlessly through the channels.

"I've got guests coming out from London for the next six months, as far as I can see," I said.

"Really. There's one other thing you should know," he continued. "Our High Commissioner has not been well. Nothing serious but he's not getting any better."

"Has anyone seen him? From the centre?"

"Not yet. He says it's just something he ate."

"Should I call him?"

"Leave it until tomorrow. He's out tonight, anyway." Jamie paused, unnaturally, in that way someone did when they had more to say. "How do you find him, anyway?"

"Who, Sir Ian? Very accessible. Down to earth. A safe pair of hands."

"The Indians love him, think he's wonderful. The MEA can't believe its luck. There hasn't been an Indophile in the job for years."

"You make it sound like there's a problem."

"I just heard a bit of Whitehall talk the other day. The word is he's getting a bit too friendly."

"Troppo," I said, mocking his own phrase. "Donned the turban."

"Exactly."

"What do you think?" I asked, wondering why he was sharing gossip with me, someone whose loyalties the Club had already called into question. I could only assume he was trying to establish how close I was to Sir Ian, whether there was evidence to link us.

"My opinion isn't important. I'm just offering some friendly career advice. He's not the most popular man in Whitehall at the moment. Don't get too close, that's all. He sucks people in, uses them." He looked at me for a moment, letting his words linger. I returned his gaze, trying in vain to believe that he didn't know Sir Ian had sent me to Cochin.

"I'll bear that in mind."

Jamie walked towards the kitchen. "I'll let myself out," he said, "seeing as I let myself in. By the way, I suggest you get your guard changed."

He threw me some keys, the spare set I kept in the guardhouse, and then he had gone.

It appeared Sir Ian was right. Jamie needed more

evidence before he could formally bring me in. In the meantime, he was prepared to sit back and watch me seduce Priyanka. It was a perverse test, a last bit of sport for Jamie before he delivered his damning report arguing against ever employing British Asians again in the security services. At least, that was what I assumed he was going to do, once the details of my father's supposed treachery had been clarified, and my own dubious conduct confirmed.

My record didn't look good when you saw it from Jamie's point of view, from the warped perspective of the Club: young British Asian lands sensitive job with the Foreign Office after much lobbying from Sir Ian, a High Commissioner who is known to be soft on India. On his arrival in Delhi, he immediately falls in with the wrong crowd, mixing with people like Frank, a former Bolshevik revolutionary. It quickly goes from bad to worse: there is sufficient evidence, in the hands of their own revisionist historian, to argue that his father, a man privy to state secrets, was a militant member of the freedom struggle. At the very least, he represents a security risk, no matter how old he is, given his sensitive work at Dounreay and with the UKAEA. He may even be a spy, which doesn't reflect well on his son, a man who is about to be entrusted with his own important intelligence work.

The Club must have been weeping with joy. Their case was almost complete, a job well done. All I had to do now was demonstrate that my affection for Priyanka, one of my "own people", prevented me from doing my job properly, from turning in her father, a very senior officer in RAW. I would then be held up as an example to all, to the security services, to local government, to the nuclear industry: employ British Asians at your peril, it is not just cricket that divides their loyalty.

Unless, of course, I could explode the secrecy of the Club, its unconstitutional influence, its febrile paranoia about all things Indian. And Dutchie's return might just be the break that I needed, providing he was conscious enough to talk.

Because Dutchie had seen the files.

CHAPTER EIGHTEEN

I WAS LOOKING forward to being back at the clinic, to dealing with routine medical problems again: malaria, dengue, gastroenteritis, dysentry, pneumonia, perhaps even some cholera. It had rained last night and the trees in the republic looked scrubbed, renewed. Even the barbed wire along Mr Jain's front wall, across the road, was sparkling with optimism. I remembered the extra-ordinary wedding I had watched there, shortly after I had arrived. Someone with a television camera had been shouting instructions to the bridegroom, who ducked his head, ran across to a small helicopter perched on the lawn, and climbed inside. The helicopter rose two feet into the air, hovered unsteadily and returned to earth again. The groom then stepped out and walked over to his wife-to-be. Later the wedding video would record that he had arrived by helicopter. All was *maya*, illusion.

Mr Jain regularly rented out his house as a wedding venue, helicopter included. It was still there, behind the wall, ready to rise up to meet the aspirations of Delhi's social climbers. I smiled as Ravi drove up onto the road outside, its surface so high that it felt as if we were on our own private flyover. I wouldn't be making this journey for much longer. Something had to give soon and I was determined it wasn't going to be me.

As we passed the Country Club, another misnomer, my pager hummed in my pocket. I pulled it out and read the following message: "HC very ill – please go to Rajaji residence. Urgent."

I told Ravi that we had to go first to Rajaji Marg, the road where Sir Ian had his official home. I wondered who had sent the message, presumed it was the clinic, and rang them. There was no answer. I tried to relax. Middle-aged women were sitting quietly in groups in the shade, knees drawn up, waiting to collect grass cuttings from the republic's well-watered lawns and sell them to the city's cowherds. We passed others, walking slowly in the heat, who had already bundled up their suburban harvest in grey plastic sacks bulging on their heads.

As we drew closer to Chanakyapuri, I became increasingly convinced that it was Jamie who had paged me. By the time we were on the roundabout, outside Sir Ian's house, all doubt had gone. I told Ravi to go round again as we slowed to enter the gates. Something was not right. Ravi looked puzzled as he accelerated back onto the roundabout, watched suspiciously by a Gurkha guard standing at the entrance to the residence. When we approached for the second time, the gates were open and I could see some activity in the porch. One of the figures was Jamie.

I told Ravi to turn off down a road just before the gates, and then immediately right into a side road where he had parked before. We pulled up next to two other cars, both of which had British High Commission number plates. Two drivers were leaning on the bonnet of one of the cars and I asked Ravi to inquire about Sir Ian.

"The High Commissioner, he is ill, sick," I told him, unfairly frustrated by his confused face. "Ask them if he is in the house, inside."

Ravi dutifully got out and started talking to the two drivers. After a few moments he climbed back into the car.

"Gone, sir. Airport."

"He's gone?"

"Eight o'clock, morning time," Ravi said, pointing at his watch. My pager had gone off at around 8.30am. I suddenly felt very vulnerable, too close to Jamie for comfort. *I could be recalled to London tomorrow if the wrong people find out that I sent you to Macaulay*. Behind the two cars, on the other side of the wall, lay the back garden where I had been barely two weeks ago, standing under the lanterns in the trees, blissfully unaware of what lay ahead, of the consequences of my short conversation with Sir Ian in the dhobi room, accompanied by the great Vinayakrao Patwardhan from Madhur.

"We must go, *abijust*, " I said to Ravi, unsure exactly where. As he turned the car round, a Gurkha guard appeared on the corner of the street and pointed excitedly down the road at us.

"Go, *challo*," I shouted at Ravi.

The back wheels spun as he completed the turn and accelerated down to the main road, where the guard was standing, but before we could pull out, away from the roundabout, Jamie's Land-Rover had blocked our way. Ravi hooted and then swerved round the square bonnet, before crossing in front of the oncoming traffic onto the main road.

"Where, sir?" Ravi asked, driving at last at the sort of reckless speed he had expected of foreigners. (I remembered his face on my first day in India when I had told him to slow down. "You don't like speed?" he had asked, incredulous.)

"Anywhere. Just go. *Challo*."

Ravi glanced in his rear mirror. I turned round, fastening my seat belt. Jamie had managed to cross the traffic and was now on our side of the road, about eight cars behind. He was driving fast, swerving as he overtook cars on the inside and outside.

"Connaught Place?" Ravi asked.

"No." I paused. "Dharamsala."

"Dharamsala?" he repeated, pronouncing my "s" like "sh", his voice going up a tone.

"Yes. Dharamsala." I copied his pronunciation, relishing the sound.

"*Abi?*"

"Now," I confirmed, glancing around again at the Land-Rover, which was still gaining on us.

"First we go my village," Ravi said. He looked happier than I had ever seen him before as he settled down into his seat. "Very near. No problem?"

"Okay, okay, *koi baat nay*. Just lose the Land-Rover."

Thanks to some anarchic driving by Ravi, we had left the Land-Rover far behind by the time we reached the Inter State Bus Terminal. We drove on through the day, stopping for food in Chandigarh, and for a short sleep in Una. I was warmly welcomed in Ravi's village, which we eventually reached after nightfall. Ravi immediately walked taller, commanding more respect than he had done in Delhi. Working for a foreign high commission ranked as one of the best jobs for a driver and here, in the village of Kandhi, all the men were drivers. They knew. Ravi's three brothers were drivers, his cousins were drivers, but his one-year-old son, Abishek, was going to be a government officer with a pension.

I had noticed that Ravi sent money back every month to his wife, queuing patiently at the post office to fill out the form, unlike other drivers in Delhi who squandered their salaries on Bagpiper whisky and rummy. His wife greeted Ravi with a warm, toothy smile, her head covered with a *chunari*, but she seemed quite unsurprised by his unannounced arrival, taking it in her modest daily stride, even though he normally returned only once a year. I liked that, envied her outlook.

We left early the next day, after a simple breakfast of *bindi*, chapati and cardamom tea, and reached Dharamsala by late morning, twisting our way up from the Kangra valley. The town was set precariously on a mountainside, its buildings fighting with pine forests for a foothold, clinging on for a view of the mauve-misted valley below. Immediately above the town stood the brooding rock faces of the Dhauladhar range, and behind them the snow-peaked Himalayas: immutable, reassuring, more silencing than I had imagined them to be.

I almost missed the Shambhala café as I walked along Jogibara road in McLeodganj, the upper part of Dharamsala. For some reason, I had it down as a large meeting place, teeming with backpackers, but instead it was a dark, cosy joint with six small tables, three down either side. I was early for lunch and Dutchie had not arrived. The only customers were a Western couple who had two small children. One was eating a plate of chips, the other, a baby, was being passed, asleep, through to the kitchen at the back of the restaurant, where an elderly Tibetan woman wrapped it in her arms and disappeared.

To the left of the kitchen door was a glass food cabinet where a collection of white, yellow and pink rolls of lavatory paper was on display. There was a mug on top of the cabinet full of coloured pencils and a pile of small sheets of scrap paper. On the walls were various posters calling for a free Tibet, and two faded posters of the Dalai Lama. A young Tibetan man welcomed me with a smile, handed me a well-thumbed menu and gestured at the paper and pencils.

I sat down at a table to the side of the cabinet, facing the door, and glanced idly down the menu. I was not hungry, but the smells coming from the kitchen stirred something and I settled on vegetable fried rice. This was the sort of place I should have come to if I had taken a gap year. Instead I had studied, which I realised now was a mistake. But I could never have sold the idea to my father, even if I hadn't mentioned India. "What do you want a year off for?" he would have said. "A holiday, at your age? You haven't even started work."

I glanced up at the Western couple with the children. They were English, in their thirties, and didn't have the rushed look of people on a brief holiday. Their clothes were too smart for them to qualify as travellers. Instead of rucksacks, they had two Karrimor baby carriers, propped up neatly in the corner. I envied their lifestyle, their freedom to travel. It was all about choices, that was becoming clear, and I was beginning to accept that I had made some wrong ones in the past few months.

I had no regrets about joining the Foreign Office, or coming to Delhi. I would never have met Priyanka if I had stayed at home. And I stood by my friendship with Frank, one of the few decent people I had met out here. It was living with the consequences of a wrong decision that troubled me: in that respect life could be very unforgiving. I had once been given a rare second chance in love and perhaps I had helped Priyanka to avoid a wrong decision, too. But I could never undo what had happened here in India. The shadow of MI6 would always fall across my life, even if I did manage to persuade someone – who? – of the existence of the Club. Frank was right: spooks stayed with you for life. And it was not stubbornness or pride on my part – I would have left tomorrow if I could – but an inability to do anything about it, which was far more frightening.

I wondered if my father had ever questioned his decision to leave India. And if he had, what had stopped him from returning, from unpicking his life? Was it obstinacy, a refusal to admit a mistake, or something else? Dharamsala was the first place in India which had made me think I could settle here. Perhaps it was the Tibetan presence. I would feel like an exile, too, in the first few months, far away from Scotland and not fully at home in India. But the feeling was not strong, not least because it was exactly what the Club would have wanted: repatriation. And what I wanted was to send the Club back to where it belonged, buried deep in the history books.

The only man who could help me walked into the café a few minutes later. Dutchie was looking sallow and withdrawn, more so than he had done at the clinic, his shaven head adding to the look of emaciation. He was wearing purple and orange striped trousers, troppo sandals, an off-white (dirty) collarless tunic, and a cotton shoulder bag, out of which a bottle of Himalaya mineral water was sticking. He still wore a nose stud, but his ears were less adorned than I remembered, a solitary gold ring hanging from his left lobe.

There was no reason why he should have recognised me – he had been barely conscious the last time we met – and he sat down at the corner table to the right of the door. He was looking down, as if he were shielding his sunken eyes from the brightness of the day, from the world, and when the owner approached, he mumbled a barely audible order. The man was not well, but at least he was here in India, which must have required a certain amount of cogency. I was amazed he hadn't been pulled over by Customs.

I climbed out of my narrow seat and walked across to his table.

"Dutchie? I'm Raj Nair. Paul in Cochin said you would be here."

He still didn't look up, giving the impression of a scolded schoolboy. I stood there: this was going to be harder work than I had thought. But then he began rocking his head slowly from side to side and a broad smile lit up his face. It couldn't be described as a direct response, but at least the lights were on. I pulled back the chair opposite him and sat down, becoming aware of a pungent damp smell rising from his clothes. Dutchie turned suddenly to look out of the window, his hunched body animated, as if an electric shock had passed through him.

"Oh, man, there he is again."

"Who?" I asked, following his gaze out of the window onto the busy street. I could sense the Western family looking at us.

"Did you see him?" Dutchie asked.

"Who?"

"He's been following me everywhere."

I looked for someone, anyone, who might fit the bill, but the street was quiet except for a couple of children playing with sticks and an old bicycle tyre. Dutchie relaxed and he turned back to face me, although his eyes were still looking down. We had yet to make eye contact.

"Who's been following you?" I repeated.

Dutchie waved an arm carelessly in the air and stayed silent. If there was someone pursuing him I might not have long. I watched as he pulled out a pouch of tobacco and a packet of Rizlas, and started to roll a cigarette.

"Paul said you saw the files. On Macaulay's island, in Cochin. Is that right?"

"Did you speak to Paul?"

"On the phone. He rang me two days ago."

"You must help him. You're a doctor, right? Such pain, every hour of every day. Man, can you imagine that?"

I was momentarily taken aback by his concern. Naively, I had dismissed him as a self-centred traveller, solely concerned with his own journey, spiritual or otherwise.

"We might not have long, Dutchie. Can you tell me what you saw?"

"You want to know what I saw? I'll tell you." For the first time he looked up, fixing me with his wasted, frightened eyes. He tried to hold the stare, but his head was wavering, as if he were drunk. Whatever he had seen was still trapped inside, burnt onto the back of his bloodshot eyes. He finished rolling the cigarette, struck a match and lit up with an unsteady hand.

"I saw a young boy, the same age as him." He nodded in the direction of the Western family, blowing out some smoke. The little boy grinned at us for a moment, his mouth smeared in ketchup, and then returned to his few remaining chips. "First he tied him up, taped his mouth, then he hung him upside down from a meat hook on the ceiling."

I swallowed hard, hoping my food was still a long way off. I had meant him to talk about the files but he clearly had something else to share first. It was important that he continued. He was talking loudly now, and I glanced round to see who was listening. The mother threw me a concerned look. I managed a thin smile, an apology. Mercifully their meal was over and they were getting up to leave, the mother putting her head round the kitchen door and being handed back her baby.

"They cut his eyelids first, sliced them off with a pair of surgical scissors. Then they took a carving knife to his ears and nose. You've never seen so much blood, never thought someone so little could kick and fight like that. When he was still, they cut out his tongue. They collected the blood in a dish and offered it to Kali."

I thought of the man who had waited outside the clinic. Tinkoo had met with a similar end. *Angrez*, the man had said. An Englishman. My stomach tightened. The implications were too far-reaching, too odious.

"Who did it?" I asked.

Dutchie drew on his cigarette, his hand shaking badly. Neither of us wanted to say the name.

"Macaulay?" I eventually said, almost whispering the word, thinking back to the dinner on the island, how I had sat next to him, so close. Dutchie's head began to tremble, small vibrations, nothing more. I pressed my teeth together. It made sense, in a diabolical way. There had been something unexplained about Macaulay when we had met, something acutely disturbing. Priyanka had felt it, too, and she hadn't seen the attack on the boy, or the shrunken head.

"I never saw his face," Dutchie said, his head more still now. "It was covered with a mask and no words were exchanged. Whoever it was made me watch the whole show. First he tied my hands and feet to a chair, then he taped my head to a pole attached to the back of the chair so I couldn't move it. Finally, he wedged matchsticks here and here" – he pushed his eyelids wide open with a finger and thumb – "so I couldn't close my eyes. I tried to roll them but I saw everything. He sat me down in front of the child, barely two feet away from where his face was swinging. I thought he was going to kill me." Dutchie faltered, his eyes welling up. "I wish he had, instead of the boy."

The family walked past us out into the street. We both looked at the boy, who smiled shyly at us as he passed, the corners of his mouth still daubed with red.

"Maybe I could have done something to stop him, coped better, but I'd shared a chillum with Macaulay barely five minutes earlier. At least I thought it was a draw, but it wasn't. It was some weird shit. I fell asleep on my bed. Next thing I was strapped to the chair, the taste of plastic in my mouth. Some mornings I can't even remember my own name."

"Where did this all happen?"

"Just across the border, in Tamil 'Nard', as Macaulay called it. We were meant to be going to Periyar, but we kept going. Driving all night. Macaulay was in a shit-mad mood, had been ever since he found me looking at the files. Never let me leave his sight. Always swearing at me. I don't remember the name of the village where we finally stopped. Next thing I knew I was lying on a railway platform in Ernakulam."

"What about the files? Can you remember anything about them? They were in his house on the island?"

"Yeah, a kind of secret library. Revolving bookcases and all that."

"Really?"

"Nah. It was in the basement. I was one of his special guests. You know, the ones who walked around with no clothes on. We got to go private side. Man, what a privilege that was."

"But you were there because Sir Ian had sent you?"

"Yeah. I was. Kind of. Then things gained a momentum of their own. I was broke. Sir Ian kept promising to wire me money but it never came. Macaulay took me in, fed me, then he started paying me to wear nothing under my *lunghi*." Dutchie laughed to himself. "Jesus, what a pervert. But hey, I needed to live. The money was good."

"And you just had to be decorative? Nothing else?"

"Pretty much. There was another guy there who went further, did the business, you know. But he also got beaten up. It was part of the package. I guess when Macaulay tired of him, I would have been asked to fill the gap." He laughed to himself again.

215

I kept him company with a nervous, encouraging laugh. "But you fell out of favour when you saw the files."

"That's one way of putting it. I'd visited the library a couple of times before Macaulay found out. The first time Paul caught me, but he said nothing."

"Did you find out anything?"

"The library was divided into two parts. The first consisted of files from 1913 to 1947. The second was from 1955 to the present day."

"1955?"

"Yeah. Although the files got thicker around 1960, when the government first announced the Commonwealth Immigration Act. There was a bit of a stampede between '60 and '62, when the Act was finally passed. Sir Ian's told you about the Cardamom Club, right?"

"He has, yes," I said, concluding that he had told more to Dutchie than he had to me. "Is that when the Club was formed, then? 1955?"

"It depends what you mean by formed. Macaulay never stopped. Someone in Whitehall began to listen to him in the early Sixties, read his reports. There was a lot of paranoia in those days. It's never been official, though, has it? So who knows?"

"What sort of people were in the files?" I asked, desperate to inquire about my father.

"Pre-1947, it was all original IPI material, the usual suspects. Post-1955, it seemed to be anyone who had left India for Britain."

"Did you look at any names in particular? The more recent files?"

"A few. But it's a waste of time, man. There nothing there. Innuendo, speculation."

Dutchie glanced round at the window as he said the words, checking up and down the street.

"And it's all in Cochin because you wouldn't be allowed to keep that sort of shit on people in Britain."

CHAPTER NINETEEN

DUTCHIE AND I must have made an odd couple as we sauntered down through the pine trees from McLeodganj to Dharamsala. Dutchie the archetypal Western traveller in his dishevelled Indian *khadi* clothes, and me, the Indian, looking like a stockbroker on holiday, wearing my Western chinos, Lacoste shirt and Timberlands. The stony track we were on zigzagged its way down the steep side of a valley, its progress occasionally broken by recent landslides that had left gaping holes in the stony earth. There was always an alternative route, though, a precarious higher path that had been quickly established by the monks who walked this way daily. We passed a few in their flowing robes, all smiling openly at us as they shuttled backwards and forwards across the hillside.

Dutchie's health troubled me. He was suffering from a degree of post-traumatic stress disorder, a legacy of what he had seen and perhaps of what he had smoked that night. At times, he was as coherent as I imagined he ever got, at other moments he was a mess, convinced that someone was following us, crouching behind rocks when he heard a bird call, or a stone falling away beneath us. But it was the student monks perched on the hills all around who troubled him the most. To me, they were a beautiful, numinous sight, sitting cross-legged in their maroon robes as they looked out across the valley, a book on their laps, lips mumbling sacred Tibetan texts. But for Dutchie they stirred up something deep inside him, as if the sighting of each one were confirmation of another pair of eyes watching him.

Once, after he had suddenly noticed a monk high up above us on an outcrop of rock, he started to shake so badly that I had to restrain him with a hug. If I hadn't, I feared he would have slipped and fallen down the valley. We sat for a while and I encouraged him to talk about his life before he came to India, something to root him to a less traumatic time. I was also curious to discover how he had come to work for someone like Sir Ian, how their wildly different paths had ever crossed. After a few minutes, I gave up searching for something stable and reassuring. His past was all too turbulent, too extreme, way beyond the parameters of my sheltered life in Scotland. I sat there, listening in appalled disbelief.

After dropping out of public school and a comfortable middle-class background, Dutchie had become a New Age anarchist, mixing it with the likes of Class War until he had fallen for a hippie traveller from Cornwall called Annalese. He had agreed, at her insistence, to drop the violence but then she was killed in a terrorist bomb blast in London, leaving Dutchie demented with rage, desperate for revenge. Through Walter, the American uncle Sir Ian had mentioned, Dutchie managed to contact the intelligence services and had offered to go after Annalese's terrorist killers in return for a clean police record. They had agreed, he eventually tracked them down and his police files had been given back to him.

"It should have been a triumph, a moment of pure satisfaction," Dutchie said, looking out across the valley. "But it turned out that she had been cheating on me. My file was full of her own reports."

"Really?"

"She had been working for the filth all along. An informer, snitch. Five years later and I still can't get over that. I thought we really had something going. And I was never able to challenge her, give her the chance to reply."

"Perhaps she began as an informer, and then genuinely fell for you. It happens. You start off out of a sense of duty, and then something else takes over."

"She filed up to the day before she died," Dutchie said, throwing his cigarette stub away.

"She could have been under pressure. Had no choice," I said, thinking of Priyanka and how Jamie had perversely tried to get me to pursue her. That was all irrelevant now.

"Maybe. I still hang on to that." Dutchie was looking fragile again.

"Sir Ian says he knows your dad," I said, quickly changing the subject.

"He knew Walter better. Ex-CIA."

"And Sir Ian sent you to India."

"I was here already, in an ashram. You know, one of those free-love, get-your-kit-off places."

"Really?" I looked at him with surprise, wanting to know more.

"No. I tried. There's a great place in Kerala where they have sex all the time, no questions, right in front of everyone. Mixed dormitories, that kind of thing. But they wouldn't let me in. Suspected my motives. I ended up over in Pondicherry, at the Sri Aurobindo. When Ian got to hear I was in India, he came down to see me, told me all about Macaulay. He didn't know about the Cardamom Club then, nothing specific, anyway. He just wanted me to hang out, sniff around."

"And you agreed."

"Yeah. I liked him. Believed in what he had to say about India. Macaulay seemed to represent everything that was wrong with Britain. Keep India down where it belongs in the world, Tebbit's Cricket Test, all that stuff. It was a chance to do something about it."

"He sent me down to Cochin after you. Only in my case he knew about the Club but omitted to tell me."

"Right," he said. It took a few moments but a different level of comprehension began to spread across his face. "Macaulay must have loved you. Ha! Very clever. I get it. A real live British Asian. That's the side I don't like. Ian'll use someone for his own ends. He knew you'd get further than me. I don't suppose Macaulay had ever actually met a British Asian before."

"Foreign Office, too."

"Love it. He must have choked on his flaccid moussaka. You work for Ian in Delhi, then?"

"Not exactly. I'm a doctor, at the High Commission. I am also meant to run occasional errands for MI6. I was just helping Sir Ian out. He got me my posting here."

"Ian's a one-off, you know, a genuine Indophile. Of course, he's interested in trade, like the rest of them, but there's an understanding there, a real love for this place."

I contemplated whether it was safe to tell him about Sir Ian's departure.

"I'm afraid he's been recalled," I said, taking my chances.

"Recalled? When?" Dutchie's eyes immediately started to flit from one side to the other, almost as if he were blind.

"Yesterday. Packed him off in an ambulance to the airport."

"Jesus. Why?"

"Officially he was ill. Unofficially the Club was onto him. They must have got wind of his inquiries."

"Us, you mean. Got wind of our inquiries."

Dutchie was standing now, and starting to shake uncontrollably again. I wished I had brought some of the sedatives I had in my room.

"He always said that might happen. I'm dead if they know I'm back. I'm dead or another child's dead. What does it matter? You've never seen a child kick out like that. Seen so much pain trapped inside such a small body."

"Dutchie," I said. I was standing up as well now, gripping his shoulders tightly. "Dutchie, listen to me. They don't know you're back. Okay? Nobody knows except me."

"What about you? Ian sent you to Cochin. They'll be after you as well."

I looked around, not so much out of fear as to see whose peace we were disturbing. A monk on a distant hillock was looking our way but he turned his head when I caught his eye.

"We must be careful, of course we must, but they don't know I'm here. All right? We're safe."

I glanced around again, scanning the countryside. The monk had disappeared.

By the time we reached Dharamsala, Dutchie was feeling more relaxed, less paranoid. My own anxiety, however, was mounting. Dutchie wanted to check his emails and I decided to do the same, in case my father had sent more details about his interrogation. There seemed to be internet cafés on every corner, interspersed with shoe shops, cheap hotels and meditation centres. We headed for the nearest, and both settled down in front of terminals.

I logged onto Hotmail and retrieved two messages. The first was from Frank. I opened the second one, which was from Priyanka. It read as follows:

"Where are you? M's internet café has closed and his house on the island is shut up. I found Paul, badly beaten up in Mattancherry. He said M had gone up country. I'm coming back to Delhi. Magazine is holding story. Miss you. x"

I looked across at Dutchie, who was reading a message on his screen. The café was empty apart from us.

"Any luck?" I asked.

"One from the missus."

"You're married?" My voice was too loud, too full of surprise. "What's her name?"

"Charlotte."

"Very . . . nice," I said, uncertainly, not sure if he was winding me up.

"Not what you would expect, huh?" He gave me a deranged grin that could have meant anything.

"I didn't mean that," I said, apologetically. "Not at all."

"Yes you did."

"What does she do? Class War?"

223

"Very witty. She's a spook. One of the good ones."

"Right," I said, returning to my screen and clicking open the message from Frank. It was becoming clear Dutchie was less out of his depth in all this than I had thought he was. "How did you meet her? Through Sir Ian?"

"Stop calling him 'Sir', would you? She used to work for Walter. You?"

"Me?"

"Are you married?"

"Not yet," I said, scrolling through Frank's message. He had been busy. "Take a look at this." I went back to the top of the email, which read as follows:

"Raj, eventually tracked down my old contact. Yes, your man in the south is ex-IPI. He was recruited in 1944 and returned to Britain after Independence, pushing papers around for MI5, before moving back to India for good in 1955. Sometime in between he managed to get his hands on IPI's more sensitive files. He's still sending in a steady stream of useless chatter from Cochin to London about Indian scientists, doctors and academics who have emigrated to Britain.

"As for our mutual friend, we know all about his touching approach to global harmony. Back in the early 1980s, the bad old days when he was following me around, he also became convinced that India was trying to infiltrate the more sensitive corners of the kingdom, ie Britain's nuclear weapons programme. He believed New Delhi would try anything, even penetrate CND, to share its secrets.

"After the Pokhran tests in 98, he was given the dubious responsibility of undermining India's claims to a place at the nuclear high table and a permanent seat on the United Nations Security Council. 'Spook with special responsibility for Pokhran propaganda.' Don't we just love these people? More later, Frank."

"I've got to make a call," I said, deleting the email. "I'll be back in a minute."

I knew I shouldn't ring Priyanka, but I almost ran across the street to the nearest phone booth. A few seconds later and I was talking to her at *Seven Days'* bureau in Delhi.

"I've been trying to ring you," she said. "Where are you?" For a few moments I couldn't concentrate, couldn't think of anything. The sound of her voice was electrifying, completely fusing everything in my mind. I had been a child the last time I felt this happy.

"Out of Delhi," I managed to say, pressing the receiver close against my cheek.

"Are you all right?"

"Fine. I'm fine."

"Listen, Macaulay's news service," she continued. "It's not just an email circular to friends. It's a major wire operation. Can you look at it now?"

"In a few minutes. Why?"

"A story's just been flagged on its breaking news channel. Half an hour ago. About a case of *sati* in U. P. – Bijnor district." I thought back to the etchings of *sati* in Macaulay's house. "It says the ceremony has been planned for tomorrow evening. It's going to be a media circus."

"Are you going?"

"Of course. It's unprecedented. Getting advance warning of something like this. Sensational. It must be a hoax. The police will be all over the area."

225

I could see the East India Company official, standing under his umbrella. "If they haven't already been bought off," I said. "I'll ring you back in a few minutes."

"Raj?"

"Yes."

She was adjusting the receiver in her hand.

"I've missed you."

I walked back across the street to the internet café, unable to resist a small skip as I stepped inside. Dutchie was still there, composing a long email to Charlotte.

"Did you ever discover anything about Macaulay's news service?" I asked.

"A little. Why?" Dutchie was concentrating on his screen.

"How much?"

"That he was circulating shite stories about India to all his pals. Things that amused him. Child labour, bride-burning, that kind of thing."

"It's more than just a circular," I said, booting up the browser. A few moments later I was looking at the home page of the Cardamom Café. I pulled out my wallet, selected a credit card and clicked on the Cardamom News icon. It took a few minutes to sign up – it was too late to worry about Macaulay now – and then I was looking at a list of stories from the last few days. Priyanka was right: it was a comprehensive databank. I was annoyed that I hadn't checked it out earlier. I clicked on the breaking news icon. The top item was about the *sati* case.

SATI *FEARS IN U. P. VILLAGE*

A sati is to be performed somewhere in the remote Bijnor district of Uttar Pradesh, according to local reports.

226

Twenty-two-year-old Kalawati was widowed two days ago and has been under mounting pressure from her husband's family to perform the illegal ceremony. The medieval practice involves throwing herself onto his funeral pyre, an act that followers believe will transform her into the goddess Sati, the consort of Shiva.

India's most celebrated case in recent times was in September 1987, when an eighteen-year-old widow called Roop Kanwar died in Deorala village, Rajasthan. Her death shocked the world, but prompted a revival of sati *worship in India.*

Sati, *also known as* suttee, *was outlawed by the British in 1929.*

I browsed through some of the other stories. "Naked swami seeks world peace, bathes in boiling butter"; "Eunuch castrates himself"; "Bam Ram, the flesh-eating swami of Bihar" (80 per cent of his devotees driven insane by "burping" corpses). There was even an entire section dedicated to animals: "PM says it's monkey business as usual" (marauding monkeys break into government offices and ransack sensitive filing cabinets); "Holy cow has bags of stomach" (four thousand plastic bags retrieved from the stomach of a cow in Bhuj); "Drunken elephant kills five in Assam"; "India's dancing bears on their last legs" and so on.

I clicked on the search facility and typed in "child + sacrifice". A few seconds later a long list of items appeared, the earliest dating back several years. I scrolled through the stories, looking at the more recent ones.

"When did you witness the sacrifice?" I asked Dutchie. He stopped typing, still looking down at the keyboard. "March," he said slowly. "Some time in March."

I returned to the list, searching for a corresponding date. Then I saw it.

CHILD SACRIFICED NEAR PERIYAR

The mutilated body of three-year-old Pradeep was found in a well outside Kumily yesterday, amid reports that he had been sacrificed to the Hindu goddess Kali. Police said they were treating the death as murder, but the nature of the boy's wounds – his tongue, nose and ears had been severed – has convinced locals that it was a ritual killing.

I became aware of Dutchie standing next to me. I pointed at the screen where I was reading but he was already looking at the copy.

"That's it, isn't it?" I said quietly, monitoring Dutchie's reaction.

"He's crossing the line. Making stories happen."

"Have a look at this," I said, clicking on the *sati* story. I waited while he read through the text. "I put money on him being behind this one as well."

"Jesus. What's he playing at?"

I thought about Sir Ian's morning news cuttings. "Spinning," I said quietly. "Altering perceptions. Presenting India in a particular way to the outside world. Look at this lot: snake charmers, child labour, naked fakirs. You'd think India was medieval if you only read this."

"He's a frigging spin doctor, too," Dutchie said, walking outside to have a cigarette. He sat down on the edge of the doorstep, unfolding a patchwork pouch of tobacco. "And I thought he was just a witch doctor."

I smiled at Dutchie through the open doorway, warming to him, pleased that I had met him now rather than in his Class War days. I kept an eye on him as I searched the site for "Tinkoo". Sure enough, the story of his morbid death came up, dated in early April, shortly before the man had appeared outside the British High Commission gates with his photos. *Angrez*, he had said. The *tantrik* had been English. Macaulay. It had to be. I glanced through some of the other stories: "Dead man to contest Indian general election", "Indian village sealed off amid renewed fears of plague", "Dowry deaths alive and well in India'. The true extent of Macaulay's activities, and presumably the Club's, was becoming increasingly apparent. Sir Ian was right: the Cardamom Club was against the very notion of a developed India. Someone must have felt very threatened.

It was impossible to tell from the site what effect, if any, such a drip-feed diet of stories might have on the West without knowing who was buying into the service. The breaking news channel boasted two hundred foreign clients, which was a not insignificant number. Far more worrying was Macaulay the *agent provocateur*. When the figures dropped for child sacrifice, he stepped in, intervened, propped up the barbaric trend. Did Whitehall know? Sanctioning propaganda was one thing, but bloodshed? I couldn't see it. Macaulay must have been doing his own thing, but what was he trying to prove? That India had sunk back into the Dark Ages the moment the civilising influence of Britain started to wane? I couldn't get the image of the East India Company man out of my head, watching from beneath his umbrella as the *Joogee* woman was buried alive.

CHAPTER TWENTY

I RANG PRIYANKA back, sounding more together this time, and we agreed to meet the following morning in Meerut, by an old Pakistani tank that she said was on display at a junction north of the town centre. She knew a journalist who lived nearby, a stringer for one of the national newspapers in Delhi who specialised in child sacrifice stories in northern Uttar Pradesh. I didn't tell her about Macaulay, that he was probably arranging the *sati* as we spoke, drugging some poor woman, paying off her family. I just warned her to be careful. Jamie could have gone after her, frustrated in his attempt to find me. I would explain about Sir Ian, my other work in Delhi, remove the last layer of deception that hung like a purdah between us.

Dutchie was reluctant to leave the relative security of Dharamsala but I persuaded him we would be safer on the move. It was a long drive to Meerut, and he insisted on travelling separately, riding his Enfield 350 Bullet. He had got it from another traveller, he said, in exchange for two sizeable slabs of charas from the Parbati valley. I liked Dutchie more and more, but I didn't mind not sharing an Ambassador. I would have to mention the smell sooner or later, couch it in purely medical terms.

We set off after lunch, driving back through Una, and slept for a few hours on the outskirts of Chandigarh. Ravi lay down on the Ambassador's front bench seat, and I took the back, the doors open to create a draught. Dutchie rolled out a mat next to his bike. The night was warm and I couldn't sleep. Ravi's film music didn't help, but he had the car radio on quietly and I couldn't complain. He had started to look worried, which didn't suit his laid-back style, and I needed him to hang around. More frustratingly, I had been unable to recall Priyanka's face ever since I had put the phone down. I could see her sari, her feet, her hands, the swell of her thighs, her breasts, but every time I moved up towards her face I had an annoying image of someone else, the receptionist at work, the withered old woman who was collecting money outside the internet café. The more I tried, the weirder the images became. Eventually I fell asleep thinking of the back of her head, flattering myself that she had turned away from me, sated, exhausted.

We reached Meerut just after dawn, the sunrise unable to awaken any beauty in its mundane cantonments. Meerut was a large army area, uniformly dull, with most of the boxed houses painted civic yellow. Despite the military surrounds, the Pakistani tank, with its faded star on the side of the turret, looked strange by the roadside, captured from the old enemy in 1965 and yet somehow standing guard.

Priyanka was late. Dutchie was less bothered by the delay than I was, tinkering happily with his bike, which had developed a problem of some sort. Then I saw a promising white Ambassador approaching, its number plate beginning with "DL" for Delhi. Several others with similar plates had passed, but this car drew up next to us and Priyanka stepped out. I couldn't believe that I had been unable to recall her face, now so instantly familiar, fresh, as if newly unwrapped.

"Sorry I'm late," she said, glancing past me at Dutchie, who was on his hands and knees, fiddling with the bike. "I went to see my friend, the local journalist I was telling you about."

"No problem," I said. I wanted to hold her close, carry her away to a cheap hotel, but we hadn't even kissed on the cheek. "What did he think?" I asked, moving breezily into journalist territory. The story was obviously preoccupying her. "Is he going?"

"He doesn't believe it. Says it's a hoax. He's chased up a few *sati* stories in the last couple of years, several around Bijnor, but said they were all just rumours."

Why were we talking like this, so formally? Her body language was restrained, her eye contact business-like. I was already trying to store the images.

"This is Dutchie, by the way," I said. "Friend of mine."

Dutchie looked up and nodded, giving her one of his particularly disturbing grins. Priyanka glanced at me for an explanation, some reassurance.

"He stayed with Macaulay on his island."

"Okay," she said, looking at Dutchie in a new light.

"I'm going to have to leave this here, let them strip it down," Dutchie said. He gestured across the road to a shack with some worn lorry tyres stacked up outside. "The engine's seized up."

We stood next to each other, watching as Dutchie wheeled the bike across the road and explained, in surprisingly fluent Hindi, that he wanted it fixed. I felt for Priyanka's hand. She squeezed it lightly and then let go.

"Come," she said. "The roads will be bad."

We agreed to go in my car. Priyanka paid off her driver, telling him to return to Delhi, which

233

guaranteed us some time together. I caught Dutchie's eye as he came back across the road, and nodded discreetly at the front passenger seat. He got the message and climbed in next to Ravi, dropping a small rucksack at his feet. Priyanka and I settled down in the back, our hands resting casually together on the seat between us. I didn't want to do anything that might embarrass her. Respect, she had said. Respect. This was Meerut, not Delhi or Bombay, or London. I liked the veneer of restraint here, the veil of modesty. It allowed for so many more possibilities when the lights went off.

We had only been driving for twenty minutes and I was already beginning to forget about Sir Ian's departure, the menacing presence of Jamie. Priyanka was tired from her early start, the dusty drive up from Delhi, but she was full of chat, talking about Macaulay, her article. She tried to engage Dutchie in conversation, wheedle out a few anonymous quotes for the piece, but he was not very forthcoming. He had taken my nod very seriously, it seemed, and thought that he was disturbing something by even hearing us talk in the back. I was on the point of telling her about the darker side of Macaulay, how we suspected his hand in today's events, when Ravi glanced anxiously in the mirror and then turned to look over his shoulder.

I turned too and saw a muddy white Land-Rover directly behind us, all over our bumper. It was a Defender, but it wasn't Jamie's and it didn't have diplomatic number plates. The windows were dark and the grilles protecting the lights were badly dented. There was no one else on the road, either in front of us or behind. A few seconds later the Land-Rover was knocking against our bumper. We were jolted forward

— I shot out an arm across Priyanka, trying to stop her hitting her head on the back of Dutchie's seat — and then Ravi was working the horn, jamming it down, barely letting it come up for breath.

"What the . . . ?" Dutchie said.

"Keep going," I shouted at Ravi. "Keep driving. Faster."

In Delhi Ravi would have stopped after a bump like that, stepped out of the car, and remonstrated firmly with the other driver, but he knew it was not that sort of incident. The Land-Rover hit us again, sliding us foward and forcing Ravi to break.

He was not smiling this time, not like when we had been leaving Delhi. For a terrifying moment, he took both hands off the steering wheel, clasped them together in front of his chest and nodded at the flashing Shiva on the dashboard.

"Who is it?" Priyanka said, looking round.

"Were you followed here?" I asked her. "Did someone come after you?"

"Not that I saw." The Land-Rover bumped us again, this time much harder, throwing us all forward.

"Oh man, oh man," Dutchie moaned, beginning to lose it in the front seat. "It's him, isn't it?"

"Raj, I'm scared," said Priyanka. "Tell me who's in the Land-Rover."

I said nothing.

"Macaulay?" Priyanka persisted.

I couldn't be sure, didn't want to upset Dutchie further. I nodded discreetly at Priyanka.

Ravi was driving dangerously, breaking all the rules we had so painstakingly established in Delhi. Overtaking on blind corners, not slowing for bumps. I looked behind again. The Land-Rover was still there, filling the rear window. It knocked us again and Ravi hit back with his horn.

"Sir," he said. "Very costly."

"I know, I know. Just keep going. You're doing fine." I looked ahead and noticed a police checkpoint about five hundred yards away, a yellow-painted crowd barrier on either side of the road, separated by ten yards and forming a tight chicane. Four overweight officers were standing on the left-hand side. One of them was waving us down. He had yet to clock how fast we were going, but his manner quickly changed as we approached. He tapped a colleague, and they all started gesturing, moving to the side of the road. Ravi slowed down, which surprised me. I looked back and the Land-Rover was slowing, too. But as we drew near the barrier, Ravi suddenly accelerated again, swerving past the policemen and through the chicane. The Land-Rover was stationary, surrounded by the curious policemen.

"Nice one," Dutchie said, looking over his shoulders. He then made a V sign with his arm, laughing manically.

"The English always stop for a bobby, no?" Priyanka said, still trying to make Dutchie out.

"Pretty much," I said.

"Filth," Dutchie mumbled.

"Something to do with our upbringing," I added.

"Speak for yourself," Dutchie said.

"Bijnor?" Ravi asked.

"Bijnor," I repeated.

"Small roads," Ravi said, turning off left down a dusty track.

The Land-Rover was nowhere to be seen.

As we bumped our way along a series of increasingly poor tracks, I told Priyanka all about the Club, how Sir Ian had sent Dutchie and then me to discover what we could about Macaulay, and how the Club had now removed him from Delhi. I mentioned what had happened to my father and explained my other role at the High Commission. It didn't seem to surprise her. As she pointed out, Ranjit had seen me a mile off at Frank's, kept on repeating that nobody did only one job at an embassy. It felt strangely uplifting to be transparent at last, liberating, although I didn't tell her about Jamie's interest in her father. Her anger would have given Jamie too much pleasure.

Finally, I recounted Dutchie's experience with the child, how the boy had been sacrificed by a man we thought was Macaulay. After the initial shock – she, too, felt sick at the thought of having enjoyed his hospitality – she fell very still, and then leant forward, resting a hand on Dutchie's shoulder. The gesture surprised me, but she motioned discreetly in Dutchie's direction. He was sobbing quietly. I kept going, telling her about the man who had shown me pictures of Tinkoo, the reference to *angrez*, the image Macaulay was trying to portray of India.

"So you think he's going to be here, masterminding the whole thing in some way?" she asked, sitting back, trying to take it all in.

"I'd put money on it."

"One sicko bastard," Dutchie said, wiping his nose with the inside of his wrist.

"What about the Land-Rover?" she asked.

"The Club got rid of Sir Ian easily enough." I turned to check the road behind us again. It was clear. "Now it's our turn."

I watched Dutchie for a reaction, but he had sunk back in his seat, temporarily lost in his own troubled world.

"We just have to make sure we find Macaulay before they find us," I said, unconvinced by my own words.

"What makes you think he's suddenly going to show his face with all the media in town?" Priyanka asked. "The BBC are coming, Zee, CNN, all the newspapers."

"He'll be in the shadows somewhere, in the background." *Shielded from the sun by an umbrella.* "The media doesn't suspect he's involved."

"Even if we confront him, he'll just say he's covering it for his news agency," she said. "Quite plausible, given he broke the story."

Priyanka was right, of course. Proving Macaulay's involvement wasn't going to be easy, which was why we needed to get to the area early, ask around, find out what, if anything, he had been saying to the locals. If our theory was right, he would be paying people off as we spoke, ensuring a smooth *sati*.

We pulled into Ghanshyampur village and parked next to a line of cars, trucks and jeeps, just off the dusty track that ran through a small cluster of brick houses. Priyanka's prediction was accurate: we were not alone. There were journalists everywhere. Priyanka chatted with a BBC reporter, who said that *The World Today* were going live with the story. He was leaning against a small aluminium step ladder as he talked. Behind him two BBC jeeps full of equipment were being unloaded. Technicians from CNN were setting up a small satellite dish just off the roadside, next to a stack of steel-rimmed crates. Plenty of Indian film crews were in attendance, too, including Doordashan, Zee, Jain and New Delhi TV, their wires scattered across the ground, tangled like snakes in a pit.

I stood under a tree with Dutchie, while Priyanka went off to find out what she could. She moved freely amongst a group of reporters who had gathered around a *paan* shop, a small tin-roofed shack with a half-empty cabinet of Mirinda bottles and a few plastic jars of boiled sweets. I felt odd watching her at work in a world that was alien to me, odd but thrilled. It was as if I had spotted a stranger in a crowd and knew, for once, that I had the confidence to introduce myself.

A line of locals had gathered next to the hut, a mixture of the old and young, all of them fascinated by the proceedings. Most of the reporters were Indians, but there was a posse of Western journalists too, chatting on mobile phones, complaining the Mirinda wasn't cold enough. Priyanka moved over to talk to one of them, a short man wearing glasses, who laughed, putting his hands out in mock despair. He occasionally looked behind him and joked with another Western journalist – gaunt, cigarette bobbing in the corner of his mouth – who had set up a laptop computer on a wicker stool under the shade of some trees across the road. A mobile phone was attached to the computer and he was trying, in vain, to get online. The mood was light, despite the nature of what might happen at any minute.

"Nobody seems to know when or where this thing's going to take place," Priyanka said, walking back over to us. "This is the village that Macaulay mentioned but

239

none of the locals know anything. They say nobody's died in the area since the end of last year."

She stepped back a pace as a police jeep swept by and pulled up in front of the *paan* shop. A senior-looking officer climbed out of the car. He appeared hassled but not too much so as he talked to several Indian journalists, fiddling with a brown leather belt that was half hidden under his stomach.

"That's the correspondent I met this morning," Priyanka said, pointing at one of the journalists who was talking to the officer. "He's got good contacts, knows everyone in the area. The inspector's asking him what's going on."

"But he doesn't know," I said.

"Nobody does. But no one wants to be the person who misses out."

The police officer climbed back into his jeep, held on unsteadily to the top of the windscreen, and was driven off again, no doubt to another village, checking, looking. Like the journalists, he couldn't afford to miss it if something happened. Priyanka said the feminists from Delhi would be after him, as they were in Deorala, if anything happened here, which, for him, represented a far more grim prospect than the *sati* itself.

While the dust was still settling, the man with the laptop called out. "Jesus, take a look at this," he said.

The journalists surged across the road from the *paan* shop. Dutchie and I moved to the back of the crowd, Priyanka edged further forward.

"It's happened," he said. "Already happened."

"That's just great. Where, for Chrissake?" the BBC reporter said, his voice getting louder.

"This has got to be a hoax," said another journalist. "Got to be."

"Who's writing this stuff, anyway?" The BBC reporter asked, swigging dismissively from his lemon Miranda.

"Cardamom News," someone said. "Whoever they are when they're at home."

"My editor's going to burn me alive," the BBC reporter whispered. The group seemed to consider his choice of words, mulling them over for a moment, wondering which way to go. Then it was decided.

"It's just a smokescreen," someone else said, guiltily, not looking up.

A few furtive glances, then more people began chipping in, embarrassed, unable to resist. It reminded me of my student days, the black humour of my first autopsy class.

"There's no smoke without fire."

"I've had my fingers burnt before."

"Out of the frying pan . . . "

"If you can't stand the heat . . . "

"Shit." The puns fell silent as the journalist with the laptop started to scroll down some new text on his screen. "They're running an eyewitness account." Everyone leant forward, craning to see the small screen.

"Read it out," someone called from the back of the crowd, but the journalist stopped before he had even started.

"Over there," a voice was saying quietly. "Over there." Heads turned. In the distance, about one mile away, a plume of dark grey smoke was rising into the sky.

"Dear God," someone else breathed. There was a respectful pause, then pandemonium, as journalists began moving towards their cars, trying in vain not to break into an undignified run. Technicians swore as they swung tripods and cameras into the back of their jeeps and the man in the *paan* shop started collecting half-empty bottles.

CHAPTER TWENTY-ONE

SATI – *AN EYEWITNESS ACCOUNT*

They bathe Kalawati first, soaping her bare back with a soft sponge. Her nakedness provokes little reaction from the family members who have gathered to watch in the cramped, airless room. A few moments earlier she has broken with Hindu convention and uttered her husband's name, confirming her wish to die. "My soul is with Rajpal Lachchuram Saini. Let our ashes be as one." In the eyes of the assembled, she has already become something supernatural, otherworldly. Sati *means "virtuous woman" in Sanskrit and there is no scandal here.*

A priest passes her a towel. She steps into it, drying her young body slowly, almost sensually, while an assistant waits with her wedding finery, a vermilion lengha *folded neatly over his forearm. She takes the skirt and blouse and puts them on, swaying slightly, unsteady on her feet. The priest nods anxiously at his assistant, who gives her a cup of* bhang – *marijuana mixed with milk and ginger – which she downs in one, her decorated hands trembling. It's her third cup of the morning. The first she took shortly after dawn, when her sisters-in-law had painted her hands and wrists with dark, swirling patterns, using henna paste mixed with oil, lemon juice and tea. The ritual,*

Mehndi, *was last performed on the morning of her marriage, barely ten months ago.*

One of her husband's sisters takes Kalawati's hand and sits her down on a fraying wicker stool, where she drapes gold necklaces round her neck. Another sister-in-law carefully fixes some rings through her ears, linking a chain from them to her nose, and then slides some bangles over her slender wrists, defying a custom that forbids widows to wear them. She is not a widow, she is a bride. More are slipped over her ankles.

Nobody speaks. Her appearance is breathtaking.

She stands, steadier now, turning to the priest, who daubs her high cheekbones with red minium. Earlier this morning, he mixed it with gunpowder and sulphur to hasten the end. Soon her soft skin will be exploding in the flames on the pyre outside. She takes her chunari, *a long veil, and places it over her head.*

The priest presents her with a sprig of cusa herb and some sesame, which she holds in one hand. With the other she drinks some water, cupping it briefly in her decorated palm. Then the priest gives her a silver box full of untampered ochre. She opens it and applies small marks to everyone's face. As she makes her way around the room, moving slowly from one person to the next, the priest repeats the word "Om", *over and over again,* "Om, Om". *She takes pieces of jewellery – rings, brace-lets, all of it gold – from one of her sisters-in-law and presents them to the priest and his assistant.*

Her time has come.

244

She almost falls as she steps outside the house, strug-
gling to draw breath. For the first time she sees the pyre
that will soon become her final resting place, her
wedding bed. Rajpal is already waiting for her, his
putrefying body draped in a cheap white sheet. The logs
are stacked up all round him. Two long bamboo poles
have been laid out on the grass next to the pyre. Beyond
them a group of musicians is waiting restlessly, most of
them drunk. She follows the priest, who leads her round
the pyre three times, accompanied by some barely audible
music. As she walks, trancelike now, whether in shock or
because of the bhang, *she throws rice over those who*
follow her. She takes off her jewellery, too, distributing it
piece by piece to her followers. They are looking happier,
clutching their relics, believing that a year of good
fortune is theirs with every step that they help her to
take.

She pauses after the third circle and glances around
at everyone, looking for a crack in their expressions, some
hint of a way out, but they have moved together,
mentally and physically closing ranks. The priest ges-
tures with a hand, subtly but forcibly. She steps up onto
the first log. It rotates under her weight and she slips,
letting out a small cry. The priest moves forward, help-
ing her to her feet. She climbs upwards until she is on top
of the pyre, her whole body shaking, and then she sinks
down on her knees, next to her husband.

Her movements have a certain momentum and the
priest seizes his moment, moving quickly. As she breaks
down, sobbing, one hand across her husband's chest,
kissing his sunken cheeks, the priest barks an order at
his assistant, who ignites one corner of the pyre with a

245

plastic cigarette lighter. The wood must have been soaked in paraffin because the flames flare up, knocking the assistant backwards. The woman looks up from her husband and screams, trying to get up.

The fire is spreading too quickly.

Moving like an overworked cook, the priest picks up a large tin of ghee and throws it unceremoniously in her direction, some of it reaching her, staining her skirt. He discards the empty tin and picks up a can of paraffin, throwing its contents on her, too. A few stinging drops get into her eyes. The hem of her skirt is already alight. She is standing now, her blouse torn, a breast exposed, but then she is suddenly on her knees again, knocked down by one of the bamboo poles.

The priest and his assistant have positioned themselves either side of the fire and they manage to keep her pinned down with the pole, pushing it hard against her bare back. Two more people move into position with the other bamboo pole, pressing it against the calves of her legs. Her resistance is sapping. There is no dignity, no sublimation, no exclamations of Satya! Satya! Satya! such as her predecessors are said to have made. Only fear, and a fizzing noise as the flames blister her face.

Soon her charred body is lying still, next to her husband's, just as was planned. The music trails off. The men slowly release their grip on the bamboo poles. They had been forced to keep them in place with their knees, such was her initial strength. But it is over now. Their ashes are as one.

She has become Sati.

A large crowd had gathered by the time we reached the source of the smoke. Policemen were everywhere, trying to seal off the smouldering pyre from the villagers and now from the media, as they all pressed forward. Dutchie had decided to stay behind, a good decision given what he had witnessed in recent months. The sight of charred corpses wasn't going to heal his scars.

The smell hit me first, kerosene and burnt butter and something else, far more pungent, slightly sweet. Pushed to one side in the mêlée I had lost sight of Priyanka. Initially I tried to fight back towards the centre of the crowd, from where the smoke was billowing, but then I felt the ground slope up beneath my feet. I was on the edge of a small mound of earth, a hillock, and I continued upwards, away from the crowds. There was a pipal tree at the top and a handful of people, villagers rather than journalists, standing in its shade. They looked at me and one of them said something in Hindi which I couldn't follow, stabbing at the ground with a finger, as if saying "Here". One word, though, I had no problem recognising: *"angrez"*. Was this the point from where Macaulay had watched flames consume the widow?

The scene below was unlike anything I had ever witnessed. The pyre must have been burning for a while, but it was still possible to make out the dim, shimmering shapes of two human figures amongst the charred wood. I stared for a moment, transfixed as the legs of one of the bodies seemed to crumple, throwing up a shower of sparks. The police had formed a tight cordon round the pyre but the press were pushing through from every direction. Gusts of wind occasionally blew

247

smoke through the crowds, who suddenly gasped as one of the skulls popped in the flames. Flashlights flickered down the police line. An officer grabbed a photographer's camera and a scuffle broke out as he wielded his *lathi* stick. The BBC reporter was desperately trying to do a piece to camera, standing on his aluminium ladder, back to the pyre, his cameraman being jostled. Other TV crews were attempting to do the same, some of them deciding to move back and file their reports from a safer distance. The senior officer whom we had seen earlier was talking frantically on his radio. The police were losing control, already fearing the feminists.

Then I noticed a small group of people gathered at the entrance to a hut on the far side of the pyre. It was not visible from where the reporters were massing, shielded from them by a cluster of trees. I moved twenty yards to my right to get a better view of it. There were half a dozen police officers standing outside the hut, one of them signalling to the driver of a police jeep, which was parked fifty yards away, again on the far side from the press and out of their line of sight. I watched the hut closely, trying to see what, if anything, was happening inside. For a brief moment, the policemen parted and I had a clear view. A young woman, wearing vermilion wedding finery, was sitting on a stool, a female policewoman standing next to her, one arm across the woman's shoulders. A second later and she was gone again, hidden behind the police.

I moved back to my original position, searching for Priyanka. As I scanned the crowd, I heard the sound of a jeep pulling away, coming from the direction of the hut where I had seen the woman. I couldn't find

Priyanka and decided to head back down the hillock and join the crowd. After ten minutes of pushing and shoving, I located her, calm in the midst of it all. Somehow she retained her dignity as the crowd surged sideways, almost knocking her over.

"Priyanka, Priyanka," I called, but she couldn't hear me. I was barely ten yards away. It was bedlam. I battled my way closer and tried again. The pushing reminded me of trying to buy a beer from one of Delhi's oddly named English Wine Shops on a Saturday afternoon.

"Priyanka," I said, almost shouting in her ear.

"I have never seen anything like this," she replied, as if we had been standing there having our conversation for hours.

"I've got something. Come," I said, putting my hand on her arm.

"But . . ."

"Come, please. Really." I grabbed her by the elbow and pulled. "You'll want to hear it."

Reluctantly she withdrew from the front line and we dropped back fifty yards to where we could hear ourselves talk.

"The widow wasn't burnt," I said, watching her rearrange her *salwar*, sweep back her hair.

"What do you mean, she wasn't burnt? It's just happened, barely thirty minutes ago. I've seen the bodies."

"And I saw her being driven away by the police, round the back there."

"You can't have done," she said, looking at the crowd, itching to return. "It's not possible." Her voice was losing conviction.

"I've seen the bodies and I've seen a woman in what looked like a red wedding outfit," I said, matter-of-factly. "Either there was more than one widow or that's not his wife on the pyre."

"Raj, this is the biggest story I'll ever cover. I must get back. I'm sorry. We'll meet later. Here in half an hour?"

She must have thought I was mad. I watched her walk, half run, as she returned to the fray.

"Lemmings, the lot of them," a familiar voice said at my shoulder. It was Dutchie.

"I didn't think you were coming," I said, scanning him nervously. He looked surprisingly together, unshaken.

"Once I heard the news I could hardly stay away, could I?" he said, raising his eyebrows. Something was wrong. Dutchie was positively relaxed.

"What news?" I asked.

"About Macaulay."

I looked at him, confused. "Is he here?"

"Yeah, he's here. No immediate plans to move on." Dutchie had begun building a large spliff.

"You've seen him? Where?"

I watched him lick the cigarette paper and then he looked up, nodding in the direction of the pyre. "The body on the right."

"How do you know?" I asked, my mind racing. He was right; in that moment I knew he was right.

"Unlike that lot," he said, indicating the crowd, "I asked a few questions. Spoke to the locals. It seems Macaulay had paid off the entire village, promised them loads more money if the *sati* went ahead. Only the widow's family changed their mind. Just as she was

250

ascending the pyre. A fight broke out, somebody doused Macaulay in paraffin and he was pushed onto the logs. A match was thrown before he could get up. The rest you can see for yourself."

"The woman was okay, then?"

"As far as I understand. A bit shaken up, naturally. You would be, wouldn't you?"

Dutchie struck a match and we both watched it fizz into life. Then he raised his celebratory spliff to his lips and started to walk over to the crowd, tossing the match away.

"Where are you going?" I asked him.

"One more look," he said, grinning like the devil himself. "Just to make sure."

CHAPTER TWENTY-TWO

THERE WAS ONLY one thing that mattered, now Macaulay was dead, and that was getting Priyanka's story into print before Jamie could stop us. I knew that his options were fast disappearing, but it wasn't worth underestimating a man of his menace and resources. Priyanka was the only member of the press who knew the real identity of the *angrez* who had perished in the flames of someone else's funeral pyre. As far as the rest of the pack was concerned, it was a bizarre accident involving an unknown foreign national. The story they had come for, a sensational *sati*, had failed to materialise, leaving them disappointed and annoyed with Cardamom News.

Ravi drove us all back to Delhi, where Priyanka and I holed up at a family friend's apartment in Civil Lines to write her story. Dutchie had decided to mark his personal closure by getting stoned at the source of the Ganges and had duly embarked on a tortuous pilgrimage to Gangotri, beginning at the Inter State Bus Terminal. I envied his free spirit, and we promised to keep in touch. Over and over again, Priyanka went through what Sir Ian had told me about the Cardamom Club, the IPI files, the news wire service and the information Frank had found out about Jamie in London. Frank had become a man possessed, emailing us with more and more information squeezed from his mole, no doubt sensing that Jamie, his lifelong nemesis, would never be more vulnerable than he was now. Frank was also planning to come back to Delhi shortly, a thought that kept us going in our edgier moments.

It was a difficult few days, as there was no knowing what course of action Jamie might be pursuing. Priyanka was up at first light, working away at her friend's computer, and was still writing long after I had gone to bed. Even when she did slip under the sheet next to me in the early hours, she seldom slept, her mind racing, asking me to go over certain points again with her. We sent out for food, and paid the guards extra in the vain belief they might stay awake at night. I could only hope that Jamie's powerbase had been eroded, that the sands were shifting back in Whitehall. Had Sir Ian heard about Macaulay? Where was he, and what sort of health was he in?

On the day of Frank's arrival, we agreed it was safe to break cover. Priyanka had finished her story and the first copies would be on the newsstands by lunchtime, making it too late for Jamie to try anything. Besides, he would be on the defensive, his position at the High Commission surely untenable once he had been exposed as a leading member of the Cardamom Club. In the late afternoon, Ravi drove us to the airport, where we waited behind buckled barriers with the card-carrying hustlers and hotel reps. On the way, we had stopped at the roadside to buy a copy of *Seven Days*. I couldn't bring myself to read it, not yet, but Priyanka seemed pleased as she flicked through the pages. I glanced briefly over her shoulder at the photos of Macaulay on his island with an elephant, of Sir Ian at an official function, and of Jamie staring out from what seemed like a passport photo, his eyes as searching as ever. It was all too real at the moment, too imminent.

Frank soon emerged from the arrivals lounge, weighed down by a bulging suitcase and beaming at us as he dodged out of the way of a snaking line of trolleys. We both hugged him, Ravi taking his suitcase as we walked over to our car. A couple of boys tried to relieve Ravi of the case, but he snapped sharply at them and they melted away. Above us storm clouds were gathering.

"You got your story, then," Frank said from the front seat. He turned round to us, pulling his own folded copy of *Seven Days* from his jacket pocket. "They were selling it as I came through."

"We couldn't have done it without you," Priyanka said, leaning forward to squeeze his shoulder.

"Or him," Frank said, nodding towards me, smiling broadly. "You could do worse, you know."

It was a relief to see Frank back on seemingly good form.

"How's Susie, by the way?" Priyanka asked, blushing, changing the subject.

"Okay," he said. "Actually not that good. It hit her very hard, what happened."

I knew I should say something but I didn't know where to start. The ensuing silence made me feel even worse.

"Is she taking anything? Medication?" I asked, slipping behind my professional mask. "I could arrange for something."

"She'll be fine. She's planning to bring the kids back soon, maybe in a month or two, when things here have settled down."

254

Our plan was to head into South Delhi, drop Frank off at his house, and drive over to the Press Club, where the senior management of *Seven Days* was due to hold a press conference about its story, just in case anyone had missed it. Despite my own reservations about returning to his old house, Frank was determined to get his life back to normal, make himself at home, order in some Bordix from Mr Tricky.

As we drew up at the traffic lights beside Qutab Minar, however, our plans changed. Ravi got talking with a taxi driver in the next lane, as was his wont, and then turned to us.

"Sir, big problem at British High Commission. Argy-bargy BJP. RSS."

"Khaki underpants," Frank said. I looked at him for an explanation. "Hindu nationalists. Shall we take a look?"

"Is it safe?" I asked.

"With her in the car we couldn't be safer," Frank said. "She must be a national hero by now."

"Stop it, Frank," Priyanka said, blushing for the second time. "We should go, though. It'll be interesting."

By the time we arrived in Chanakyapuri, there must have been several hundred demonstrators outside the High Commission, waving banners and shouting, but not with the passion Ravi had led us to expect. The presence of a number of Black Cats, India's elite armed guard, who were deployed in front of the gates and along the perimeter wall, probably had something to do with it, but it wasn't enough to stop one enthusiastic youth setting fire to a Union Jack and dancing

255

round it with some friends, filmed by a grateful camera crew.

We hadn't mentioned Jamie yet, but I sensed Frank could restrain himself no longer. "Do you suppose he's in there?" he asked.

"If he's got any sense, he'll already have left the country," I replied.

"What car does he drive?"

"A white Land-Rover, why?"

"Like that one?" Frank was nodding at a vehicle pulling out of the side gate, down by the medical centre, unnoticed by the crowd in the dying evening light.

"What a nerve."

I looked around for Ravi, who was leaning against the bonnet, having a cigarette. He quickly concealed it with the back of his hand when he saw me.

"Sir?"

"You see that Land-Rover?"

"Yes sir?"

I didn't need to say anything else. He smiled as both of us remembered the last time we had encountered one.

"No bumping, just follow it," I called, as Ravi turned the car round.

"I think I'll stay here," Priyanka said, kissing me on the cheek. "I'm not sure I'm Jamie Grade's best friend right now. Find me later at the Press Club. And keep a note of anything he says."

Frank and I presumed Jamie was going to the airport. Ravi closed up behind his Land-Rover. Neither of us discussed why we were in pursuit, or what we might say if we confronted him, but we were united in a desire

256

to see Jamie one more time, out of curiosity, or anger, I wasn't sure. Perhaps we just wanted to make sure he left the country.

It soon became clear, however, that Jamie wasn't heading for the airport, not yet, at least. We were moving slowly in heavy traffic along the Vikas Marg flyover, and had just passed over the Jamuna river when Jamie turned off suddenly down a side road and doubled back under Vikas Marg, bumping along a dusty track. We turned off, too, but I told Ravi to pull over, at least five hundred yards behind Jamie's Land-Rover. Ravi switched off his engine and lights, and we all sat there, peering into the gloaming. Jamie had climbed out of his vehicle and was walking over to the water's edge, where he stopped and stared across the river, towards the Indian Tax Office buildings on the far side. Behind him was a cluster of slum dwellings, *jhuggis*, a few dim lights and the occasional figure just visible within. Parked in front of the *jhuggis* was a row of ornately decorated, horse-drawn carts. High above, the traffic was inching along under the orange glow of street lights, commuters returning home from Connaught Place, oblivious of this other world below.

"*Batar*," Ravi said, cutting into our silence. "Hindi film." I hadn't noticed the music drifting across the riverbank. There was so much background noise in India that I had become adept at ignoring it. Now he had mentioned it, I marvelled that I had managed to block out the sound. As I listened, I became aware of the foul-smelling river, too, and the mosquitoes that were chewing my ankles, the sweat trickling down my back, the distant rumble of thunder. I returned to watch Jamie as he struck a match and lit up. He was too far away to see clearly, but I knew it was a *coheba*. He seemed to toss the match into the water and just stood there, a faint silhouette in the dusk, head occasionally tilting back as he exhaled some smoke.

"Have you thought what you will do when all this is over?" Frank asked, still watching Jamie.

"Not yet."

"Will you stay out here?"

"Perhaps. Sir Ian will recover, come back out and all will be well with the world. You?"

"I'm damned if I'm letting one man ruin our lives. We nearly moved when we first heard he had been posted to Delhi, but I decided then it would give him too much pleasure." He paused. "The kids are fine, but Susie needs a little more time. She's enjoying being with her family, her sisters. She didn't realise how much she missed them."

We sat in silence for a while. Behind the *jhuggis*, a large electricity pylon, weighed down with a tangle of illegal hook-ups, was shorting out, sending fits of white sparks into the night air.

"Was it strange being back in Britain?" I asked, realising that I was no longer surprised by the sight of a short-circuiting pylon.

"Strange? I was a foreigner. Kept checking my change all the time."

Jamie hadn't moved from his riverside spot. I suddenly had a horrible feeling that he was waiting for us.

"What about him?" I asked, gesturing towards Jamie. "Shall we go over? Say our fond farewells?"

"Why not?" Frank said. "Old times' sake."

As we walked down the track towards him, I became aware of a large shape a few yards beyond, close to the turbid water's edge. It was an elephant, swaying from side to side as it pushed some straw around with its trunk on the muddy ground. The animal's ankles were chained together. Beyond it I saw four or five other elephants, similarly hobbled, swaying on the shore.

"Ah, comrades," Jamie said, turning to us. For a moment I thought we had been watching the wrong person. Jamie looked different, his hair darker, the balance of his face altered in some way, too much forehead. Was he expecting us? It was hard to tell. Nothing was ever straightforward with Jamie. "I hope you're satisfied," he continued, turning back to the water. "Job well done."

"Are you flying out tonight?" I asked, noticing that the bottom of one of his trouser legs was ripped.

"You saw the mob."

Then it occurred to me that Jamie had disguised himself. He probably had any number of identities and passports, a perk of the job.

"I don't think you've met Champa, have you?" he said, looking round at the elephant. "He belonged to Macaulay, the elephant he first trained with."

I looked past Jamie at the vast animal, its chains clinking, remembering Priyanka's questions on the island about Macaulay the mahout. I wasn't sure who looked the more pathetic standing there: Jamie or Champa.

"I felt I should let him know his old master's dead," Jamie continued, more subdued. "The least I could do. Then I must tell Asif, his present mahout. He's only seventeen, less than half Champa's age." He nodded in

259

the direction of the *jhuggis* behind us. "They liked him around here, you know. Liked him very much."

"Did he visit often?" I asked, trying to picture Macaulay picking his way through the mud, wondering if it was the elephants who drew him, or the youthful mahouts.

"Not so much in recent years. But when he was younger . . . " Jamie trailed off in mid-sentence, then began again, apparently addressing Frank. "Your lot refused to see this side of India. You paid for your party elephants in the air-conditioned comfort of Khan Market, but how many expats knew where these animals had come from? It takes four hours to reach Vasant Vihar from this colony – hot work in the heat. Oh yes, you all loved their pretty chalk colours, the cameras clicked, children gazed up in awe, but who saw the mahout's bloody metal spike stuck deep into the elephant's neck?"

"What is it you so fear about India?" Frank asked, interrupting Jamie with an urgency that I had never heard in his voice before. "What is it?"

"Fear?" Jamie laughed. "It's got nothing to do with fear. God, Frank, you never cease to amaze me. Lutyens had it about right: 'Liberty is a blessing which must be earned before it can be enjoyed.'"

"Let's go. We don't have to listen to this," Frank said to me, turning to leave. "I would ring the airport, tip them off you're coming, but the sooner you're out of this country, the better."

"I remember thinking something similar when you left Britain," Jamie replied. Frank stopped and the two men glared at each other for a moment, the mutual hatred tumbling down through the years. Then Frank turned away and started walking towards our car. As I caught up with him, Jamie called: "Where's the girl, by the way?" I resisted saying anything. I suddenly regretted coming here and wanted to be as far away from Jamie as I could get. "Look after her, won't you?" he called, his voice fading under the noisy flyover.

CHAPTER TWENTY-THREE

ONE OF THE least surprising aspects of our marriage was its endorsement by the stars. Priyanka's father had told me first, letting me break the news to his daughter. In all other respects, the Pillai family had overlooked the differences our proposed love marriage had presented, the challenges to tradition, but no amount of talking would have persuaded them to waive the *thalakuri*. Priyanka had been depressed for days, knowing how unlikely it was that I would have *chovva dosham*, too, but I had been quietly more confident. Something about our whole relationship, the way we had come together, had given me hope. And in the end that hope had proved well founded.

A far greater surprise was the appearance in Cochin of my father, who arrived from Delhi in time to see me tying a sacred locket, or *thali*, round Priyanka's neck. He had watched the proceedings from a wheelchair, which he was initially cross about, but his legs were much weaker than he admitted and he later relaxed into it, particularly when he was wheeled around by a succession of Priyanka's disarmingly beautiful cousins. I was more than happy to participate in the ceremonial requirements of a traditional Nair wedding, which was a far more modest affair than the gaudy events I had been involuntarily exposed to in the republic. This was definitely a helicopter no-fly zone.

A pipe and drum had played when I tied the *thali* with a gold thread, but not the sort I was used to back home. The pipe, called a *nadaswaram*, had soared to a high pitch at the moment my nervous knot was complete. We were sitting on cushions, on a decorated dais, which we later walked round three times in front of a lighted lamp. I also presented Priyanka with a silk sari, which her sister (who had grown considerably less frosty towards me, particularly when the horoscopes had come through) had helped me to choose on the M. G. Road, together with another traditional Kerala dress.

All of which had left me profoundly moved. Priyanka had looked more beautiful than I had ever seen her, and her family had made me feel unconditionally welcome, which couldn't have been entirely easy for them. My only pang of sadness had been before the ceremony, when we went around the elders to accept their blessings. My father was wearing a white shirt and a *mundu* wrapped round his waist (he had bought it, he said later, immediately after touching down in Cochin, from a shop in Ernakulam that was still standing from his day), and it was nearly too much when Priyanka and I both knelt down before him and touched his feet. As we rose, I saw tears in his eyes and sensed, in that moment, that he regretted closing the door so hard.

It was now the evening and we had all gathered on the lawn outside the Malabar Hotel for what everyone kept referring to as Raj's Western-style reception. I had insisted on paying for something (as had my father), and a party overlooking the harbour where it had all begun seemed as appropriate as anything. My father had changed into a kilt and was regaling a crowd of people with stories about his life in Edinburgh. Dutchie was also in attendance, getting drunk on Kingfisher as he chatted up three of Priyanka's cousins, all of whom had clearly never seen anyone quite like him.

He looked a changed man (he, too, was wearing a *mundu*, with gold stitchwork round the hem, though tactfully not as embroidered as my own) and I was pleased to see him here. I had asked him to be my best man, on condition that he didn't make a speech, and he had been the model of good behaviour, taking his turn to wheel my father around and making sure my glass was never empty. I had declined his offer of a stag night – it was too terrifying a prospect – and we had settled instead on a pub crawl round Edinburgh with some old friends after Priyanka and I returned from our honeymoon. I was taking her to a remote desert island called Bangaram, which sounded expensive and far away, but which was, in fact, only a few hundred kilometres off the Malabar coast. She had agreed to live in Edinburgh (where the government had offered me a job in tropical medicine and hygiene), providing that we visited her family together at least twice a year, which seemed a fair deal.

Priyanka had become something of a celebrity in journalist circles, both in India and abroad, in the weeks since *Seven Days* had published her account of Macaulay and his fiery demise. As for the Cardamom Club, the British papers turned the story into a full-blown spy scandal, bringing Indo-British relations to an all-time low, damaging bilateral trade and severely embarrassing the government in London. By all accounts, the Club had never enjoyed any formal endorsement, but came into its own after India and

Pakistan conducted their tit-for-tat nuclear tests in the desert. Up to that point, it had been much as we thought: an entirely unofficial cell of officers within the intelligence community who had common concerns about India. They had long believed that the former colony represented a potentially grave threat to Britain's internal and external security, a subtle menace that was perceived as being quite different from the noisy Islamic fundamentalism of Pakistan. The seemingly unstoppable rise of Hindu nationalism only served to confirm their worst suspicions.

Sir Ian, in other words, had been fully justified in his fears. What he hadn't been aware of was the extent to which the Cardamom Club's unofficial existence had been tolerated by successive heads of MI6 and MI5, without the knowledge of their ministerial bosses. The Club was seen by intelligence chiefs as a useful place where their officers could safely let off steam. Messages sent between those sympathetic to the cause were nostalgically signed IPI, shorthand for a certain frame of mind, a hidden agenda that might one day be more formally acknowledged. (Interestingly, though, the existence of the Cardamom Club did appear to have become temporarily known to one or two senior members of the Conservative Cabinet in the 1980s. It was, after all, the era of the Cricket Test.)

As the original members of IPI either retired or died, the Cardamom Club might reasonably have been expected to disappear for good, but its membership swelled with the next generation of Indophobes, men like Jamie Grade, a middle-ranking MI6 officer who was against the promotion of India and "dilution" of Britain. In the 1980s, Jamie went about persuading sympathetic colleagues in MI5 to put numerous Indian immigrants under surveillance, and was in regular contact with Macaulay, calling up the occasional old file, commissioning new ones, and generally raising his profile within the intelligence community.

Macaulay couldn't believe his good fortune. For a few years he basked in his southern glory and was even sent out a few high commissioners who were known to dine occasionally at the Club. But his luck seemed to have dried up with the arrival of a Labour government and he slipped back into the shadows. Macaulay's star, though, was destined to rise once again after the nuclear tests. While the Cardamom Club's line on immigrants had been, in reality, only occasionally bought by the security chiefs, its other argument, that post-Independence India posed an increasingly dangerous threat to the new world order, suddenly found itself official government policy.

Encouraged by all the attention from London, Macaulay continued to update his database on immigrants under the cover of writing a history of modern India. The fact that he had failed to unearth a single mole in over forty years seemed to have been overlooked by the Club, but he thought his boat had finally come in when a young British Asian working for the Foreign Office showed up in Cochin. He wasn't a Muslim, which would have been a bonus in an increasingly anti-Islamic culture back home, but he did work for MI6. A quick cross-reference to his father's files (a former anti-British subversive) and bingo! A whole family of moles. It hadn't quite worked out like that, of course.

According to the government's own preliminary inquiry, the findings of which were shared with my father, his old IPI file had not been sent over to London when he was originally vetted for Dounreay. (Macaulay's reports had obviously been out of favour at the time.) Ironically, Macaulay had only learnt of my father's connection with the nuclear industry after he had contacted a Club member in MI5, presumably on the afternoon before Priyanka and I went to dinner on his island. The discovery of his sensitive career, coupled with my "penetration" of the Foreign Office and MI6, was proof enough of a major security breakdown. No wonder Macaulay had been waiting many years for someone like me, as Paul had said.

Jamie had evidently managed to slip out of the country the night that we confronted him on the Jamuna riverbank because he was given a lowly job back in London, working on the Antarctic desk. Despite considerable pressure from the Indian government, he was not sacked, after it was claimed that he had no knowledge of Macaulay's different, more macabre, understanding of news management.

I wanted to pay him a visit when we returned to Britain, offer him an exploding *coheba*, but Priyanka had talked me out of it, said it wouldn't serve any real purpose. She was right, of course, but she did promise that she would investigate dark rumours of Jamie's preference for small boys on the beaches of Sri Lanka, and write it up in the *Scotsman*, which was to be her new employer in Edinburgh.

She was standing at my side now, looking out across the harbour as the sun set beyond the fishing nets. In front of us our fathers were chatting together, Mr Pillai's hand occasionally touching my father's arm as he crouched on the grass next to him in his wheelchair. Under some coconut trees by the water's edge, Paul was talking with Dr Gopalakrishnan. Dutchie was there, too, still standing, although looking increasingly as if he were going to be the official wedding drunk. There could have been no better cure for his nightmares than seeing Macaulay being consumed by his own nightmares.

Dutchie staggered over to join Frank, who was lying back on a swing, still recovering from his journey. He had travelled with Susie and the children by train from Delhi, an epic voyage that had taken a total of four days, beginning badly at Delhi railway station when they turned up to see a sign announcing that their train had been delayed by thirty hours. Frank and Dutchie had hit it off straight away and I wondered if he saw some of his younger self in him.

As for Susie, she had bounced back from the problems of the past few months, and she was now shuttling across the lawn from one group of people to another, purring with all the pride of a bridegroom's mother. If it hadn't been for her, of course, I would never have met Priyanka, but in truth our relationship was not as close as it had been, although she would never have admitted it. Her *joie de vivre* had been dimmed, the unshakeable optimism was no longer there, which upset me. She would cope – she was that kind of woman – and she was laughing now with Sir Ian and Mrs Pillai, both fully recovered. Sir Ian had stayed in London for a month, helping the government with its inquiry, before resuming his duties in Delhi. I had promised Mrs Pillai and Dr Gopalakrishnan that I would look into courses in ayurveda when we were back in Edinburgh.

Mr Pillai had spotted his daughter and was now walking over towards us. We chatted for a few minutes and then I took the opportunity to slip away and talk with my father, who was sitting on his own, staring out across the harbour. The fishing fleet was returning, racing in with the tide and streaming between us and Mattancherry on its way up to the market.

"I think you should know something," he began, as I sat down next to him.

"I don't think I should," I replied, sensing what he was about to say, my heart filling with dread. I couldn't help thinking of Dutchie and how he had been given back his police file, most of it compiled from reports supplied by his girlfriend.

"I was asked once—"

"Dad, please."

"Are you so afraid that you don't want to hear the truth?" He had not spoken to me or to anyone else about Priyanka's revelations in *Seven Days*. She had kept him out of the narrative, at my request, but I knew he had his own story to tell. I just wasn't sure I was ready to hear it.

"I *was* asked once to report back to Delhi," he began again, his hands fiddling with his sporran. I closed my eyes, rolled my head back onto the seat, and listened to the call of a nearby barbet. "It was just after I had started working at Dounreay, in 1965. I was the in-house doctor, bloody remote place, the only medically qualified person within a hundred miles. Now, of course, after all the scandals, it's got its own fancy occupational health department. A man rang me up late one night at home. We were living in Melvich Bay at the time, about seven miles from the site. It was an

269

Indian voice and he said it was too dangerous to meet in person. He told me to find out all I could about the secret supply of plutonium and highly enriched uranium that was making its way from Dounreay down to Aldermaston, where Britain's nuclear weapons were being manufactured. China had conducted its first nuclear test the previous year and India was feeling a bit jumpy, exposed. He promised large and regular payments. Well, you can imagine I was stunned and needed time to absorb the implications."

"Did he give you a number to ring back?" I asked. I was sitting up now, leaning closer. His voice was growing tired, a little hoarse, and I passed him his whisky, which someone had placed on the grass beside his feet.

"He said he would call again. I don't know what it was exactly, but something about the call didn't ring true. He sounded Indian all right, but I became suspicious, made inquiries of my own. I had a friend in Whitehall, someone who had been involved with positive vetting at the site. There was never any proof, of course, but it became increasingly clear that the call had originated in Whitehall rather than New Delhi. I was being tested, or set up, whichever way you wanted to look at it. It didn't matter to me. I was scared to death. Terrified. Everything, my job, my new life in Scotland, all that I had worked for, was suddenly in jeopardy. From then on I vowed to have nothing to do with India. I severed all contact."

He cut one hand across the palm of the other, making me jump. I looked across at him. His eyes were clear, brighter for sharing the story, and I realised he was telling it as much for his own benefit as for mine.

"Your mother didn't like it, of course. But we had no choice. I was being scrutinised by someone and I was determined never to give them an excuse to ring me again. In some respects, I still think I did the right thing. It wasn't long before rumours started circulating about uranium going missing, enough for twelve nuclear bombs."

"Did you tell Mum everything?" I glanced up at the fading sky, my lucky stars beginning to shine through.

"No. I overreacted, felt I couldn't trust anyone. I think I told her something about the importance of blending in." He paused. "The man never rang back."

I wanted to ask more about my mother, but it wasn't the time or place. As I had listened to his voice, it became clear that he was much more sick than he was letting on.

"What about before you left for Scotland?" I asked, hoping the question wouldn't set anything off.

"What about it?"

"Were you a . . . "

"A young and passionate man?" He chuckled gently at the recollection. "It was a long time ago. I had always wanted to study medicine but we were all swept up by the events leading to Independence. They were heady days. It took time to remember that what I really wanted in life was to be a doctor, not some self-serving politician."

I felt Priyanka's hand on my shoulder.

"May I join the men?" she said, putting her other hand on my father's shoulder.

"Of course, my dear," my father replied, quick as a flash, putting a hand up to pat hers. He was quite taken by Priyanka.

"What were you talking about? State secrets?"

My father hadn't heard her properly and covered himself with a neutral grunt.

"That sort of thing," I said.

"Have you told him ours?" she asked, looking around to check that no one was listening.

"Not yet. I thought it was a secret."

"What are you two talking about?" he asked, mildly irritated.

I checked with Priyanka that it was okay – she was still smiling – and knelt down beside my father, balancing myself on the side of his wheelchair. I wasn't sure how he was going to take it, but I desperately wanted him to know.

"You're going to become a grandfather," I whispered close to his ear, my hand on his.

"Ah," he said, touching the side of his nose. "Now that's the sort of secret I don't mind keeping."

It was then, at perhaps the happiest moment of my life, that I first began to watch my own wedding reception from afar, not from above, but at a safe distance, the man beneath the umbrella. At first I felt like an impartial witness, but then, as events unfolded, like a helpless observer smacking against the glass.

Priyanka spotted the dancer first, a young woman from Rajasthan. We hadn't asked for any entertainment, other than a Kathakali show, which had been provided by the hotel and was not due to start for another hour. The Rajasthani dancer, hands pressed together in front of her, was stamping her splayed feet, bells jingling on her ankles. On her head was a large silver bowl of burning oil. It should have been a happy spectacle, the sort tourists pay good money to see, but her fixed smile, the aggressive stomp, those flames (should the oil be burning so fiercely?), started to ring other bells. I remember thinking Priyanka must have similar thoughts, because she glanced across at me for assurance, the first hint of fear creasing her eyes, the last look I would remember.

I left my father's side and stood in front of him, moving a few feet towards the dancer. Instinctively, I held out my hand for Priyanka's, which I folded into my own. The hotel manager was coming towards us — from afar (or was it with hindsight), he seemed to be slowing up, reaching the end of his day. He smiled, handing me a card.

"Is there a problem?" he asked. "She is a surprise wedding present — very costly. A performance by one of Rajasthan's finest dancers."

"Who sent her?" I asked, not taking my eye off the burning bowl, or my hand from Priyanka's. She was barely five feet from us now.

The manager shrugged his shoulders and held out an envelope, which I took from him. Why were my hands shaking as I slit it open? I pulled out the cream card and read the handwritten note: "Satya! Satya! Satya!" Did I look up at the dancer again? Did I have time to show Priyanka the card before the dancer stumbled and fell towards her? All I remember is the arcing of the flames as the bowl toppled forward, spilling its infernal fuel. And I can see Priyanka's face, questioning, terrified, alight, as she tried to shield herself with her arms. But I can't recall who rushed to her help first when the hem of her dress ignited and new flames danced into life.

To my everlasting shame, it wasn't me, for I was far away on the other side of the lawn, beneath my umbrella, watching her roll on the grass. Someone braver – Frank? – tried to smother the flames with a *sherwani* coat, a sister desperately threw jugs of water on her, and was it Dutchie patting helplessly with his bare hands? Whoever these courageous people were, their actions were in vain, as the oil – it must have been something else – had covered her from head to toe, and her sari had been woven from the finest, most flammable silk. She had bought it with her sisters in Ernakulam, on yet another shopping trip, one of the few I had been allowed to attend. I remember being served plastic cups of sweet tea on a lonely chair in Seemati, an air-conditioned emporium at the far end of the MG Road, watching her pick up sari after sari, and thinking how lucky I was as she occasionally turned to me, holding one up against her chest, smiling.

When the flames finally abated, I knew she lay too still, half hidden beneath a mound of wet tablecloths and coats. I was there by her side, late, I know, although others were kind enough to say afterwards that nothing more could have been done. With blistered hands, I searched for a pulse, but she was too hot to hold.

Even then, at the end of our life together, she possessed the calmness that had drawn me to her at its beginning, back at Frank's house on that warm evening in his courtyard. Slumped by her side, I began to realise that she would never breathe again. Our chance had come and we had grabbed it, only for her to be taken away. In one sense I could have no regrets: there had been no missed opportunities, no what-ifs. But in every other sense the numbing regret was bewildering, the loss too swift and complete to contemplate.

I thought for a moment about Macaulay, Jamie, the Club. They had managed to burn their bride in the end, shaped another story that would percolate slowly outwards, twisted perhaps into a dowry death or something more macabre.

Dutchie appeared by my side, and steered me gently towards an ambulance that had drawn up at the front of the hotel. We hugged as the tears came, tears that stung our seared cheeks: the retching sorrow, anger, futility of it all. After everything that Priyanka and I had striven to achieve together, had we actually made a difference? The thought that we hadn't, that her death had in some way been inevitable, was almost too much to bear. The Club's files might have been destroyed, Macaulay was dead, the department closed for a final time, but I knew now that it would always be there, its doors open, just a different name above them, waiting for the next generation, ours and theirs.

THE END

Jon Stock

Riot Act

"A darkly sparkling, new millennial crime thriller" – *Sunday Times*

"The most off-beat hero of the year is a fully-fledged street-fighting anarchist ... violently politically correct and amoral, but written with real power" – *Daily Telegraph*

"An exciting talent" – Val McDermid, *The Times*

OTHER BLACKAMBER TITLES

Qaisra Shahraz

Typhoon

Three women, one man, one night!

'A gripping, hugely involving and very satisfying read.'
Kate Mosse

'Full of vivid detail about the lives and loves, the duties and desires in Muslim family life few people in the West know. Begin that adventure with this novel.' *Yasmin Alibhai-Brown*

A riveting family saga of deceit by the best-selling author of
The Holy Woman.

Chiragpur is a traumatised village, warped in time and space, haunted by what happened there some twenty years earlier in a courtroom in Kacheri. *Typhoon* is a tragic tale of three young women, each one demonised by her past: Naghmana – the glamorous business executive from the city; Chaudharani – the village land baron; and Gulshan – the wronged wife. One caught in the arms of another woman's husband in the middle of the night, the second raped in her youth, and the third loses her husband to a total stranger.

Reshma S. Ruia

Something Black in the Lentil Soup

'Ironic humor and a fierce wit combine in this haunting tale of East meets West wannabe Indian poet.' Gary Pulsifer, *Arcadia*

This is a comical and irreverent portrayal of three parallel cultures – British, Indian, and British-Indian. Penetrating insights into social mores and conventions.

The novel follows the changing fortunes of a virginal middle-aged Indian male in search of literary fame and romantic glory. Kavi Naidu arrives in England, a contender for the prestigious Commonwealth literary prize. A pompous, sentimental figure, he is suddenly catapulted from the sleepy humdrum routine of Delhi, into the heady distractions of London.

Naidu's arch rival and nemesis is the enigmatic, suave Seth, a distinguished man of letters whose sophisticated pose and ennui is a perfect foil to Naidu's clumsy, eager naiveté. Readily shrugging off his vows of chastity and temperance, Naidu succumbs to the charms of Naina Mistry, the Indian High Commissioner's sultry wife, with her jamun-red lips and plunging neckline.

All BlackAmber Books are available from your local bookshop.

For a regular update on BlackAmber's latest release, with extracts, reviews and events, visit:

www.blackamber.com

.